I MARRIED A DRAGON

Prime Mating Agency

REGINE ABEL

CONTENTS

Chapter 1	1
Chapter 2	8
Chapter 3	20
Chapter 4	35
Chapter 5	52
Chapter 6	67
Chapter 7	76
Chapter 8	85
Chapter 9	97
Chapter 10	107
Chapter 11	118
Chapter 12	131
Chapter 13	143
Chapter 14	159
Chapter 15	175
Chapter 16	191
Chapter 17	204
Chapter 18	215
Epilogue	234
Also by Regine Abel	271
About Regine	275

I MARRIED A DRAGON

He's a beast only she can tame

When a dark portal spewing shadow beasts opens into a research facility, Kaida's unit is dispatched to destroy them. The last thing she expects is for the massive dragon amidst the creatures to claim her. To avoid an intergalactic conflict, and to perform an important mission, she consents to a temporary marriage of convenience with the Shadow Lord Cedros. But with each passing day, she finds herself drawn to the sweet and socially awkward male who lurks within this strong and fearsome protector of his realm.

She's his peace and his salvation

For decades, Cedros searched in vain for the one female who would silence his growing madness, take away the pain torturing his body, and end the loneliness and isolation that is the curse of a Shadow Lord. Who would have thought she would be an off-worlder? And yet, here she is, his little Kaida, a human so fragile, so delicate, and yet so strong. Her mere presence brings him divine peace. Her simple embrace awakens feelings and emotions he never thought possible.

How can he convince her to stay with him in this world so ill-adapted to her species, and when she didn't come to him by choice, but out of duty?

DEDICATION

To those who speak and think with the candor and the innocence of a child. To those who look at the world with the same curiosity, open mind, and eager heart. To those who accept that there is an infinity of possibilities, and that it's okay to explore them all.

Clinging to a belief, an opinion, a way of life, rejecting any other possibilities just because that's how it's always been done, or how it's been taught to you, is a self-inflicted slow-acting but lethal poison. Change is the foundation of evolution and of life itself. Do not fear it. Embrace it.

There is no shame in changing your opinion or in admitting you were wrong. The only shame is the harm you do to yourself and your loved ones, and everything you missed out on or deprived yourself of because you were too afraid of leaving your comfort zone.

Reclaim your inner child.

CHAPTER 1
KAIDA

Shouts, screams, and the thudding sound of countless feet stampeding out of the research facility greeted us the minute we entered the building. Panic and terror too often brought out the worst in people. My heart constricted at the sight of some employees getting blindly shoved, falling, and getting trampled by their colleagues attempting to flee whatever beasts emitted the dreadful roars and screeches further in. But once survival instincts kicked in, rational thoughts usually went on a hiatus.

I fought my natural urge to assist the fallen, since my colleagues would handle them. As part of the main strike team, it fell to my teammates and me to contain whatever mess awaited ahead. I'd taken part in countless hairy missions, but never with anything that sounded like those things.

Hot on the heels of Tedrick, our squad leader, I adjusted my blaster to the highest stun as we reached a first set of security doors. They gave access to the long corridor leading to what the facility's map on the interface of my armband described as Engineering. As soon as they parted, all wandering thoughts of the panicked civilians vanished. I shuddered at the sight of the two abominations that had been trapped in the corridor when the security lockdown kicked in.

Their bodies vaguely reminded me of a nightmarish greyhound with twisted legs. Their heads had no visible eyes, only a flayed, long maw of dagger teeth. Thick spikes covered the area where their eyes and foreheads should have been, tapering off along the nape. Above what appeared to be an ethereal set of shadow wings, and extending off their shoulders, they had a pair of snake-like appendages that attempted to strike their target whenever within range. The long tail, covered in spikes, ended with a spiked-mace-like bulge with a sharp blade at the tip.

"Eliminate the aqrats," Tedrick shouted. "Shoot to kill!"

He didn't have to say it twice. My teammates and I switched our blasters' setting to lethal and unloaded mercilessly on the two creatures that were charging us with rabid fury. To my utter relief, they were no challenge to our combined fire power. Still, it blew my mind that, instead of a gaping wound where the blaster shots hit the beasts, chunks of flesh tore up before dissolving into smoke. When they died, each creature simply evaporated, as if it had never existed. However, the deep claw marks on the walls made it clear they had been real.

"What the fuck are they doing in this place?" Oleg asked, echoing the thoughts each of us undoubtedly shared.

"Veladeem's scientists didn't create these horrors," Tedrick said in a tense voice through our com. "They just messed with shit they shouldn't have and let these bad things come in."

I wanted to ask more questions, but knew better. Tedrick wouldn't give more details than he was allowed or willing to. Anyway, now wasn't the time. He gestured for us to follow as we ran up to the end of the corridor. A massive set of reinforced doors barred the access to Engineering.

"Overriding the security locks," Maeve said through our com.

She hooked her hacking device to the biometric lock, then tapped a few keys. Seconds later, the massive vault doors were parting before us. As Enforcers—agents of the United Planets Organization's peacekeeping force—we had the best of everything the galaxy had to offer. Our hackers also had backdoors in far more places than the public would be comfortable knowing.

We found more of those dreadful creatures swarming inside, flying around what looked like a giant power core.

The target? A ginormous gold and bluish-black dragon with a shadowy aura.

It only took a second to realize the smaller nightmarish creatures were attacking the magnificent—yet terrifying—dragon. Although he was wrecking them, a single well-placed swipe of his massive paw all but tearing one of the creatures in half, with so many of them attacking him from all sides, the fiends were still getting several hits in.

"Protect the dragon!" Tedrick shouted in our com.

Despite the billion questions firing off in my mind—and undoubtedly in my companions' as well—we quietly complied. With his security clearance level, Tedrick knew a lot of classified information, little of which he could share with us. I'd never heard of an aqrat, let alone seen one before. What the fuck were they, and where did they come from? And a freaking dragon?

While his body had all the characteristics of a dragon, I absentmindedly noticed that he mostly appeared to stand upright —almost bipedal—instead of on all fours. He was fighting on the circular platform around the power core. The tall railings offered little safety for him should he get knocked over. There was at least a fifty-meter drop, not that he wouldn't be able to fly back up.

To my shock, a shadowy portal—halfway down the shaft the power core was erected on—seemed to be the doorway through which these nightmarish creatures had entered the research facility.

My team and I spread along the outer walkway while shooting at the aqrats. Although it required multiple shots to the body to slay one, a single shot to the head had them shattering in an explosion of shadows before vanishing.

A handful of the aqrats we targeted redirected their attention towards us, but most remained focused on the dragon, making our job of thinning their numbers easier. The dragon dove from the platform, spraying a flock of aqrats below us with purplish shadow flames. Instead of burning them, it appeared to make them swell and bloat, as if they were absorbing the shadows. Their flight patterns became erratic, almost drunken. The dragon flew around, smashing a bunch with his tail and lacerating others with his claws. Either option had the same outcome of making them shatter, then dissolve into smoke.

The remaining aqrats following the dragon down the shaft forced us to move on some of the ramps leading to the platform of the power core in order to get a proper angle to fire at them. Four of us stood by ourselves on our respective ramp, while Maeve and Oleg stood together on the southeast ramp.

"What do we do about the dragon once we're done with the critters?" Oleg asked as we were taking out the handful of stragglers.

"Fall back to the exit at the end of your ramp," Tedrick replied. "If all goes well, he should simply return to his realm through the portal."

"And if all does *not* go well?" I asked.

"Then it's going to get ugly real fast. Find a place to shelter, but *do not* harm or kill the dragon," Tedrick said in a tone that brooked no argument.

My curiosity further spiked as to what was so special about the creature… beyond the fact that he was a freaking dragon.

As the last couple of aqrats dissolved, we all started running back towards the doorway at the end of our respective ramps.

However, an enraged roar from the dragon had my blood turning to ice. He didn't seem appeased *at all,* but he appeared to be itching to fight a bit longer.

Arms and legs pumping, I dashed towards my exit, only to stop dead in my tracks and throw myself backward when the dragon breathed a powerful stream of shadow flames directly in my path. The flames shot upward through the grids of the ramp while the dragon flew up.

"Fuck! It's blocking my way!" I exclaimed through the com. "I'm going to circle through the platform towards another ramp."

"Run!" Tedrick shouted. "Everyone else, blasters to stun. Aim for his throat!"

I never reached the central platform. Like a deadly monster emerging from the depths of a dark ocean, the dragon soared above the ramp, breathing his shadow flames in a sweep in front of me. Flying overhead, he reached the central platform and, with a powerful swipe of his enormous claws, he destroyed the connecting paths towards the other ramps.

While he was savagely wrecking any means of exit that way, I tried to go back towards the doorway. But seconds later, I heard a loud flap of wings before he fired his flames again in front of me. In my attempt to come to an abrupt stop, I tripped and fell onto my stomach. My teeth rattled in my head from the force of the impact. I turned onto my back and immediately pushed myself up on my feet, only to see the giant beast land on the ramp directly in front of me.

My stomach dropped to my feet. Heart pounding, I could barely breathe as the creature roared again, its golden eyes filled with madness. It appeared to be foaming at the mouth while a shadowy substance—likely blood—dripped from the countless lacerations and wounds the aqrats had inflicted.

As if in slow motion, I raised my blaster and aimed at his throat, knowing I wasn't making it out of this one. I stared at his massive maw opening to countless razor-sharp giant teeth as he roared again and lunged for me. My shot went off at the same time his hand closed around me, knocking off my weapon.

I vaguely heard Tedrick barking orders through the com, but the deafening sound of my blood rushing in my ears drowned it all out. Like a brick wall, the golden chest of the dragon came at me at a dizzying speed as he lifted me up. I thought he would toss me into his gaping maw, but he slammed me against his chest. I gasped, the wind knocked out of me.

"Ejaya!"

The foreign word resonated loudly in my mind. It hadn't come through my com, and I hadn't heard it through my ears. It had been spoken to me telepathically. But by whom? The dragon? And what the fuck did it mean?

I knew it was important, and that I should focus on it, but that stupid survival instinct I'd mentioned earlier kicked in with a vengeance. I wiggled and fought to free myself from his crushing hold. That only made him tighten his grip, his second hand joining the fray.

"He… he's crushing me," I said to my team.

"Ejaya!" the foreign voice repeated.

"No fucking way!" Tedrick whispered in a disbelieving voice through the com. "Kaida, stop fighting! He won't hurt you. He's calming down. Don't fight him!"

As I tried to listen, my body had gone into flight mode. I was being crushed. I couldn't breathe. My skin tingled, and my head felt light. In that instant, I knew I would lose consciousness. Maybe it was a good thing. Then I'd stop fighting. Then, maybe, he'd loosen his grip.

But even as that thought entered my mind, I realized it was no longer his hand holding me, like King Kong holding Ann Darrow. It was now both of his arms. I couldn't say if my mind was playing tricks on me, but he seemed to be shrinking down to a more human size. However, I would never know. Just as a veil of darkness descended before my eyes, a massive sedative dart embedded itself in his neck.

CHAPTER 2
KAIDA

Sitting in one of the smaller meeting rooms of the UPO Enforcers' HQ, I shifted restlessly while waiting for whoever would interview or debrief me. The barren room contained a rectangular table for ten, a whiteboard on one wall, a giant vidscreen on the other, and nothing else.

At least, this isn't an interrogation room with a two-way mirror.

At this point, it wouldn't have surprised me all that much. Forty-eight hours had gone by since I'd lost consciousness in the research facility, and I still didn't know what the fuck was going on.

The morning after, I'd awakened in a medical pod in the infirmary. Why I'd been out so long, when I normally should have recovered from getting squished in a few minutes, still baffled me. Although Dr. Bailey had given me a clean bill of health, she still kept me in isolation for twenty-four hours to make sure the toxins the aqrats had passed on to the dragon during the battle hadn't infected me.

For some reason, I didn't quite buy it.

Nobody would answer my questions. Tedrick didn't even

come see me. They only asked me to write up my report from my isolation room. This morning, they'd finally released me only so that I could come to this meeting room. That two guards escorted me here from the infirmary seriously freaked me out. What did they fear? That I'd run? Why would I?

The sound of the door opening startled me. I immediately straightened, wondering which suit was coming to debrief me and, hopefully, give me some answers. To my shock, instead of the head of our department, a stunning female Temern entered the barren room. Typical of her avian species, she had a beak that made it harder to see when she was smiling, although she undoubtedly was right now. Her white feathers, with dark specks on her wings and sprinkled on her chest, reminded me of those of a snowy owl. She had a majestic pair of wings that almost trailed to the floor, and a long, fluffy white tail that vaguely reminded me of that of a bird of paradise.

"Hello, Ms. Daigo. My name is Linsea Voln. I'm sorry for making you wait," the Temern female said in a sweet and melodic voice that immediately felt soothing. She took a seat in the chair across the table from me. "This case has been rather insane. I'm sure you have many questions, and I will endeavor to answer them for you."

"Hello, Ms. Voln," I replied, feeling more confused than ever. "I don't believe we've ever met. Which department are you from?"

"Oh, right, I'm sorry. I am an ambassador with the UPO. I handle mostly critical foreign matters—basically political conflicts that might devolve into an interplanetary war."

My jaw dropped as I stared at the female. It was shocking enough that the UPO would send a Temern to speak to me. As some of the most powerful empaths of the galaxy, Temerns were highly sought after by the legal system, governments, and corporations, whether as mediators, negotiators, or merely to help assess if a person was being deceitful in their dealings. But now she was implying that I was somehow involved in something that could cause interplanetary war?

"What do you mean by 'war potential'? And what in the world does it have to do with me?" I asked, rolling my shoulders to loosen the tension quickly building in my back. "I'm guessing it has to do with that portal and the dragon? Was that a foreign attack?"

"I understand your shock," Ms. Voln continued. "And I promise to answer all of your questions. But first, may I ask that you call me Linsea? We Temerns aren't too big on formalities."

I nodded absentmindedly. "Sure. And you can call me Kaida, if you wish."

She beamed at me, her smile more visible in her stunning blue eyes than in the stiffness of her beak. "Excellent. But to answer your question, no, it wasn't a foreign attack. That portal resulted from Veladeem Research overstepping their boundaries and illegally performing unsupervised research with shadow obsidian stones. They shouldn't have had the stones in their possession to begin with. And using one of them created a rift into the void—you could almost call it a parallel universe—from whence came the fiendish creatures you fought."

Linsea shifted her wings and clasped her long, slender fingers on the table in front of her before continuing.

"However, the 'dragon' named Cedros Qhelian—who is in fact a Derakeen—is indeed at the heart of the issue. He is a rare breed of his species, which resembles what humans call dragons. His people live in the shattered world of Dramnac."

I recoiled in surprise. "Wait, what? I thought an anomaly had opened in the center of that planet, and it had somehow imploded."

Linsea smiled and nodded with an amused expression. "An anomaly did shatter Dramnac into a million pieces, but it still thrives in fragments that exist in different phases of reality held by their core. All Derakeens can shift phases to travel between the dimensions of their world."

"Wow, okay. That sounds both messed up and super cool," I said, intrigued.

"It *is* a fascinating world. However, only Shadow Lords like Cedros can open portals between dimensions and between worlds," Linsea explained, taking on a serious expression. "Therefore, their people revere them almost like gods."

I nodded pensively. "Yeah, I can see that. Such insane power would be in high demand but is also extremely dangerous."

"Agreed. As recent events demonstrated, Derakeens aren't the only ones to travel in the shadows. There are entire realms that evolve in parallel to our own reality. Many are peaceful, but other shadow dwellers aren't so much."

"Like those aqrat monsters," I said, barely repressing a shudder.

"Correct. On top of opening portals and guiding back to their home travelers who get lost in the void, Shadow Lords fight the monsters that pierce through the veil to keep the shadow pathways safe," Linsea continued. "Certain pathways are safer than others. But the one that Veladeem tried to create is the worst possible one."

"Where were they trying to go?" I asked, more intrigued than ever, my detective instinct kicking into high gear.

"To the shadow obsidian mines of Dramnac," she said matter-of-factly.

I frowned and pursed my lips pensively. "That's the second time you mention shadow obsidian. I thought this whole thing about portal opening stones was a myth."

Linsea shook her head. "No, shadow obsidian is real, and it allows regular Derakeens to open portals like the Shadow Lords, but for a shorter duration. Each stone must first be engraved with a destination so they don't end up in some dreadful place. As you can guess, the governments of every advanced world would love to get their hands on these precious pebbles, which we cannot allow."

"In shady hands, it could be a complete disaster," I concurred.

"Exactly."

"Okay, while this is all really fascinating, what does it have to do with me?" I asked, more confused than ever.

She gave me a sympathetic smile. "I'm getting to it. As you likely noticed, Cedros entered some kind of rage after the battle. It is common for Shadow Lords when they spend too much time out of phase or traipsing in the void. It messes with their heads. But worst still, wounds from aqrats—among others—accelerates the process. Their saliva and venoms actually infect the Shadow Lords with a form of... well, something akin to rabies. It can take weeks and even months to burn it out of their system, a very long period during which they're all but feral."

I frowned again, my eyes going out of focus as I replayed the events in my mind. "Yes, he seemed to be foaming at the mouth. But then, before I lost consciousness, I got the distinct impression he was calming, maybe even shrinking. Does that make sense?"

Linsea grinned at me and nodded. "Absolutely. While there is no medical cure for jokraz—the Shadow Lord rage—there is a natural one in the form of an Ejaya."

"Oh, my God! He said that!" I exclaimed, leaning forward with excitement. "It was like I could hear him—or at least I'm assuming it was his voice—speaking telepathically to me and repeating that word, almost like a prayer, like he was in shock. But then Tedrick shot him. The dragon is fine, right? It was just a sedative?"

"Oh yes, he's absolutely fine. Believe me, things would be far more tense right now had Cedros been harmed. It would be a full out war," Linsea said reassuringly. "But yes, he did telepathically speak to you. In their battle form, Derakeens cannot use words like we do. However, your presence triggered his accelerated healing process and calmed him. You are the first human Ejaya."

"Come again?" I asked, disbelievingly.

She chuckled and nodded. "You are Cedros's Ejaya. Just being around you, and especially in close physical contact with you, triggers a physiological response that makes him secrete loads of endorphins and an immune response that acts as a potent antiviral agent. So instead of taking weeks or months to fight jokraz, they fully recover in a few days, sometimes even just hours, depending on how extensive the infection runs."

"Whoa… Okay. That's different. I guess that's why he was squishing me to get that close contact," I mumbled, remembering how not particularly pleasant that bone-crushing hug had been. "But I'm still not seeing where the problem is."

"The problem is that an Ejaya is unique to each specific Shadow Lord. Cedros can only establish that connection with a single person in the entire universe, and that's you," Linsea explained carefully. "Therefore, the Derakeen Council demands that you fulfill that role with Cedros."

My stomach dropped as I stared at the Temern in disbelief. "Demands?"

She nodded with an apologetic expression. "Under Derakeen law, an Ejaya may not refuse the call of her or his Shadow Lord. That means they want you to go live on Dramnac with Cedros and to see to his welfare."

"You've got to be kidding?" I asked, raising my palms questioningly. "And what if I refuse? Which I obviously want to do…"

"If you refuse, they threaten to launch a war against the member planets of the UPO," Linsea said in a soft voice. "So, as you can guess, we need you to consent, but not only to avoid a war."

"What else is there?" I asked, still in complete shock.

"While on Dramnac, we want you to also take on an undercover mission for us."

I froze for a split second, my stunned outrage temporarily taking a backseat while my Enforcer instincts surged to the fore. "Mission? What kind of mission?"

Linsea grinned, knowing she had piqued my interest. "Veladeem Research received the shadow obsidian stones from anonymous smugglers. We need to find out who they are, how they are acquiring the stones, and put a stop to their business. If they bring those stones on to penitentiary planets, they could break out the most violent and hardened criminals in one fell swoop and take them halfway across the galaxy without the guards being able to do a thing about it."

My brow creased as I nodded. I could see a million different ways to misuse these stones. If they fell into the hands of a warmongering species, they could open portals into unsuspecting neighboring planets and commit genocides. Pirates, thieves, and slavers could also wreak havoc with such a tool.

"Right, that does sound like a worthy mission. But what does that mean as far as Cedros is concerned?" I asked. "Once the mission is done, do I get to just pack and leave Dramnac, or am I expected to stay there a specific amount of time? And what of him? What are his expectations where I'm concerned?"

I didn't have to spell out what worries gnawed at me.

Once more, Linsea looked at me with compassion. "These are all very valid questions. However, I will let my husband answer them for you. He has already discussed the situation with Cedros, and he's currently negotiating with the Derakeen Council."

"He's an ambassador, like you?" I asked, genuinely curious.

She chuckled and shook her head. "Not exactly, although one could say that a lot of his work ends up having important diplomatic and political ramifications, mainly with primitive worlds."

I narrowed my eyes at her in reaction to her evasive

response. But before I could probe her further, she suddenly perked up. Her face taking on a soft, almost timid expression, like that of a blushing bride, had me intrigued.

"Please, excuse me for a minute," Linsea said, rising to her feet.

My eyes widened as she nervously smoothed her feathers, then exited the room. Burning with curiosity, I leaned over the table and stretched my neck to look into the hallway through the door left halfway open. My heart melted when I saw her extend her hands to a male Temern, about one head taller than she was. He had golden feathers with maroon wings.

A pang of envy coursed through me as he gently took her hands, looking at her like she was the greatest wonder of the universe. He drew her to him, and they gently stroked their beaks against each other's before embracing. She melted in his arms, her wings flattening against her body while his massive ones wrapped around her. Eyes closed with an expression of pure bliss, the male rested his cheek on top of Linsea's head. I couldn't say for certain, but I could have sworn one or both of them was cooing.

With obvious reluctance, the male—who I assumed to be her husband—released her. He caressed her cheek with infinite tenderness, which elicited that same almost timid expression from Linsea. After rubbing beaks with her one last time, he took her hand and led her towards the room I was sitting in.

I swiftly leaned back in my chair, feeling a little guilty for spying on their moment of affection. What I wouldn't give to share that kind of connection with someone. I'd been single for far too long. It wasn't like the Enforcers didn't have plenty of great males of every species to pick from, but none of them stirred me the right way.

"Kaida, please meet my husband, Kayog Voln," Linsea said as soon as they entered the room. "My love, this is Kaida Daigo, Cedros's Ejaya."

"Miss Daigo, it is a pleasure to meet you at last," Kayog said, his silver eyes sparkling with both kindness and amusement.

My face immediately heated. Although he wasn't a mind-reader, I strongly suspected he knew I'd spied on them. If he hadn't seen me, he'd more than likely felt my emotions. The subtle broadening of his smile seemed to confirm my assumptions.

"The pleasure is mine, Mr. Voln," I said as they both took a seat in the chairs across the table from me.

"I understand you are on a first name basis with my beloved," Kayog said in a sweet and cheery voice. "May I be so bold as to ask for the same privilege?"

"Sure, I'm also not big on formalities," I said with a grin, instantly liking him. "But I have to say that it's quite adorable seeing the two of you working together."

They both chuckled. Kayog cast an affectionate glance at his mate and caressed her cheek with the back of his hand. He then refocused his attention on me.

"Believe me, Kaida, it is far too rare a pleasure. Our respective careers force us both to travel a lot, often to opposite ends of the galaxy. But we seize every opportunity to be together."

"Right. Linsea said you aren't an ambassador like her. May I ask what you do?" I asked.

By the look he gave me, Kayog was not fooled by my less-than-subtle attempt at finding out how the heck he fit into this whole dragon mess.

"I am the founder and lead agent of the Prime Mating Agency," Kayog said.

My brain froze. "You're a primitive alien matchmaker?"

I flinched as soon as the words left my mouth. I hadn't meant to sound derogatory or disrespectful. To my relief, Linsea chuckled while Kayog burst out laughing.

"I certainly am that, among other things," the Temern said in an amused voice.

I smiled back before quickly sobering. I licked my lips nervously as I carefully chose my words. "Look… uh… I'm not sure how you fit into this entire situation. However, while I'm quite willing to take on the mission Linsea was mentioning earlier, I have absolutely no intention of getting shackled into a marriage of convenience with some stranger."

"A very understandable and reasonable response," Kayog conceded, sobering as well. He cast an inquisitive look at his mate. "How far had your discussion gone before I interrupted?"

"Your timing was perfect, Kay. We had just reached your part in this," Linsea said.

"Excellent," he replied, turning back to me. "As my Linsea probably mentioned to you, I've had discussions with both Cedros and the Derakeen Council. While he's very open to anything that would be agreeable to you, the Council not so much. They are pretty adamant about you complying with their laws as Cedros is one of their most powerful Shadow Lords. A marriage of convenience was the only temporary commitment they would agree to."

"Forcing me to play wife to a stranger?" I exclaimed.

Kayog raised an appeasing hand. "While it would indeed be a legal marriage, in this specific case, we would void the intimacy clause. Cedros has agreed to it. He only requests the peace and healing that only you can provide him."

I nervously tucked a strand of hair behind my ears, a million thoughts firing off in my mind while I wondered why the heck I was even considering any of this.

"He is a very good male who you will definitely grow very fond of. Once that temporary period is up, I suspect you may be the one unwilling to leave."

I narrowed my eyes at him. "How temporary is temporary?"

He gave me a sheepish expression. "According to the Prime Mating Agency's rules, it is six months. However, I will never lie to you. And I can already say with conviction that the Derakeen

Council will try to challenge your potential desire to leave once that time is up."

"Challenge or stop me altogether?" I insisted.

"Challenge. They cannot coerce you to stay," he specified.

"But they are *coercing* me to marry him," I argued. "Once my six months are up, or however long I take to complete the mission, I will absolutely want to leave. Cedros's problem still won't be solved, if he cannot find a replacement Ejaya."

This time, Linsea intervened in a gentle voice. "You are correct. However, while they demand for you to go to Dramnac now, you will have six months to build a friendship with Cedros. Six months to come up with a solution that will allow you to reclaim the life you choose, while also catering to his needs."

"Such as what?" I insisted.

"Such as him coming to you whenever he needs a hug," Kayog said in a teasing voice. "After all, he can open portals to pretty much anywhere in the galaxy. You wouldn't even have to leave your house."

I scratched my nape and slowly nodded. "Okay, yeah, that could work. Assuming he doesn't show up needing a 'hug' right in the midst of a mission. But what exactly are we talking about in terms of hugs?"

Kayog laughed. "The Shadow Lords need contact with their Ejaya. Typically, they will hug you, rub their faces over you, and just cuddle *a lot* with you. Although there is *absolutely nothing* sexual about it, the more direct the contact, the more effective it is."

"Why does it sound like you mean naked?" I grumbled, frowning.

Kayog grinned while his mate chuckled.

"Because he does," Linsea said.

"Indeed, I do. After all, like us Temerns, Derakeens do not wear clothes. So, for now, I would suggest you pack bikinis, short shorts, and crop tops for all the cuddling until you feel comfortable enough to do it without clothes."

My brow further creased. "You're assuming I'm going to accept."

"I *know* you're going to accept. I can read your emotions, remember?" Kayog said smugly. "Do not glare at me, my dear Kaida. Your sacrifice will allow us to avert a war, provide the UPO with a local detective that could prevent the proliferation of a dangerous tool, and bring peace to a kind male and protector of multiple realms. You will have six months to get to know him and find the perfect solution for the long term. But after talking to both of you, I can tell you with absolute certainty that you will not *want* to leave Dramnac or Cedros… ever."

CHAPTER 3
CEDROS

Four days. Four long and excruciating days since I'd last held my Ejaya… since I'd smelled her divine scent. Every cell in my body ached with need. Even my scales hurt from the brutal withdrawal. Holding her in my embrace had given me such peace, such delightful peace, like I'd never felt before.

But a human?

I still couldn't wrap my head around the fact that my Ejaya belonged to a different species. In all the history of the Shadow Lords, none had ever been paired with an off-worlder.

Then again, some of my brothers died insane from never finding their Ejaya.

Could theirs have also been a human or born of a different species altogether? I didn't even want to contemplate such a terrible thought. There are infinite worlds, physical and ethereal —countless shadow realms whose existence the dwellers of the physical worlds couldn't even begin to imagine. No Shadow Lord could explore them all in a lifetime to find his Ejaya, if she truly could be from any species.

I could only praise the gods to have finally put my little human in my path. I had begun to believe I would die insane, for

I had explored every phase and area of the fragmented world of Dramnac, never finding the one meant for me.

It still chafed that Kaida had required a couple of days to wrap up her previous life and pack her things before she came to me. While reasonable, it had prolonged my agony. Once she arrived, it would take every shred of my willpower not to throw myself at her and bask in the ecstasy of her embrace. She wasn't Derakeen. She didn't know the ways of an Ejaya. I had to be careful not to scare her and drive her away with my constant needs.

Although Kaida's delay in coming here was so that she wouldn't have to leave again, she'd only committed to stay with me for six months. Her departure after that was simply unacceptable. I would find a way to bind her to Dramnac. I held little hope that I could make her love me. On top of being nothing like her human males, I was awkward and socially challenged. But I would spoil Kaida, see to her every need, and make her fall in love with Dramnac. I could only hope she wouldn't find my appearance too off-putting.

Councilor Gavyr heaved another sigh. Judging by his constant pacing on my terrace, you'd think he was the one awaiting his Ejaya's arrival. As was often the case with red-scaled Derakeens, he had a swift and impatient temper, odd traits for a Councilor. You'd think that age would have calmed him, but at fifty-six, he remained easily inflamed. And yet, I couldn't complain in this instance.

His impassioned demands that my Kaida settle on Dramnac had played a major role in convincing her to come to me. A part of me felt guilty to have somewhat coerced my Ejaya to my side. But she had been created for me. I fully intended to make it up to her. Any minute now, Kayog would send us the call for me to open the portal that would bring her to me.

Soon, the sun would reach its zenith over the private floating plateau upon which I had erected my lair. As one of the most powerful Shadow Lords of the Oddran region—if not all Dramnac—I was entitled to prime real estate. While many of the nobles and wealthy members of our society often exhibited their hoard with flamboyant decorations, paved grounds with rare stones or gems, I had kept mine elegant but mostly natural. I loved the feel of grass beneath my feet, and the natural beauty of the world. I could only hope my Kaida felt the same.

But I will change it all, if it will make her happy.

Gavyr sighed again and cast an impatient glance at his armband. I shifted my wings while trying to think of something clever to say to at least entertain him with conversation. But as always, my tongue turned to lead. Anyway, what did one discuss with a Councilor? If nothing else, his pacing kept him at a comfortable distance from me. Regular Derakeens like him all failed to properly control their phasing abilities, which made standing near them quite unpleasant.

"Finally!" Gavyr exclaimed, startling me. "Kayog sent the signal. You may summon the portal."

My hearts leapt. The oddest mix of excitement and fear surged through me. I forced the thoughts of all the things that could go wrong out of my head as I called the shadows to me. They flowed through my body, growing in strength like a gathering storm in my chest. The world blurred around me as I focused on the destination. The fabric of the world ripped before my mind's eye, taking the dark shape of a giant vortex until the center cleared into a window through space, which allowed me to see my Kaida next to Kayog.

I fired the shadow energy gathered in my chest at it, opening a giant portal a few meters in front of me, with the entrance light years away from here in front of my Ejaya. As with each time I opened a portal, it burned as if a part of my soul was getting torn out. But this time, I welcomed the discomfort.

The Temern came out of the portal first, a human female I didn't know behind him. And then my Kaida, followed by a small hover cart carrying a pair of crates and a large bag that I assumed to be her belongings.

By the Gods! Her divine scent slammed into me with a violence that made me dizzy. My mouth watered, my scales and every nerve ending ached with need. To my shame, I could feel myself trembling from the effort it took to silence my urge to rush and embrace her. However, whatever expression Kaida saw on my face appeared to frighten her as she took what I presumed to be an involuntary step back.

Ashamed, I closed my eyes and took in a deep breath, only to jerk them back open. What a stupid idea! I'd only inhaled more of her scent, exacerbating my burning need to touch her, to wrap my body all around her. She wasn't even attractive by Derakeen standards. And yet, I had never longed more fiercely for a female.

"Master Kayog, there you are at last," Councilor Gavyr said, his displeasure at the wait barely veiled.

"Actually, Councilor Gavyr, I believe we are four minutes early," Kayog said in a cheerful voice. "But I can understand your eagerness."

Under different circumstances, I would have been amused by the skillful way the Temern had set the grumpy Councilor straight. But my brain was focused on keeping me from throwing myself at my Ejaya like a rabid beast.

"Right," Councilor Gavyr responded.

"Councilor, Cedros, please meet Isobel Biondi, a human priestess recognized by the United Planets Organization," Kayog continued with the same carefree tone. "She will officiate the human union. And this is your Ejaya, Cedros. Meet the lovely Kaida Daigo. Kaida, this is Cedros Qhelian and the Derakeen Councilor Gavyr Strono."

I pressed my palm to my hearts and bowed my head deeply, feeling almost faint as I did so.

"It's a pleasure to meet you, Cedros," Kaida said, her voice sweet and musical, sending shivers down my spine.

"It is an honor of a lifetime to meet you at last, my Ejaya," I said, surprised that a single intelligible word managed to cross my lips. "Thank you for consenting to come to me."

Her face softened in the most delightful way, and she almost seemed timid for a moment.

"Welcome, Ejaya Kaida," Councilor Gavyr said, breaking the magic of the moment. "I am pleased you made the right choice. It is a great honor to serve a Shadow Lord."

I flinched inwardly and cast a worried glance at Kaida. To my relief, aside from looking unimpressed, she didn't seem otherwise offended by his haughty ways.

"Well, if we're all ready, we may proceed with the ceremony," Kayog said with the same enthusiasm. I made to dispel the portal, but he raised a hand, stopping me. "Unless keeping it open is a strain on you, it will not be necessary to dispel the portal. This ceremony is very brief, and merely a formality to make it legal and binding for the UPO."

"Very well," I said.

"Please stand face to face and hold each other's hands," the human priestess said.

Kaida approached me with determined steps, and I met her halfway. I shouldn't be so surprised that she wasn't skittish. After all, she was a UPO Enforcer, a protector of her people, like I was. She cast a distracted glance at the breathtaking view of Oddran. Although it seemed to awe her, Kaida swiftly returned her attention to me.

I liked that.

Lightning struck me when she placed her small hands in my much bigger ones. My mouth went dry, and my throat warmed. The heating chamber located there filled with hydrogen, ready for me to ignite as a loud purr of delight escaped me.

Mortified, I clenched my teeth and swallowed hard to silence the unwelcome sound. Kaida's eyes widened. I couldn't say if shock, confusion, or a mix of both had prompted this response. But the way her gaze locked on my throat, I already knew its golden scales were glowing from my repressed urge to breathe fire in bliss.

"Forgive your Shadow Lord," Councilor Gavyr said in a bored voice. "He's still recovering from jokraz. The lack of an Ejaya has been torturing him, and now he's struggling to control his physiological response from the overdue relief your presence procures him. It shall pass in a couple of days."

My scales burned with humiliation to have the Councilor thus expose my weakness. Worse still, he'd done it in such a dismissive and cavalier fashion. An out-of-control addict was not the first impression I wanted to give my human Ejaya. Our females understood well the state I was currently in, but Kaida wouldn't.

To my surprise, instead of looking at me in a worried or disappointed fashion, Kaida glared at the Councilor, as if to express she'd felt his comment had been inappropriate—which it had been. She then turned back to look at me with sympathy. She smiled, then gently squeezed my hands in what I could only interpret as encouragement.

A wave of warmth filled both my hearts, even as they constricted with a grateful emotion for my Kaida. She might not know the way of the Ejayas, but she clearly had the soul of one.

"We are gathered here to celebrate the union of this woman, Kaida Daigo, and this Derakeen male, the Shadow Lord Cedros Qhelian, in the sacred bond of marriage. Such union must be entered into freely, with honest intentions, a genuine commitment, and not for financial gains or deceptive purposes," the priestess said. "Kaida Daigo, do you freely and willingly take this Derakeen male, Cedros Qhelian, to be your lawfully wedded husband, for better or for worse, through good times and hardships, in sickness and in health, until death do you part?"

"I do," Kaida said, the firmness of her voice pleasing me beyond words.

"Cedros Qhelian, do you freely take this woman, Kaida Daigo, to be your lawfully wedded wife, for better or for worse, through good times and hardships, in sickness and in health, until death do you part?"

"Yes. I wholeheartedly do," I replied with far too much eagerness.

"Kayog Voln, do you bear witness that this human female, Kaida Daigo, and this Derakeen male, Cedros Qhelian, freely committed to be legally married to each other in accordance with human and galactic laws?"

"I do," Kayog said.

"By the power vested in me by the Clerical College of Earth and the United Planets Organization, I declare you husband and wife. Cedros Qhelian, you may kiss the bride," Priestess Biondi said.

I knew what a kiss was. I also knew what kind of mostly chaste kisses humans exchanged at the end of their wedding vows. Over the past few days, while waiting for my Ejaya to finally come to me, I had rehearsed a million times how I would impress her with the gentle and respectful way I would kiss her. But the moment she stepped closer to me and lifted her face towards mine, the burning hunger her mere presence ignited in me returned with a vengeance. The second our lips touched, every rational thought fled my mind.

I couldn't recall picking her up, but the sudden feel of her supple body in my arms drove me insane. I vaguely felt Kaida's gasp against my mouth as I pressed her to my chest. Her lips were soft, warm beneath mine, and awakened an odd flame in the pit of my stomach. But a greater need superseded my curiosity about this unexpected physiological response to my Ejaya.

Kaida stiffened in my arms, but neither fought me nor

attempted to free herself from my embrace. I broke the kiss, rubbed my face all over hers and along the length of her slender neck. Soft... so insanely soft! I deeply inhaled her scent, the divine aroma making my head spin. My heating chamber warmed, and a growling purr surged from my throat as my nezarone hormones began to flow through me. I felt drunk, the throbbing ache in my scales and nerve endings giving way to a blissful tingle.

"My Ejaya..." I whispered in an almost pained voice.

I needed to release her before I scared her away, but I couldn't just yet. One minute... just one more minute, and I would. To my shock, Kaida wrapped one arm around my neck and gently caressed my hair with her free hand. A wave of peace washed over me as I tightened my embrace around her.

"It's okay. You're going to be okay," Kaida said in a soothing voice. "I'm here, now."

"My Kaida..."

I spoke the words in the crook of her neck and pressed a grateful kiss against her palpitating artery as a thank you. Summoning all of my willpower, I forced myself to release her. I still felt dizzy, drunk from this far too brief taste of the divine. Instead of immediately moving away from me, Kaida took a single step back and gave me a gentle smile. The worry I felt instantly vanished, and I smiled back. Yes, my little human truly had the heart of an Ejaya, even if she likely didn't realize it.

My scales darkened with embarrassment at the sight of the other people present staring at the spectacle I'd just made of myself. Councilor Gavyr seemed excessively bored and annoyed. Priestess Biondi looked mightily uncomfortable, keeping her eyes averted. But Kayog had tilted his head to the side while giving Kaida and me an assessing look. Although I couldn't read his expression, I got a strong and distinct impression that whatever his empathic abilities had perceived from us pleased him.

Isobel Biondi cleared her throat and took a couple of hesitant steps towards Kaida and me, while extending some kind of tablet. "If you would both be so kind as to press your thumbs in your respective signature box, we can complete the final formalities and give you… privacy."

Kaida's cheeks reddened, and my eyes widened in sudden understanding. Of course, the human priestess would have interpreted my behavior as an uncontrolled libido. I couldn't decide if that thought amused me or made me feel even more mortified. My Ejaya pressed her thumb in the appropriate box, and I did the same.

"Well, that concludes it," Kayog said while tapping something on the interface of his armband, putting us all out of our collective misery. "We will now leave you both to get better acquainted. As a reminder, a Derakeen wedding ritual isn't required."

"Be that as it may, I'm sure a binding will take place between them before the six months are up," Councilor Gavyr interjected in a tone that spelled trouble.

"Time will tell," Kayog replied in a non-committal fashion.

He turned to look at the portal with an expectant expression. To our shock, a human male came through carrying a medium-sized crate that he placed on my Ejaya's hover cart.

"Thank you, Culvert," Kayog said in a friendly fashion to the man, who nodded in response before leaving through the portal. "My dear Kaida, this is your dowry. I hope you will find these few items helpful in making your new life here more enjoyable. Do not hesitate to reach out to me if you need anything."

"Thank you, Master Voln, for everything. Please give my best regards to Linsea," Kaida replied.

The face of the Temern melted in a tender expression I instantly guessed was in response to the name Linsea. His mate?

"I most certainly will. I wish you the best as well, Cedros," Kayog continued.

"Thank you, Kayog."

After exchanging farewells with Councilor Gavyr, the Temern and the human priestess left through the portal. At the same time I dispelled it, Gavyr took flight, leaving me alone at last with my Ejaya.

My gaze immediately locked on her, my body still aching for sustained contact with her. Kaida shifted uneasily on her feet and wrapped her arms around her waist while eyeing me warily.

"You look like you want to eat me," she said with a nervous laugh. "You guys don't eat people, I hope?"

I swallowed hard and shook my head at her obvious attempt to defuse the tension with humor. "Apologies if my stare makes you uncomfortable. I just *really* want to hold you."

Her eyes widened slightly. "But you just did."

I snorted. "I need more… A *lot* more. The aqrats inflicted many, many wounds on me during that battle, and I'd already been on the verge of falling to jokraz before it. I have a large amount of toxins left to eliminate."

"Oh, okay. Hmm… Can we get my stuff inside first, and then you can hug me again?" Kaida asked.

I didn't know how to read her response. Her voice didn't sound annoyed or resigned, but it also lacked any type of enthusiasm.

"Of course," I replied.

To my relief, she gestured in a way that set the hovering platform in motion. While we had similar technology, I had no clue how hers worked. In truth, we hardly ever used ours since most of us simply moved objects with our telekinetic abilities.

I stole glances at Kaida as we approached the massive glass doors that led into my lair.

"How much do you hate being my Ejaya?" I blurted out, immediately kicking myself for it.

Kaida's jaw dropped, and her steps faltered as a strange

expression laced with guilt flitted over her features. "Wow, you're blunt."

"A Shadow Lord and his Ejaya openly discuss any topic. But I can try to adjust, if it isn't the way of humans," I replied.

"No, it's fine. I like honest discussions. I guess you took me by surprise," she said as the doors parted before us onto the large open floor plan kitchen and living area. She stopped to face me. "And no, I don't 'hate' being your Ejaya. I love the idea that my mere presence can heal someone and bring peace to them. But I've just been uprooted from my life. I'm on a foreign planet, with a complete stranger, who needs frequent, very close contact with me. It's… a little overwhelming."

A sense of guilt washed over me. "I understand. I *am* sorry for the inconvenience but *not* for finding you."

That same odd expression crossed her features. Her gaze then roamed over me before locking back up with mine.

"Are you in pain? You are trembling," Kaida asked in a soft, slightly worried voice.

"Yes. I'm going back into withdrawal."

"Withdrawal?!" she exclaimed.

"I've already used up the nezarone hormone that holding you earlier had produced. I need much more to fight the infection," I explained.

I felt twitchy. Speaking of my current state only exacerbated my discomfort. The sooner I got Kaida settled, the sooner I could hold her again.

"This is the kitchen," I said, pointing at it. "I rarely use it but had it adapted to your needs. I will show you how to operate it later. And over there—"

"Cedros, stop," Kaida said, startling me. I gave her an inquisitive look. "You can give me the tour later. There's no reason for you to remain in pain, if simply holding me can relieve you."

My hearts leapt, and I almost jumped on her offer before

reining myself in. "It… it may take a while. I mean, I will have to hold you for an extended period, not just a couple of minutes."

"I see…," she said, sounding slightly deflated. Kaida took in a deep breath and straightened her shoulders. "Well, that's what I'm here for. Let's get you feeling better. Where do you want to do this?"

My hearts melted with affection and gratitude for the female. "This way, my Ejaya," I said, gesturing towards my nest.

Kaida followed me quietly, her eyes flicking this way and that as she took in the interior of my lair. To my delight, she seemed to appreciate what she saw. But that would have to wait until later. My entire body was vibrating with anticipation.

I opened the large, intricately ornate wooden doors to my nesting chamber, and gestured for Kaida to come in.

"Oh, wow!" she exclaimed, looking awed as she took in the place. "This is stunning!"

My chest swelled with pride at her reaction. Floor-to-ceiling reflective windows surrounded the circular room. Looking outside, it felt as if we were hanging in the air, which wasn't entirely false. Overhead, a glass dome gave us an unimpeded view of Dramnac's shimmering opalescent sky. It could actually open, allowing me to fly directly into or out of my nest. The circular, recessed nest in the center of the room ate up more than half the space.

"I have built a space on this wall for you to put your coverings in," I explained, pointing at it. "I have also added this chair here, as I understand humans always have one in their nesting chambers."

"That's very considerate of you," Kaida said, looking a little nervous.

"This is where we lay," I added, fighting not to lose the battle against my growing need to hold her.

"Okay," she said. Taking another deep breath, she walked

towards the chair, removed her feet coverings, and slipped them under it, then looked at the nest. "Should I just go in?"

I almost said yes, before frowning at her body coverings. I needed far more direct contact than this. All covered in black, the top exposed part of her chest and neck in a V-shape, but the fabric hid everything else, all the way to her wrists. Similarly, her lower coverings of the same color hung a little loosely around each of her legs, down to her ankles.

Catching my disapproving stare, Kaida grimaced, and her shoulders slouched.

"Right, that part," she mumbled.

To my pleasant surprise, she immediately proceeded to remove her upper coverings, only to reveal a smaller under covering which hid the two mounds of her chest. To my dismay, removing her lower covering also exposed a shorter bottom covering. Both hugged her body like a second skin.

By the look I gave her, Kaida immediately understood my expectation that she would remove those as well. She frowned and took on a defiant expression.

"My undies aren't going anywhere. This is as far as I'll consent to undress to accommodate your need for greater contact," Kaida said in a firm voice.

Despite my burning urge to argue, I held my tongue and gave her a sharp nod. This was already a significant improvement in comparison. I could finally see what my Ejaya truly looked like. Gods, she seemed so delicate and fragile. Her pale skin, almost translucent in places, looked like it would easily tear if handled even with the tiniest roughness. She possessed no claws, only softly rounded nails, and no other visible natural defenses. Even her teeth were blunt. Kaida looked like a piece of art or collectible one kept safely inside their lair, too helpless to fend for herself.

And yet, she's a decorated Enforcer of the UPO.

I liked the softness of her long, dark brown hair, the same

color as her eyes. They were strange eyes, a round circle of color with a centered round pupil instead of a vertical slit like ours. The also roundish, flappy appendages that served as ears for humans really looked bizarre. And yet, they were cute in their own way. For all that, Kaida had a strange but pretty nose and very nice lips that would make many a Derakeen female envious. Her straight legs and odd feet would take a bit longer to get used to. But in the end, her unsettling appearance was irrelevant. I didn't need her as a mate, but as my Ejaya. And right now, I was going to revel in the silky contact of her fragile human skin against me.

I extended a hand towards her. Kaida licked her lips nervously then willingly came to me. I pulled her into my embrace, and a blissful growl escaped me as searing heat enflamed my scales and nerve endings everywhere her naked skin came into contact with me.

"My Kaida…" I whispered as I picked her up and buried my face in her neck.

She yelped and hung on to me when I flapped my wings to carry us right over the nest and settle us down in its center. Walking on the thick and plush cushion could be a little awkward alone. With the two of us, it would be a disaster.

Without releasing my embrace, I laid down, wrapping myself all around her soft body, unable to stop the endless rumbling moans pouring out of me. Kaida wiggled, once, twice, then slightly pushed back, which had my arms instinctively tightening around her.

"You're squishing me," she complained, pushing back harder.

"Oh, I'm sorry," I said, quickly loosening my hold.

"It's okay, but you're very strong," Kaida replied in a concil-iatory tone. "You can hug all you want, but be careful how tightly you hold, and try not to smother me. I need to breathe, too."

Although embarrassed how thoughtless my greed had made me, the small chuckle in her voice as she spoke those words softened the very valid underlying reproach.

"Feel free to poke me here or to bite my neck if I hurt or squish you again," I said in the same playful tone, pointing at a sensitive spot along my side.

"I'm sure it won't come down to me having to maim you," Kaida replied, while settling into a more comfortable position against me.

I wrapped myself around her again, making sure she was all right. Gods, her skin was so soft! I'd known holding my Ejaya would be wonderful, but nothing prepared me for this sensory overload.

"My Ejaya..."

"It... it's helping you? Your hormones are flowing again?"

Her voice was almost timid when she asked.

"Yes. It is wonderful. You smell like the freshest of morning breezes. Your skin against mine feels like the caress of the first rays of light when I emerge from the cold darkness of the void. Holding you is like embracing the divine," I said, my voice slurring on the last words.

"Wow... That's a very nice thing to say to a woman."

Her voice was hushed, almost a whisper like my own had been. I attempted to smile, but I couldn't swear she would have seen it. My head was spinning, and a growing grogginess was overtaking me as nezarone increasingly flooded my system. I didn't fight it and let my consciousness be swept away.

CHAPTER 4
KAIDA

Under different circumstances, I'd be offended to find myself in bed—in my undies at that—with a dude who fell asleep less than two minutes after we got in. It still was awkward as hell to be in such a state of undress with a strange male obsessed with rubbing all over me. And yet, I wasn't minding it as much as I dreaded.

Sure, I wasn't allergic to cuddling with a fine, muscular specimen of manhood, alien though he was. That he had the sexiest lips in the galaxy, rather pleasant features—even though his dragon eyes slightly freaked me out—and chiseled abs just the way I liked them didn't hurt, either. At first, I'd worried about his scales and the spikes on his arms. I figured I'd get scraped to hell and back with all the hugging. Yet, despite their hardness, they remained quite pliable to the touch.

Cedros smelled good, like untamed wilderness. When his throat glowed, it diffused the most pleasant heat that warmed me to the bones, making my muscles deeply relax. But above all, Cedros seemed sweet. He had an aura of boyish innocence about him. From what little I'd been able to find out about his species,

I suspected he interacted little with others, which could explain his awkwardness.

I didn't doubt whatever toxins those monsters in the lab had infected Cedros with were hurting him. In my line of work, I'd too often seen the reaction of people suffering from substance abuse finally getting their fix after a brutal withdrawal. Cedros had behaved the same the minute he held me. It still boggled my mind that contact with me and my scent were all he needed. While the compassionate side of me certainly loved bringing him this peace, I couldn't deny it also stroked my ego.

But right now, I needed to cast compassion aside and attend to my own needs.

I shifted to look at Cedros and immediately regretted it. I couldn't tell how long he'd been asleep, at least for a couple of hours. During that time, I'd dozed off once or twice. But this lengthy immobility had made my limbs go numb. They awakened in the most unpleasant rush of pins and needles in my feet and hands. Although annoying, that wouldn't have been so bad. But the shift had also put undue pressure on my over-inflated bladder.

I'd been trying to ignore it for a while, but I'd reached my breaking point. Wetting Cedros's ginormous bed on the first day didn't feature on my to do list, today or ever… I began shaking Cedros to wake him up, already picturing the embarrassing penguin walk I'd do to reach the hygiene room to avoid making a mess.

Right on cue, Cedros tightened his hold around me and snuggled further, adding pressure to my already very pissed bladder —pun intended. I squealed and squeezed my legs together, barely repressing the urge to shake him again. If he tightened any further, my bladder would flip us both the bird and show us who's boss.

Feeling slightly guilty, I tapped the 'sensitive' spot he'd shown me earlier, which matched the general area of a human's kidneys. Nothing. I poked it again a bit more forcefully, still nothing.

Sorry buddy, but I'm not peeing myself to spare you a bit of discomfort.

This time, I balled my hand and gave him a solid jab—not the bruising type, but strong enough he'd feel it.

And feel it, he did!

His eyes jerked open, and his embrace around me loosened. His dilated pupils narrowed back down to a slit in his fiery orange eyes as he stared at me in shock.

"Sorry for hurting you," I said sheepishly, "but I *really* have to pee."

"Pee?" he repeated.

Although confused by the term, he was surprisingly alert for someone who had just been abruptly awakened by a punch in the kidney.

"I need to relieve my bladder," I explained.

"Relieve your…? Oh! You have to urinate! Yes, I've read of human physiological needs."

Without missing a beat, Cedros got up, lifting me at the same time, and flapped his wings, flying the short distance to the wide set of doors on the left side of the bedroom's entrance. To my surprise, the doors parted long before we were close enough for any kind of motion detector to kick into action.

Once again, the view from the room took my breath away. Like in the bedroom, giant reflective windows covered most of the walls, giving us a stunning view of the outside world. As there was no visible land in this section of the house, it felt as if we were floating in the clouds.

The room possessed a humongous shower area in a slightly recessed circle taking most of the space. On the left side, in the only section of proper wall instead of windows, a large toilet sat close to a floating sink. It didn't have a backrest or water tank, but had two square pillars on each side. The design accounted for sufficient space behind it to accommodate a Derakeen's tail. However, the hole looked wide enough that I could probably fall into it if I didn't take care. Freakier still, there wasn't any water inside it, but a dark void that had me instantly wondering if it wouldn't try to suck me in like a wormhole.

But such wandering thoughts had to take a backseat. As soon as Cedros put me back on my feet, I squeezed my legs shut as the urgent need to pee came back with a vengeance. It was like my bladder *knew* that liberation was imminent, and it just couldn't wait anymore.

"Thanks," I said to Cedros, my voice strained from the effort.

He beamed at me, his hand still resting on the small of my back as he looked at me expectantly. I stared, wondering what he was waiting for, and he just stared right back at me. I blinked, thinking to myself he couldn't possibly expect me to pee in front of him. He frowned, looking just as confused.

"You just have to lower your bottom undies and sit to relieve yourself. I will hold you so you don't fall in," he finally explained, as if he was addressing a clueless child.

"I know how to use a toilet," I said, dismayed. "But I need you to leave now. I'm not peeing in front of you."

"Why not?" he asked, looking genuinely confused.

"Because it's not done. This is something we do in private!"

"But it's a natural function that—"

"CEDROS! I *really* need to pee right now, and you're keeping me from relieving myself. Please, JUST GO!"

If my bladder wasn't torturing me right now, I'd feel bad about the hurt look on his face, which he quickly hid before clearing his throat.

"Very well. Please, be careful not to fall in. The hole is wide. You will find silk paper in the casing next to the waste seat. Just press your hand on top," Cedros said in a chastised voice, pointing at the pillar left of the toilet.

Without waiting for my response, he turned around and left, his shoulders and tail stiff.

Guilt gnawed at my insides. He was just trying to take care of me. I'd apologize and explain later after I'd taken care of my little problem.

But now that the door had closed, my bladder became an even greater bitch. Each time I tried to spread my legs to lower my boxer shorts, it threatened to let go right there and then. Grinding my teeth, I dealt with a few false starts before deciding on a course of action. Positioning myself right above the toilet, I slid the waist of my boxers as low on my hips as possible without spreading my legs, then I swiftly yanked them down while sitting on the toilet.

Niagara Falls instantly shot out of me. I yelped while trying to hold on to the right pillar to keep from falling in. I closed my eyes, and a blissful moan escaped me at the utter relief. Who would have thought peeing could be such an orgasmic experience?

It went on… and on… and on. The absence of the sound of my urine hitting water inside the bowl disturbed the heck out of me. Naturally, my stupid mind—with my twelve-year-old humor —started imagining where all of this was going. A very vivid image of a poor group of Derakeens traipsing through the void, suddenly getting drenched by an unexpected golden shower, popped into my mind. I snickered at the same time I flinched at that visual. Obviously, the Derakeens would have a smarter system than that. I'd have to ask Cedros how it all worked.

As I was finally finishing relieving myself, I tapped the top of the stone pillar on my left. A lid folded open, revealing a thick stack of what at first glance looked like tissue paper. I picked one up, and my lips immediately parted in shock. The damn thing was so soft and silky, I actually wondered if Cedros had literally meant that this 'paper' was made out of silk. It felt like a crime to use this to wipe myself with, but it indeed appeared to be tissue paper.

I grabbed a couple to take care of business but never got around to it. Just as I was about to do so, a gushing sound resonated behind me. Half a second later, I felt as if I'd just been kicked in the ass. A powerful blast of water slammed into me, propelling me forward. I shouted in shock and fear before landing flat on my stomach a meter away.

"Kaida!"

Cedros's muffled voice, filled with concern, reached me through the closed door right before it slid open. He rushed in, his jaw dropping at the sight of me. I lay sprawled on the floor, belly down, my boxers wrapped around my ankles, and my bare ass, drenched in water, staring at him. Mortified, I glanced at him over my shoulder. Of all the undignified positions after making such a fuss about not stripping in front of him! I scrambled to get back on my feet and got even more tangled in my boxers. I didn't even have a long t-shirt on to pull down and cover my modesty.

"My Kaida! What happened?" Cedros exclaimed, coming to my rescue.

He got me up on my feet with an ease that screamed of his tremendous strength. Under different circumstances, his confused and dismayed expression would have been hilarious as his gaze flicked between the toilet and my messy self.

I slammed my hand, still clutching the silk paper, in front of my cooch. With Cedros standing mostly in front of me, my naked butt could keep mooning the windows. To think I'd managed not to pee myself only to still end up dripping between my thighs and down my legs.

"I don't know. The toilet attacked me with a blast of water," I said, outrage seeping into my voice at the toilet's betrayal.

"That was just the cleansing water!" Cedros exclaimed,

stunned. "Humans have them. You call them beet... hmmm debee..."

"You mean a bidet?"

"Yes!"

"That's no freaking bidet! It might as well have been a fire-hose at full power! I'm shocked it didn't send me flying through the windows!"

By the amused look Cedros gave me, he realized I was exaggerating a bit... just barely.

"I will adjust it to significantly lessen the strength of the water from now on," Cedros said in a conciliatory tone. He cast a glance towards my groin, which had me closing my legs even more tightly and placing my second hand in front of my nether region. "I'm guessing you want privacy again?"

"Yes, please," I replied instantly.

I didn't need to read minds to understand he found me baffling. Thankfully, he didn't argue and simply walked out of the room. I cleaned myself the best I could and washed my hands in the sink. Thankfully, my boxers weren't drenched, only damp in a few spots. When I returned to the bedroom, relief flooded through me not only to find Cedros gone, but that he'd brought my belongings into the room.

Swiftly rummaging through them, I got myself a fresh pair of undies. I glanced at the clothes I had left on the chair earlier and seriously considered putting them back on. Finally, I decided against it. Cedros had not awakened from his healing sleep by choice. I suspected there would be a lot more cuddling happening soon.

While I hated that I'd been somewhat coerced into this role, I genuinely wanted to help Cedros and fully intended to hold up my end of the deal. The greater the contact I gave him now, the sooner we could get to a semblance of normality where he wouldn't constantly need to be wrapped around me.

Just as I opened the bedroom door, the most delicious aroma

of cooked meat greeted me. My stomach instantly rumbled in approval. I walked down the very large hallway and past a few doors before reaching the living and kitchen area. It struck me then that the corridor's impressive width and the ceiling's insane height probably served to accommodate the massive size of Cedros in his dragon form.

I loved the slightly rough texture of the pale stone that shaped the walls. I couldn't fathom how they had gotten such huge slabs so perfectly cut and lined up seamlessly. But then, that choice of material made perfect sense. Imagine a Derakeen losing his cool and breathing fire inside a house made of traditional materials with a greater risk of being flammable...

As I reached the kitchen and living area, I once more marveled at the stunning beauty of Cedros's house. It truly felt like living in a castle in the sky—which, technically, wasn't false. The massive windows all around made the space wonderfully luminous and gave the impression it was even bigger than in reality.

However, Cedros busying himself in the kitchen drew my attention. For all his alienness, he was truly a stunning male. At least seven feet tall, with the right level of bulging muscles everywhere, without falling into overly bulky, he had the type of imposing stature I always found sexy in a male. His reptilian legs and feet, not to mention his tail, didn't bother me. I'd lived and worked alongside enough aliens to appreciate the beauty in non-human aesthetics. And that purplish-blue hair of his made me want to sink my fingers into it.

My 'husband' was undoubtedly attractive.

On some sort of grill, Cedros had big chunks of meat sizzling, although there didn't seem to be any flame beneath them. He answered that question moments later when his chest swelled, as if he was taking a deep breath, then a steady stream of fire shot out of his mouth. As the flames licked the meat, he used a long, BBQ fork type of utensil to turn the pieces so they could cook on all sides.

I stared in both fascination and disbelief as some flames grazed over his hand. But he didn't flinch or otherwise react. Where my delicate human skin would already be blistering from the heat, his appeared utterly unaffected. My gasp drew his attention to me.

Cedros immediately stopped breathing fire at the meat to first beam at me, then take on an almost timid expression. He shifted on his feet and cast a nervous glance at the meat.

"I am preparing food for you," he said, sounding sheepish. "I read that humans should eat once every four hours or so. The cooking surface isn't fully operational yet, so I improvised."

"That's very nice of you. It smells amazing," I said, approaching.

His beaming smile returned. He placed one of the chunky pieces of meat on a clean dish on the island the grill was embedded into and gave me a set of 'utensils' comprising a two-prong fork and a much-too-big, sharp knife that his people would probably deem average-sized.

"Taste and let me know what you think," Cedros said with enthusiasm. "I have marinated the meat overnight with the spices I believe match the most what humans use in their cooking. It's *pranar* meat, a favorite among my people. And I have vegetables cut up for you, too."

Cedros clamped down after this flurry of words, probably more than I'd ever heard him say in one go since my arrival. This apparent shyness from this mountain of muscles was quite endearing.

I ogled the meat, my watering mouth silencing the little voice at the back of my mind, warning me this might taste foul. I picked up the massive utensils. To my delight, the knife cut through the meat like butter. It was nicely pink inside, the exact shade of medium I liked. I brought a tiny piece to my lips and braced for it.

My eyes nearly popped out of my head, and a rapturous moan rolled out of my throat at the wondrous explosion of flavor on my taste buds. The meat was tender and juicy, spiced to perfection. I could have sworn I was eating a prime rib steak. Cedros grinned from ear to ear, exposing an impressive pair of fangs I hadn't really noticed before.

He piled a bunch more meat on my plate as well as a mix of vegetables, some steamed, others raw in a salad. I followed him as he placed my dish on the circular dining table with chairs that didn't quite seem to know if they wanted to be normal chairs or bar stools by their odd heights and lack of backrest.

Nonetheless, I dug in, my hollow stomach welcoming the delicious sustenance. The flavors were messing a bit with my mind as the greens that resembled lettuce tasted like carrots, the reddish things that vaguely looked like tomatoes tasted like cucumber, and the purple root-like raw vegetable actually tasted like cherry tomatoes.

After a few bites in, I realized Cedros was just sitting next to me, staring at me with a silly grin. I immediately felt self-conscious.

"You're not eating?"

He shook his head. "We eat our meat raw, often a live catch that we hunt in our battle form. Although, when in a hurry—or not in the mood to hunt—we will sometimes go buy live chattels at the market."

"Oh… So you never have social dinners sitting around the table?" I asked, taken aback.

"Not in the way humans do. Our battle form allows us to consume larger animals, which spares us from having to eat for days, maybe even up to a few weeks, unless we exert ourselves a lot during that time. But we share small bites in social settings."

"Small bites like what?" I asked, fascinated, while taking another bite of my meal.

"Any foods and drinks that ferment fast," Cedros said matter-of-factly. "We can usually eat them in a single bite. We serve trays of them, and people eat the ones they like."

"You guys serve each other gas-inducing amuse-bouche during social events?" I said, my disbelieving tone more a statement than a question.

Cedros smiled. It softened him in the most amazing fashion. "We do not get 'gas' that way," he said in an amused tone. "We produce hydrogen as a byproduct of most of the things we eat. It gets stored in our primary hydrogen storage chamber at the back of our stomach."

He rubbed his hand over his neck, and it glowed, diffusing some heat.

"Some of it gets transferred to the heating chamber along our upper chest and throat. It is a smaller hydrogen chamber. We can preheat the hydrogen there before igniting it to spit fire, or simply to diffuse heat. It is practical to warm us up, or a youngling. And it is both soothing and a display of affection to warm others who we embrace with it."

"That is wicked cool," I said, genuinely impressed, after swallowing my mouthful. "But how do you ignite the hydrogen?"

He grinned, then pulled his tongue out at me. Beyond its impressive length that awakened far too inappropriate thoughts in my mind, its raspy appearance reminded me of a feline's tongue. To my surprise, he scraped it against his sharp upper teeth, and a tiny spark flickered.

"Oh, my God! It's like a flint!"

He nodded. "As we control the amount of hydrogen we release, we can control the size and intensity of the flame. So when our chambers grow too full, we might breathe out tiny flames to burn some of it."

I tilted my head to the side and glanced at one of his arms on the table. "Speaking of burning, your own flame licked your arm earlier while you were cooking the meat for me. And yet, you seem unscathed. Are you immune to fire?"

A glimmer of approval crossed his fiery eyes. "Good observation. No, we are not fully immune to fire. We just have a high tolerance and resistance to it. This little flame, for a few seconds, will not bother me at all. Considering how often we accidentally breathe fire, it could be problematic, like because of a powerful sneeze. We'd incinerate people nearby. But if we were to be exposed for a sustained period to our most concentrated fire, we would reach the point where damage would occur, and we would burn."

While fascinated by all of this, my mind had remained stuck on the fact that they could accidentally breathe fire because of a powerful sneeze. Judging by Cedros's sudden air of confusion, my face was undoubtedly showing how freaked out I now felt.

After a beat, his face lit up with understanding, and he burst out laughing. "Do not fret, my Kaida. I will not breathe fire on you. This was just an exaggerated example. I could almost count on one hand how many occurrences of people accidentally breathing fire on another have occurred in the past century. We are in control of ourselves. Usually, 'uncontrolled' fire occurs in moments of extreme emotion, like someone having an orgasm. And even then, they always aim away from their mate."

My face heated, and I shifted in my seat. I grunted an acknowledgement before shoving a big spoonful into my mouth to hide my embarrassment. I wasn't prudish, but I had a very vivid imagination. His words had immediately sparked the image of what Cedros would look like as he climaxed, head thrown back, face dissolved in an air of ecstasy, with a powerful stream of flames shooting out of his mouth. Naturally, all this with me writhing beneath him.

Fuck my life… I didn't need that visual. Especially not since

I'd be spending a lot of the foreseeable future with his hot, naked body wrapped around my barely dressed one. Still, that visual had something thrilling and exciting. You didn't become an Enforcer for the UPO without being an adrenaline junkie.

"Well, you're an excellent cook," I said, shifting to a safer topic. "How did you learn if you don't cook your food?"

Cedros puffed out his chest proudly. "While waiting for your arrival, I've watched videos and read guides on caring for the needs of a human. I had hoped it would be adequate for you."

"Aww, you're really sweet. But you don't have to do that," I said, sincerely touched. "Once your cooking plate is functional, I'll be able to make my own meals. I don't expect you to take care of me."

Cedros frowned as if I'd said something offensive. "It is my duty *and* my honor. A Shadow Lord caters to the needs of his Ejaya, just like she takes care of him. We are meant to be each other's best friend, trusted confidant, and devoted care-giver. Beyond my role as a Shadow Lord, my main purpose is to see to your welfare and your happiness. I've waited my whole life to finally have that privilege. I intend to enjoy it fully!"

I gaped at him, robbed of words. How did you respond to that? What possible countering argument could you give someone to 'deprive' them of the pleasure of what they considered a privilege and an honor?

"I see…" I said, for lack of a better response.

Having nearly emptied my plate and feeling too full to eat another bite, I put down my utensils. However, I resisted the urge to squirm under Cedros's gaze. He continued to stare intensely at me for a few seconds, his wheels visibly turning.

"For the first time in my life, I have felt peace because of you. Every moment spent by your side, and even more so holding you in my arms, the fog I hadn't even realized had been choking my mind has been lifted. It's the same with the physical pain that had become an almost constant companion, so much I barely even noticed it anymore."

My throat tightened as he reached for my left hand and gently squeezed it. His eyes immediately closed, an almost pained expression—that I actually knew to be of pleasure—descending over his alien features.

"Nothing and no one in this entire universe will ever make me feel this divine bliss the way simply touching your hand does for me right now," Cedros whispered before slowly opening his eyes to look at me. "There can never be another Ejaya for me. You are my one and only. I will do everything in my power to ensure you are happy and never want to leave me."

I covered his hand holding mine with my free one and turned to face him, a very serious expression on my face. "I will not abandon you, Cedros. Whatever the future holds for us, I am your Ejaya, and I take it seriously. We will work something out so that we can both be happy. I promise."

Apparently mollified by what he seemed to take as me conceding, Cedros relaxed, his frown once more giving way to a smile. He pushed back his stool and drew me to him. I went willingly as he sat me sideways on his lap and wrapped his arms around me. I didn't want to admit it, but I rather liked the way he gently rubbed his face on my nape while inhaling my scent. There was nothing sexual in the gesture, but it still felt rather amazing knowing I had such a powerful effect on someone, to be so desperately wanted.

"You feel so good," he whispered, as if for himself.

I snuggled against him and gently caressed his arm around me. "What does it feel like? That toxin, I mean."

"When freshly bitten, it feels like acid coursing through our veins. It burns like it's eating us from the inside out while it spreads. It becomes both an excruciating physical and mental pain. On the one hand, the poison is wrecking our bodies, and on the other, our mind feels like it's on the verge of fracturing. And then, our bodies all but shut down. The toxin numbs part of our organs, slowing them almost to a halt."

"That sounds horrible. But you're eventually able to fight it back, right?" I asked, my heart filling with compassion for him.

"Eventually, yes. Before you, I would be curled up in a semi-comatose state of agony for weeks, the longest bout lasting one-hundred-and-eight days."

"Oh, my God! That's terrible."

He nodded before nuzzling my nape again, his arms tightening around me in a possessive fashion. "This time would have been the same, maybe even worse. But you saved me. After they stunned me in the factory, they kept you and me together in the same medical pod. I'm afraid I fractured two of your ribs by falling on top of you," he added, in a sheepish tone.

I jerked my head up and looked at him. "I had broken ribs?"

He nodded once more. "Yes, and a concussion. Your healers didn't tell you?"

"No! I did not know what the heck happened during the first twenty-four hours except that they were mending me, and that I had made a full recovery!" I said, feeling somewhat outraged and betrayed.

"I do not know why they didn't tell you. But I held you while the pod mended you, which went a long way healing me of the worst of the toxin."

"I'm at least happy that, even unconscious, I could do that for you," I said in all sincerity, although still miffed about the secrecy.

However, I strongly suspected tremendous pressure from the Derakeen Council had played a role in the Enforcer's leadership going that route. I didn't begrudge what healing I'd been able to give Cedros, even unaware. But I hated to have been used this way without my knowledge. Had they asked me, I would have consented. They didn't have to put me in an induced coma to bypass asking me and the risk that I might refuse.

"You did. An Ejaya's scent and touch trigger a physiological response that kicks our organs back into overdrive. It causes the nezarone hormone to flood our bodies, and then it's like touching the divine. Normally, after a day of traipsing in the void, or getting a slight scratch from an aqrat, we only need contact for a few minutes, less than an hour in the worst cases. But I have a lifetime of catching up to do. So, I'm sorry that I will continue to bother you excessively in the next couple of days. But I promise it will diminish with time… Well, unless you don't mind."

I gave him an inquisitive look.

"Holding one's Ejaya feels good, sick or not. Shadow Lords cuddle often with them," he added, giving me the most adorable boyish expression.

I chuckled. "I'm sure we'll work that out, too, so you get your cuddling fix."

He grinned and gave me another affectionate squeeze.

"I'm here to help you," I reminded him, sobering. "But I'm glad you found your tongue again. You spoke little earlier."

"My brain was foggy from the toxin," he said apologetically. "Be aware that, like most Shadow Lords, I am socially awkward. We're mostly loners until we meet our Ejaya. Please be patient with me and don't be shy to call me out if I am acting weird or inappropriate. I want to learn, and I want to please you."

My chest warmed further for my dragon. While I loved a big and strong man, I also had a thing for a shy nerd or geek. Cedros was turning out to be a delightful mix of both. And oddly enough, my protective instincts were also kicking in for him.

"Don't worry about it. You're fine. I bet you will find me even weirder than I could ever find you to be," I said in a gentle tone. "We'll adjust together."

He beamed at me and kissed my forehead.

"Good! You must let me know if you have any other needs I haven't addressed or adaptations you require me to do to our lair. I have seen the liftable seats that humans put on waste seats. I will have one added in our hygiene room so that you no longer risk falling in since you want privacy. Otherwise, I will constantly worry when you're here alone."

My cheeks burned at the memory of the spectacle I made of myself. However, I welcomed the thought of a proper toilet seat scaled to my human behind instead of the gaping hole that looked like it wanted to swallow me.

"Sounds like a grand plan. As long as you lift it before you pee…" I added with a semi-false warning in my voice.

Cedros blinked and gave me a confused look.

I chuckled. "Never mind. Let's clean this up, and then you can give me that tour of the house."

"Yes, my Ejaya."

CHAPTER 5
CEDROS

My Ejaya enjoyed my meal! A million other recipes I had read about were already flashing through my mind as the silliest pride filled me. I would charm my Kaida with great food—among other things. After all, her species had a saying about winning a human male's heart through his stomach. Surely it applied to females as well?

As I cleaned the table and counter, in which Kaida insisted on helping, I realized how easy it was speaking with her. Sure, she confused me at times, but my tongue didn't get tied like it did with others.

"I had a larger cooling unit installed here so that you can have room for all the foods humans eat," I said, pointing at it by the counter. "We normally only have drinks, mostly fermented, in there. As you can see, I have filled it with fruits and vegetables for you, as well as some more cuts of meat, some of which are already marinating."

"Thank you. That was very thoughtful of you," she said gratefully.

Pleased by her approval, I gave her a tour of the living area, with the giant screen and my vast library of plays, which her people called movies.

"I usually lie down on this couch to watch. You can tilt the backrest all the way down, although I normally keep it at seventy degrees," I explained, suddenly feeling self-conscious when Kaida began browsing my library.

Her curious expression shifted to surprise, then an odd mix of disbelief and amusement as she read through the titles.

"Claiming Drusha, For the Love of Arlea, Ilze's Golden Scales, An Ejaya Like No Other..." She turned to give me the strangest sideways glance. "Most of these titles sound like romantic movies."

I shifted on my feet, feeling embarrassed for a reason I couldn't explain, and scratched the scales on the side of my neck. "I... uh... Yes. They have a strong focus on romance and love. It is fascinating to me to see how regular people interact with each other. The first courtships between juveniles to the more elaborate ones of adults... The dynamic of a normal family, from the younglings playing together to their relationship with their parents... The social events they take part in, whether purely for entertainment or as part of the courtship... It is fascinating, but not something I will ever experience."

"So you experience it through the movies," she said in a soft voice.

I nodded.

"I like family plays the most. I love seeing how normal younglings are raised by their parents," I said wistfully.

"*You* are normal," Kaida said with a frown. "You just have extra abilities."

I smiled, both touched and amused by her reaction. "I didn't mean to sound as if I believed myself less," I said teasingly. "I've been told my whole life that I am actually greater than the common Derakeen. I do not have low self-esteem because of what I am."

"Good! Nor should you," she said firmly in a way that made me chuckle.

"Still, it would have been nice to see my lair filled with life, like in those plays," I said matter-of-factly.

Kaida tilted her head to the side. "You want a big family with many children?"

"I did."

"Did?" she repeated, frowning again.

"I cannot have one unless you fall in love with me," I said with a shrug. "Most Shadow Lords remain single. But for those of us who take a mate, it is always their Ejaya."

"Oh," Kaida said, looking guilty.

"Do not feel bad, my Kaida," I said. "Although Ejaya's usually marry their Shadow Lord, it sometimes happens that an Ejaya is already mated by the time her Shadow Lord finds her. Some Ejayas meet their true mates afterward. There is no rule that states an Ejaya and a Shadow Lord must fall in love. She can be by his side during the day, then have a normal family who she returns to every night."

"And the Ejaya's mate doesn't mind that another male is hugging his female and rubbing all over her for hours every day?" Kaida asked, her eyes wide with shock.

I chuckled. "We are not 'another male' but Shadow Lords," I replied teasingly. "There is nothing sexual in those interactions. So no, their mates do not mind. Quite the opposite. It is an honor for a male to have an Ejaya as his mate. It greatly elevates his status."

"Wow. That's admirable."

It was my turn to tilt my head and look at her strangely. "Admirable? You sound like you disagree."

She shifted on her feet and tucked a strand of hair behind her ear. "I don't consider myself the jealous or controlling type, but if my partner was an Ejaya, I wouldn't be okay with them getting hugged the way you've been hugging me. Even though you've done nothing inappropriate, it's too intimate. Only I should hold my partner that way."

I reflected on her words, an uneasy feeling settling in the pit of my stomach. "So, if you were to find yourself a mate—human or otherwise—would you then abandon me to keep him from feeling unfounded jealousy?"

Kaida stiffened, her eyes widening as the greater meaning of her words dawned on her. She chewed her bottom lip before shaking her head. "When you put it that way, it's suddenly less black and white. No, I wouldn't abandon you. But man… I can't imagine explaining this to my boyfriend or husband."

My smile returned as relief drained the tension building in my back. "There's a simple solution. The day you wish for a mate, pick me."

Kaida's lips parted in shock. I chuckled, unable to believe my boldness. I had not really considered that possibility, but that thought was seriously growing on me. Not giving her a chance to respond, I grabbed her hand and drew her after me.

"Let me show you the rest of the house. I do not really use these other rooms. They are basically guest rooms right now—not that I ever have guests—and were meant to eventually become my offspring's nests."

I quickly showed her the three spacious rooms, each a smaller version of my nest, as well as the two other hygiene rooms. I then led her to the fourth room.

"As you can see, this is currently empty. I intended to make it a playroom for the younglings. However, you are free to do with it as you please, be it an office, a training room, or whatever else you fancy."

"Thank you! I could certainly use both!" Kaida said with a grin.

"Anything you need that isn't available on Dramnac, I can open a portal anywhere in the universe to go fetch it for you," I said proudly.

"You know, I could get used to that kind of first-class shopping," she said teasingly.

"You most certainly can," I said, both smug and serious. I walked back out of the room and showed her the last door closest to my lair. I opened it and waved her in. "This is technically your nest."

"Technically?" she asked, raising an eyebrow.

"An Ejaya sleeps with her Shadow Lord," I said, as if it was self-evident.

"Like mates?"

"No, to the extent they don't couple. It's just for contact, unless they become mates," I explained. "Anyway, Derakeens rarely couple inside their lair. My people mostly do it in flight. It also diminishes the risks of burning things at the time of climax."

"*You* breathe fire when you climax?"

The words no sooner left Kaida's lips than a bright shade of red suddenly crept up her cheeks. It was insanely adorable.

I chuckled and shrugged. "Me? I don't know. I've never coupled with a female. But it is common for both males and females to breathe fire when they do."

Kaida just stood there, gaping at me, a mix of shock and disbelief etched on her face.

"What? Why are you looking at me like that?" I asked, unnerved by her intensity.

My question seemed to snap my Ejaya out of her dazed state. She shook her head and averted her eyes while blushing even more. "Nothing," she mumbled under her breath. "So, you expect me to share your bed every night?"

I nodded. "Yes. Unless you really need some time alone."

"I see."

I frowned at her less-than-enthusiastic tone. "Is that a problem?"

She shook her head. "As long as you don't go back to

squishing me, we should be fine," she said, in a slightly teasing tone.

I scratched the scales below my right horn and bowed my head in embarrassment. "I was just in withdrawal. No more smothering, but I will still hug you."

The amused, almost tender smile she gave me awakened the most pleasant warmth in my chest.

"You're cute," she said in a gentle tone.

"I am?" I asked, stunned. I'd been called many things, but never cute.

"Yes, you are. It's quite unexpected seeing how badass and intimidating you looked when you were fighting those portal creatures."

That "badass" term sounded illogical to me. But I had read it enough in human literature to understand it held a flattering meaning. I loved receiving these praises from my Kaida.

"Speaking of portals, let's go down into the city. I want to show you your new home," I said with enthusiasm.

"Sweet! Let me put some clothes on and pull out my jetpack."

"No!" I said in a tone that brooked no argument. "No jetpack. I will fly you down in my arms this time."

She narrowed her eyes at me. "Is that just another excuse to hug me?"

I chuckled. "No, it's not, although I welcome that additional benefit. However, aside from the fact that it will be easier for us to talk that way, it will also be safer," I explained. "Like every other city on Dramnac, Oddran is unstable. Rifts can occur anywhere at any time. I must first show you how to recognize them so you don't get sucked into a phase shift by accident."

"Okay, that's a valid argument," she said, looking somewhat chastised. "I'll be right back."

I let her go to put on some clothes. I seriously dislike her need to be dressed. Sure, it was the way of her people, but it made little sense on Dramnac. Whether dressed or naked, she would draw attention as an off-worlder, but even more so because of her clothes. Her footwear made sense as, without them, the softness of her feet would undoubtedly result in many injuries. But our warm climate otherwise made clothes pointless, if not inconvenient.

Oh well, with time, I intended to convert her into not wearing any, at least inside our lair. I didn't want any obstacles between us when I held her, however small they were.

Kaida did quick work of getting dressed. When she came out of our nest, I groaned inwardly at the extensive amount of fabric she'd wrapped herself in. Biting back the urge to complain, I took her hand and led her out onto the terrace. At least, the obnoxious coverings that cheated me out of fully feeling her thankfully didn't snuff out her exquisite scent.

After picking her up in my arms, I pressed my nose into the crook of her neck and inhaled deeply.

Kaida wiggled in my arms while giggling. "That tickles!"

I didn't pull away immediately, rubbing my nose on her neck for a few seconds more, while she continued giggling. I eventually stopped and lifted my head to look at her, hiding none of the happiness I was feeling in that instant.

"I love the sound of your laughter," I said, my eyes locked with hers. "I love how little things like tickling you fill my hearts with joy. Merely being next to you makes me want to smile. Thank you for allowing me to finally experience what the simple happiness of companionship feels like."

The strangest expression flitted over Kaida's face. For a moment, I almost panicked at the air of sadness in her eyes, as if she wanted to cry. But then she smiled, lifted her face towards mine and gave me the sweetest kiss on the cheek.

"This is only our first day," Kaida said in a gentle voice. "I will make sure you get to experience as many of the social things you have missed out on as possible."

I smiled, pressed my lips to her forehead, then took flight, hugging her middle. Thankfully, my Ejaya didn't fear heights. Eyes wide, sparkling with awe and excitement, she marveled at the surreal landscape of Oddran.

As a Shadow Lord, my lair was among the highest floating plateaus of the city. All around us, countless other plateaus of varying sizes floated at different heights on a wide radius around the black gate below.

"Is each floating island someone's personal property?" Kaida asked.

"No. Like me, most nobles and the very wealthy have private plateaus, unless the plateau is too large to house a single lair. Then there can be multiple owners sharing it," I explained, pointing at one such example below us. "You see this one? There are twelve families sharing it, but that plateau has a surface of nearly two-hundred square meters."

"Right. So having twelve families on the same plateau means they are poor?" Kaida asked.

"Not necessarily," I replied, loving her genuine curiosity about the city. "The fewer people on your plateau, the higher your status. However, the height of your plateau is even more important than its size or how many people share it. There are twenty-six levels, my lair being located at the highest one with only four other plateaus. The plateau of these twelve lairs is on the seventeenth level. They have a higher status than those two lairs sharing a plateau on the sixteenth level."

"Okay, I think I get it. But that means that whoever is at the top will forever remain there, right? No chances for anyone else to climb socially—both physically and figuratively—unless someone sells their home?"

I smiled and shook my head. "Actually, the highest level continually climbs, although it is strictly regulated and extremely costly. People can make their plateau float higher with shadow obsidian dust. But the bigger and the higher your plateau, the more dust it requires."

Kaida nodded in sudden understanding. "And because it requires less for lower and smaller plateaus, it gives the people in lower levels a chance at trying to catch up."

I grinned. "Correct. But it is a complex, and potentially dangerous process. Abusing it is what caused the shattering of our world. So while everyone stockpiles shadow obsidian dust, they can only start injecting it to the base of their plateaus during specific time periods and after obtaining a series of demanding permits."

Kaida frowned, her eyes flicking in every direction, before lingering on a family flying up from the black gate towards their plateau.

"I get the whole status thing with being the highest, with the least impeded view, but it also feels like a chore," my Ejaya said pensively. "I mean, it's a really long way to fly up to the twenty-sixth level. That looks almost like a little over one kilometer vertically, not to mention the horizontal distance from the gate. Shouldn't the plateaus closer to the gate be the prime real estate as you have easier access to everything? Usually, living down-town is noisier but more expensive because of all the convenience."

"Fair point, my Kaida. But people who can afford the higher plateaus can also afford marked shadow obsidian stones to open portals directly to and from their homes. However, most are too stingy to actually use them and fly instead so that they can keep their wealth to build their hoard."

As we approached the black gate, the gaping vortex surrounded by the largest plateau of Oddran, Kaida began to understand the downsides of the lower levels. Aside from the people flying everywhere, goods being transported by hand, on flying devices, or merely by telekinetic powers cluttered the air.

The closer to the gate, the less privacy you enjoyed, and the greater the noise.

Above all, while she couldn't put it into words, Kaida could feel something off about the air surrounding us. It was, in fact, the instability in the world's fabric. It grew the closer we got to the black gate.

"The land around the gate seems extremely vast," Kaida mused out loud.

"It spreads for many kilometers in every direction. However, there are some gaping holes scattered in its midst," I explained. "Nobody lives there. You will only find merchants and commercial businesses lining the circumference of the gate, and a few farms and factories behind them. But the further inland you go, you will only find wild creatures and untamed land that we occasionally hunt in."

I landed in one of the least crowded areas of the commercial street in the market sector. With much reluctance, I put Kaida back on her feet. I kept my hand on her waist and, to my delight, she didn't reject my touch.

Every eye locked on us, although people mainly focused on the strange Ejaya that was my Kaida. They'd never seen a human in the flesh before, and for many, I suspected not even on an image. Thankfully, they kept a respectful distance. My presence no doubt played a part in it. You didn't approach a Shadow Lord unless you had business with him, or if he came to you first. And even then, they made sure not to invade our personal space.

While it was mainly to protect us from their inability to properly control their phasing powers, I believed fear also played a big role. You never knew when jokraz would take over one of us. Nobody in their right mind would want to face off against a rabid Shadow Lord.

I looked at my Ejaya with a bit of confusion. "You do not seem disturbed by the attention you're drawing."

She shrugged. "As an Enforcer, I'm used to the locals

gawking at us whenever my team and I go in for a mission. I expected your people to be extra curious about an off-worlder in their midst. I doubt you guys get too many visitors."

I nodded, once more pleased to find her nowhere near as skittish and delicate as her fragile appearance led me to believe.

"Anyway, I'm gawking right back," she said with a mischievous smile. "They all look so different in their scale colors and horn shapes. But they all only have four horns, whereas you have eight plus that kind of crest in the middle of your forehead."

I smiled while leading her towards one of the kiosks of the open market. "Accurate observation. Those four extra horns and my crest constitute my shadow crown. It is what identifies me as a Shadow Lord. You will see a few other golden Derakeens like me, but they will have a pair of golden wings instead of dark ones like mine and only four golden horns."

"That's really cool. Do they have a purpose?" she asked.

Her genuine curiosity pleased me tremendously. I had not dared hope she would find me interesting enough to want to talk about what I was.

"Yes. My crown amplifies my control over the shadows and makes it easier for me to see beyond the various pathways of the veil," I explained.

We stopped in front of a kiosk. It had samples of various fruits and vegetables people usually bought for their pets or to feed the chattel they intended to eat later.

"This store, and the other two on the right, sell fresh fruits and vegetables. Whenever you need something, you just come here and select the ones you like in the amounts you want, and they will deliver it to our lair. Don't worry about currency. They will directly charge my account."

Kaida immediately frowned at that last comment. She opened her mouth to argue. A single look at my face silenced whatever obscenity she'd been about to say. I'd read enough about humans to know both males and females contributed equally to the wealth and needs of their family unit. While Dera-keens also did with various aspects, providing *sustenance* was foremost a male's duty for us. But above all, one of an Ejaya's principal forms of compensation was to have all of her needs provided for by her Shadow Lord, on top of an additional mone-tary compensation.

I should have specified this to Kaida. I kept forgetting she knew very little about her role, including its benefits and duties, beyond letting me rub all over her.

Although taken aback, the merchants proved quite gracious when I requested they allow Kaida to sample the fruits and vegetables I hadn't been able to match to any human ones. To both our delight, my Ejaya identified many she liked, and the merchants took notes—as did I. I loved the enthusiasm and bold-ness with which she tried everything, even those odd-looking to her. The way her face lit up when she stumbled on something pleasant to her taste buds filled my chest with warmth. Until now, I'd never had someone to care for, and the joy of doing it for her exceeded my wildest hopes.

I pointed to the left path around the black gate. "This way, you will find the furniture and decoration stores. The other way, you will find the chattel vendors. On the other side of the gate, you will find most of the trade and administrative businesses, from builders to lawyers. As my lair is your lair, I would like you to redecorate it however you see fit. We can go have a look at—"

"Excuse me, Shadow Lord Cedros," an annoyingly familiar voice called behind me.

I turned to face the intruder. Chegan, his mate, and their two younglings were looking at me expectantly.

"Sorry to pester you during your time with your Ejaya, my lord. But could I trouble you for a portal to the Kairns of Alja?"

My face hardened, my patience running thin with those stingy nobles always looking for a free ride. "In case you haven't noticed, the black gate is right behind you."

He slightly recoiled at my stern response. His blue scales darkened, and he had the decency to look embarrassed to be thus publicly called out. "Of course, but with two restless younglings, traipsing the void can turn into a real headache. Not to mention it will leave us a non-negligible flight distance from our destination. Whereas, with your assistance, it would spare the little ones an exhausting flight."

That he would use his offspring as an excuse only further aggravated me. "That's what shadow obsidian stones are for," I replied in a clipped tone.

His mate Tyvea took a step forward and bowed her head in a pitiful and submissive fashion, drawing her young closer to her. "You are right, my lord. Sadly, we just realized we've already used the last marked one. We were about to take the flight to the other side of the gate to buy more when we noticed your presence. We figured it was a sign from the Gods. But do not fret. We will not trouble you further and go fetch more stones."

I clenched my teeth, not in the least fooled by her false commiseration. She was as stingy as her mate. I didn't doubt if I asked them to empty their purse, I'd find a handful of stones in there. It suddenly dawned on me that I'd never bothered arguing with people like this before. Normally, I would either just open the gate upon request to be rid of their unpleasant presence, or I would pretend not to hear them calling me and take flight.

But my Ejaya's presence is blocking their unpleasant aura!

That realization further made me notice the complete absence of nausea I'd otherwise normally feel right now for being this long in the market, surrounded by so many people. No fogginess was taking over my mind. For once, I could experience what it was to feel normal in a public setting.

I cast a look at my Ejaya, my hearts filled with gratitude, only to find her staring in turn at the stingy nobles and me. I immediately felt embarrassed. Did she think me cold and lacking compassion that I would deny them something I could do so easily?

Without thinking, I summoned the portal. I barely acknowledged Chegan and Tyvea multiplying their thanks as they ushered their progeny inside the portal. I dispelled it as soon as they were through and eyed my Kaida warily. My abdominal muscles tightened with worry when her frown deepened as she gave me an assessing look.

"You're too kind for your own good," Kaida said pensively. "Granted, I don't know how much effort it would have taken them to fly to the other side of the gate to buy some shadow obsidian... especially for the kids. But it sounds to me like they were just being lazy and entitled."

Relief flooded through me as I nodded. "They were indeed being entitled and stingy. This is one of the many reasons we don't mingle with the general population. If they had their way, they'd use us as their personal portal summoner at every opportunity. That is not the purpose of a Shadow Lord. We stabilize gates, rescue the lost, and kill monsters."

"Well, you might need to remind them of—"

"Shadow Lord Cedros? Could I bother you a moment?" an unfamiliar voice said, interrupting my Ejaya.

I turned to look in disbelief at the male standing next to a female I assumed to be his mate. By the absence of urgency in his demeanor, he wasn't here asking for help for a lost soul or an ongoing attack. That could only mean one thing.

"Yes?" I answered, my voice frigid.

"My mate and I need to go to the Rodova Mountains. Would you be so kind as to—"

"Surely, you jest?" I interrupted, anger surging through me.

The male shifted on his feet, visibly intimidated by my anger. And yet, he lifted his chin defiantly, standing his ground. "Using the gate can be fickle when going to the Storm Lands. Reliable stones there are rare and their cost prohibitive. If you can open a free gate to the stable Kairns of Alja for wealthy nobles, surely you can extend a similar courtesy to poor commoners traveling a much longer and perilous journey?"

Kaida rolled her eyes and turned around, walking back towards the kiosk. I suspected it was to keep herself from commenting in a way that might be deemed offensive.

This was specifically why we didn't offer free portals. By the way others were eyeing us intently, if I complied with his request —valid though his arguments were—many more would come ask for a free ride. I needed to take my Ejaya away from the market.

She'd only walked a few meters away from me, but already the familiar nauseous feeling was coming back, settling in the pit of my stomach. I wanted to tell the commoner to piss off and pretend he hadn't run into a Shadow Lord today. However, this could devolve into a lengthy argument, and I didn't want to give the impression that I gave preferred treatment to nobles. I should have told Chegan to get lost.

Annoyed to no end, I summoned the portal to get rid of them, intent on picking up my Kaida immediately thereafter and flying away from here. However, the moment the shadowy doorway formed before me, a cold shiver ran down my spine. The roots of my scales tingled as I felt an unstable rift forming a short distance to my right.

A sense of dread crashed over me as my head jerked in its direction... in Kaida's direction. Staring absentmindedly at the goods on the stalls, she kept walking right, seconds before she vanished from view, swallowed by the invisible rift.

CHAPTER 6
KAIDA

No words could express the extent of my annoyance. The minute Cedros had opened that first gate, I'd known some other mooches would come asking for a free ride. As an Enforcer, I'd too often been in a similar position where civilians thought to use me to take care of their personal vendettas or issues. I couldn't open portals, but they figured since I could shoot stuff, I could rid them of an annoying neighbor or the giant worm rats infesting their basement.

Did I look like a freaking assassin or exterminator?

The argument that male had so thickly laid on Cedros to guilt trip him into doing his bidding had pissed me off beyond words. If I'd stuck around a moment longer, my sharp tongue would have likely gotten me in trouble. This was my first day on Dramnac. I didn't know the local culture and couldn't afford to alienate the population so soon after my arrival.

I went back to browsing the goods on display, secretly hoping Cedros would tell them to take a hike. I needed to find out more about that Ejaya business. If I was here to take care of him, did that include the right—if not the duty—to tell people taking advantage of him to fuck off? I sure hoped that was written somewhere in the fine print. I'd have no problem doing it. While I was usually sweet, I could be a ruthless bitch any day of the week.

A sudden cold draft took me by surprise. It wasn't so much a draft as it didn't flow by. It felt more like a column of cold had appeared out of nowhere near me. An odd, almost nauseous feeling settled low in my belly, and the urgent need to move away overwhelmed me.

Wanting to walk past whatever this was, I took a couple of steps forward. A powerful tingling spread all over my skin, and my stomach flip-flopped like in a much-too-fast elevator ride. In a flash of understanding, I realized too late what was happening. My vision blurred, and so did the world around me. For a split second, I felt faint, then my vision cleared only for me to find myself standing in the middle of a dark space.

The oscillating smokiness of what I could only call walls told me I'd somehow crossed the veil and was now standing in the void between worlds. The total panic I expected to rob me of any rational thought never came. I was transfixed, fascinated by the strange environment. I could only credit my Enforcer training for keeping my head in this stressful situation.

I didn't understand how I could see in this complete absence of light. And yet, I could clearly make out the small circular space—approximately a three-meter radius—in which I stood. Eight corridors branched off of it, headed in every direction. But even as I contemplated which one to follow, two of them collapsed. The others shifted, making way for the formation of a different, larger pathway.

I almost headed down that way, but remembering the abominations we'd faced off against in the Veladeem research lab cooled my ardors. Without weapons or a clear map out of here, going on an exploratory tour without a guide sounded unhealthy.

I took a couple of steps backwards, hoping it would take me out of the anomaly I'd stepped into and back to the open market.

Nothing happened.

This time, a sliver of fear entered my heart. What if I got permanently lost in this void? What if something came at me from one of the dark corridors that led to who the fuck knew where? What if…?

But I immediately squashed those thoughts before they could fester and lead me to panic. Cedros would find me. Not only was that his job, but I was his Ejaya. He'd move Heaven and Earth—in this case, all of freaking Dramnac—to get me back.

The larger pathway that had opened after the other two collapsed seemed to swell further. Then, at the very end, maybe twenty meters away, a light sparked, growing bigger by the second. I squinted, trying to see what it was. It looked like the shimmering sky of Dramnac. Could it be a doorway back out into the real world?

I headed that way, hoping that Cedros had either noticed my vanishing, or that someone traipsing around the market had noticed what had happened to me. After barely five meters towards the luminous doorway, its light quickly began fading. The fifteen meters remaining of my original destination shrunk before me as the pathways shifted, new corridors opening all around, including one overhead. I was only grateful one hadn't opened beneath me, making me fall to my death or who knew what else.

Once more, I silenced the fear trying to take root as more corridors lengthened and others shortened. I nearly jumped out of my skin when Cedros's voice shouting my name suddenly resounded everywhere at once. I couldn't even begin to guess which direction it came from. But hope soared in my heart. He knew I was lost in the void. He was looking for me. I shouted his name back. To my utter dismay, the void appeared to swallow the sound. I almost felt it getting snuffed out barely a few centimeters in front of me.

Another bright doorway opened to my right, a mere two-meters away. On instinct, I hurried through it as I recognized the sky and some trees. But as soon as I exited the void, my heart seized in my chest. Instead of the black gate's open market, I'd landed on a tiny floating rock covered in moss, no bigger than two-meters in diameter. Floating islands of varying size—but none large enough to hold a house—surrounded me. The larger ones that would have given me a bit more safety all hovered out of range, either too far up, sideways, or below.

To make things worse, a powerful gust of wind nearly knocked me off my tiny refuge. I shouted in fear and dropped to the ground, trying to make myself as small as possible so the wind wouldn't get me. I couldn't see a single soul. Way down below, at least a couple of kilometers down, small moving dots hinted at potential wildlife roaming a valley.

I couldn't even run back inside the void that had led me to this death trap. Any sign of an anomaly had vanished the minute I'd appeared here. I shouted Cedros's name at the top of my lungs. While my voice carried, there was no one to hear it.

This time, the panic I'd kept at bay while traipsing between worlds finally took root. I never should have exited the void. In there, Cedros could have found me. But now that I was back out in the real world, could he still track me? Who would come to this forsaken place and find me here?

My teeth chattered under the chilling cold that swirled around me with the gusting winds. I should have brought my jetpack. At least then I could have flown down to the surface and maybe found a proper shelter or some village or dwellings. I shouldn't have allowed my temper to make me wander off. Cedros had warned me anomalies could happen at any time. If only I had remained next to him, this wouldn't have happened. I should have—

A violent ripping sound, akin to a thunderclap, interrupted my string of self-recrimination. As if in response to my silent prayers, a giant black vortex opened vertically about fifty meters above me and maybe a hundred meters away. It no sooner finished forming than a gold and midnight-blue dragon shot out of it with a powerful roar.

Tears welled in my eyes, and my heart soared upon recognizing the beloved being.

"CEDROS!" I shouted, jumping to my feet.

I didn't think he could hear me from such a distance, but the name no sooner left my lips than his head jerked towards me.

"My Kaida! I found you!"

A teary laugh poured out of me when I heard his telepathic voice resonate in my mind as he dove towards me. But it quickly turned into a terrified shout when another gust of wind knocked me off my feet. I tumbled over the edge of my small island, barely catching myself on an overhanging rock. However, the moss covering its surface gave me little to no purchase.

And then my hands slipped.

I screamed as I started tumbling down. It was a short fall. With a few powerful flaps of his wings, Cedros reached me in seconds. His massive paw closed around my body as he caught me. I felt no bigger than a Barbie doll in his palm as he brought me up to his chest, covering me with his other hand.

Weeping with relief and gratitude, I pressed my head against his wide chest, listening to the hammering of his twin hearts. Cedros threw his head back and fired the most impressive stream of shadow flames. In that instant, I knew beyond any doubt he was expressing an excess of joy and relief to have rescued me.

"I have found you, my Ejaya. You are safe. Do not be afraid anymore. I have found you," Cedros kept repeating to me in his telepathic voice.

A rumbling sound further up drew my attention. The portal through which he had arrived appeared to fold in on itself and inside out before stabilizing again. At a subconscious level, I surmised he had reset its destination. Holding me tightly against his heart, Cedros flew through the portal.

To my shock, we came out half a second later on the terrace of his house. He landed, the portal unraveling behind us with a slight swishing sound.

"I'm sorry... I'm so sorry, my Kaida..." Cedros telepathically said, even as his size steadily shrunk as he shifted out of his battle form.

Still holding me, this time with his arms instead of his hands, once back to his normal form and height, Cedros gave me a bone-crushing hug. When his ability to speak returned, he multiplied the apologies for his perceived fault in this.

"I never meant to put you in danger, my Ejaya. I should have paid more attention. I promise never to be so negligent again. I—"

"Stop, Cedros," I said, taking his face between my hands. "You weren't negligent. I brought this upon myself by walking away while you were dealing with those people."

A flash of anger crossed his alien features. "I should have told them to get lost and kept my focus on you," he ground through his teeth. "Instead of looking at fruits and vegetables, I should have warned you about what to do if this happened."

"Aww, sweetie, please stop berating yourself. You did nothing wrong. I don't blame you for any of this," I said in a gentle voice. "It was an accident. Thanks to you warning me about that possible occurrence, I didn't panic when I inadvertently stepped into that rift. But more importantly, I didn't freak out because I knew you would look for me and that you'd find me. And you did. You rescued me, Cedros. You brought me home, safe and sound."

"Always, my Kaida. I will *always* come for you and save you," he said fervently, before covering my face with kisses.

I started giggling. "It tickles!"

That didn't stop him. After a while, he picked me up and carried me to the living area. He sat down on the massive couch and settled me in his lap.

"Should you ever be caught in another rift, do not move, unless you have a compass with you," Cedros explained. "Tomorrow, I will not only teach you how to use it but also how to travel in the void—not that you should ever do so on your own. However, making sure you know how to find your way out by yourself will give me peace of mind. Had I not seen you enter that rift, you could have spent a long time on that rock, since you traveled so far."

"Traveled far?" I exclaimed, stunned. "I didn't! I barely walked five meters inside the void."

Cedros smiled and caressed my hair. "Distances are different in the void. In there, each step you take is a little over five hundred meters in the real world. I found you over eighteen kilometers away from the market. Thankfully, you were still in the same phase as Oddran. But if you had shifted to another dimension of Dramnac, tracking you down would have been more challenging."

"Oh wow! That's crazy!" I said, bewildered. "I tried to step backward at first, hoping it would take me back out the way I came in, but the pathways only shifted around me."

Cedros shook his head. "Once you're in, there is no backing out, unless you have the power to open a doorway through the veil, like most Derakeens do. You were in an unstable rift. Therefore, its pathways kept shifting, leading to random destinations. Had you entered a stable rift, they wouldn't have moved."

"How did you find me? I heard your voice at one point, but it was coming from every direction at once," I asked, fascinated.

He leaned in, his nose brushing against my neck, then inhaled deeply. It tickled, making me giggle again. He lifted his head back to look at me with a tender expression that did funny things to me.

"I followed your divine scent, my Ejaya. As a Shadow Lord, I can see any rift, where they are going, where they came from, and even what they were before they shifted in the case of unstable ones. Therefore, I explored each one where your scent was the strongest. But then it cut off, and I knew you had exited the void. My hearts nearly stopped in fear of where you might have landed."

"On a freaking tiny rock with crazy winds looking to blow me off," I said with a shudder.

His arms tightened possessively around me. "Never exit a rift unless you can see a substantial amount of solid ground through the window. We can fly, you can't."

"Believe me, that lesson has been properly learned," I replied, refusing to think what might have happened had I stayed there much longer in that icy wind.

"Still, I found you by exiting in the general vicinity of where those unstable rifts would have led."

"How many did you exit before you found me?" I asked, genuinely curious.

"Sixteen," he replied.

"Damn, you're fast!"

He puffed out his chest with pride. "I'm one of the greatest Shadow Lords of Dramnac. Of course, I'm fast, especially where saving you is concerned."

"I'm still baffled how you orient yourself in there. It was just a bunch of shadowy corridors. Most of them looked the same, a few were wider, and some longer. Choosing which way to go felt like a leap of faith."

He smiled with a commiserating look. "Actually, each path has a clear signature to guide you. Main pathways act almost like street signs for us. Unfortunately, as a human, you cannot feel the phases. But if you could, once you recognize it, you automatically know that the path left is destination X while the path right is location Y."

My heart sank. "So I'll forever get lost in there…"

He shook his head. "Maybe not. Like I mentioned, there is a

compass we give our younglings and impaired Derakeens who cannot properly detect phases."

"Oh right! You mentioned a compass!" I replied, my excitement resurfacing.

"Yes, it should hopefully work for you. We will try it in the morning, my Kaida. But should this ever happen to you again without a compass, please stay still. If you had remained exactly where you were, I would have found you right away. Sometimes, the rift can be so brief that you can get kicked right out of it when the phase shift ends. Instead, it shifted with you. There are stones to exit a rift, but *you* have to be careful using them."

"Why?"

"Because, if the rift shifts, you could find yourself exiting over a chasm," Cedros said matter-of-factly.

"Ugh. Are all the portals this tricky?" I asked, feeling discouraged.

"No. The black gate is very reliable, with stable, marked doorways. You will also find permanent portals around every city that are just as safe. And then the ones we summon, whether with a shadow obsidian stone or with our powers, also have a clear and trustworthy destination."

"Well, that's reassuring," I mumbled, still feeling somewhat dejected.

Cedros chuckled and kissed my forehead.

I smiled, but my mind was stuck on my mission. I needed a safe and reliable way to explore the void in order to complete my assignment. I eyed Cedros, considering bringing it up, but decided against it. Now wasn't the time. I had no intention of hiding anything from him. In truth, I could use some of his assistance and knowledge. However, I could only hope that, once he found out, he wouldn't go all caveman, overly-protective on me.

CHAPTER 7
CEDROS

My hearts still hadn't settled from the ordeal my Ejaya had just faced. Had she been a Derakeen, I would have been embarrassed at best not to have warned her of it. Then again, she would have felt it first and stepped out of the way. But my Kaida was a human. So damn fragile and helpless when it came to heights.

I couldn't hold her close enough to reassure me she was indeed safely back in my arms. The sight of her falling off that floating rock would haunt me forever. If only I could give her wings… But of all the new abilities I might give Kaida, should we become true mates, her growing a new pair of wings sadly didn't feature on the list.

Still, the affection that had steadily been blossoming in my hearts for my Ejaya only increased further as I once more kissed her forehead. She had every right to be mad at me for failing to protect her, yet she had fully absolved me and only displayed gratitude that I had saved her… as was my duty.

She was perfect.

"Tell me, what's it like to be a Shadow Lord?" Kaida asked,

lifting her face to look at me while snuggling sideways in my lap.

I thought about it for a second before answering. "It is extremely rewarding, but also quite lonely. Now, I'm used to it, but my first years as a fledgling were extremely hard."

"How so?" she asked, her voice filled with commiseration.

"I was just five years old and had never been separated from my mother and two siblings before."

"Five?! What happened? Did you start showing your powers, and they sent you to some Shadow Lord training school?"

I chuckled and shook my head. "No. I wish. When Derakeens reach the age of five, both male and female younglings go into the void with a compass and food for thirty days. We must remain inside the black gate for at least ten days and follow the Shadow Trail. It's a special path with a series of beacons that we must mark to prove we have completed the journey. Most fledglings will come out after ten to thirteen days. A Shadow Lord will remain for at least a couple of years."

Kaida straightened and stared at me with disbelieving eyes. "What?! Two years?"

I nodded gravely. "I actually remained for three years. While difficult, it benefited me. The longer you stay, the more powerful you grow."

She frowned, giving me an assessing look. "So, you *chose* to stay that long?"

I smiled and shook my head. "No. Nobody *chooses* to remain that long in darkness. Our body tells us when it's time... when we're done. It normally coincides with when our shadow horns finish growing, although sometimes you can remain there a few weeks longer after they do."

"But... you were just a child! You only had food for thirty days. How did you eat? Who raised you? Who looked after you?" Kaida asked, flabbergasted.

"I raised myself, and I hunted for food," I said with a shrug.

"There are entire realms and complex civilizations that exist in the void. They wouldn't qualify as a traditional species by the UPO's standards, but they are organized peoples. And there are also wild creatures to feed from."

"The aqrats?" she asked with a shudder.

I chuckled. "You only eat aqrats out of desperation. Not only do they taste foul, they often give you stomach aches or can even trigger jokraz if you inadvertently eat one of their toxin sacs."

"But how would you even successfully eat one of them? Don't they turn into smoke and dissipate when killed?" Kaida asked, looking slightly confused. "The chunks of flesh we shot off with our blasters in the research lab just evaporated."

"Good observation, my Kaida," I said proudly. "But that was because they were in the physical world, where they shouldn't exist. In the void, they remain whole. Thankfully, there are many other creatures to hunt, mostly inoffensive and easy to capture by a fledgling."

Kaida shifted in my lap and chewed her bottom lip as she reflected on my words. "I still can't imagine a five-year-old in such a situation. You must have been scared."

I shrugged again. "At first, yes. But the trail is quite safe. It was only once I went beyond it that I became scared, as this was uncharted territory. Mostly, though, it was loneliness that plagued me. I used to be very close with my siblings. I no longer had anyone to play with or talk to."

"Jeez! How did your parents handle it? They must have been sick with worry."

"Not really. I mean, any good parent would worry about their child, but I had to interact with the beacons at least once a month. So my mother knew I was alive."

"Your mother? What about your father?"

"He died when I was three," I said, matter-of-factly.

"Oh! I'm so sorry!" she exclaimed.

"It's okay, don't be. It is common for Shadow Lords without

an Ejaya to die young from a particularly virulent case of jokraz. When a Shadow Lord grows close to fifty years of age and still hasn't found her or isn't mated, our people expect him to reproduce with at least one female who has the highest control of her phasing so their coupling can be more tolerable for him. That's how I was conceived. Therefore, I didn't really get to know my father, although I've met him a few times."

"I see," Kaida said pensively. "Honestly, I don't think I could handle my young child disappearing for three years like that. I'd probably freak out after a single day and run through the void looking for him."

I chuckled and caressed her hair affectionately. "If you and I were to have offspring, there is a good chance that one of them would be a High Shadow Lord. But since I have you, my Ejaya, I would be able to go check up on our son or daughter and report back on how he or she fares."

She shuddered, her head involuntarily shaking as she reflected on my words. "I don't know. I really don't think I could deal with it. Still, when you returned, it must have been quite the celebration."

I shook my head. "Not exactly. My family rejoiced not only to see me safe and well, but also that there was an official Shadow Lord in our bloodline. It elevated their status. But I couldn't really celebrate with them. By then, the company of others had already become unpleasant to me."

"Because you'd lost the habit of socializing?"

"In part, although we can overcome that. But it was mostly the fact that they couldn't control their phasing."

"Right. I didn't think you would already be sensitive to it back then," Kaida said sheepishly. "I thought the more powerful you grew, the more intolerable it became."

"That is also true. However, I had spent three years getting every cell in my body infused with shadow and learning to control phasing. So being surrounded by people who didn't was beyond jarring. It's like your reality is always about to tilt. Like walking or standing with a lean, always feeling on the verge of toppling over. It's quite nauseating."

"Ugh, sounds like having a hangover. What did you do then? Could you still share the same roof?"

"No. The Council awarded my family a larger piece of land with enough space to build a separate lair for me so their proximity wouldn't inconvenience me. I lived there, my mother providing for my basic needs, and I studied with a virtual tutor both in academics and combat."

A stricken expression descended over her alien features, and she rubbed my chest in a soothing gesture. "Oh, my poor Cedros. It must have been so hard."

I smiled. "Do not be so saddened, my Kaida. It wasn't that bad. Sure, I struggled with envy at seeing my siblings playing together. But mostly, I enjoyed being alone. It was more comfortable for me. Anyway, the older I got, the more scared people became of me—as with all Shadow Lords. They constantly worry we might involuntarily harm them if our rage triggers. And that's why you will rarely see one of us in public, unless accompanied by an Ejaya to calm us."

"Despite the phasing of people around you?" she asked, tilting her head to the side. "You seemed all right earlier, just annoyed by the freeloaders."

"I was more than all right earlier, because you silence the discomfort. My world is perfect with my Ejaya next to me."

Overcome by a wave of affection for my little human, I gave her an affectionate squeeze while rubbing my face on her neck, only to be annoyed once more by all the wretched coverings she had on. I straightened and glared at her clothes.

"What?" she asked, looking confused by my sudden displeasure.

Without answering, I got rid of her clothes. To my delight, she didn't balk and only snorted, giving me a look that said I was hopeless. It pleased me beyond words how quickly we'd grown comfortable with each other on that front. I'd feared an uphill battle.

Dismissing my annoyance at her undies, I didn't make a fuss over them. I'd eventually convince her to get rid of them. For now, I carried her outside to the terrace and settled on the lounging chair. The sun was setting over Oddran, and I wanted my Kaida to be mesmerized by the beautiful colors that would dance over our shimmering sky. She *would* fall in love with this world, despite today's rocky start.

My arms tightened possessively around her, and I purred with happiness when she willingly snuggled with me. Thanks to my contact with Kaida, the steady flow of nezarone in my blood kept me on a nice high. Fortunately, it was nothing like the brutal grogginess that had taken me over when she first arrived. Our first cuddle had handled the worst of the toxins poisoning me.

"I thought I'd never find you," I whispered, almost more to myself. "I thought I'd die early like my father, going insane from jokraz without ever experiencing this divine peace."

She lifted her head to look at me with sympathy and gently caressed my cheek. "You found me, in the most unexpected fashion… but you found me. Though I wonder how you went about looking for your Ejaya. If you mostly live isolated and mingling with others makes you ill, it must have been difficult."

I shook my head. "No, not at all. I would just visit markets and social gatherings. I do not need to be next to my Ejaya to sense her presence. The minute you entered the research lab, I felt you. It was dim at first, but grew stronger as you came closer. It nearly drove me insane with need, but also with fear that the aqrats might harm you. But simply flying over a crowd would suffice for me to know if my Ejaya was there. And believe me, I have flown over every single millimeter of Dramnac, in vain, since you weren't here."

"That, I most certainly wasn't," she said with a small laugh.

"Frankly, this is the last place I ever imagined I'd land on. I didn't even think your world could still sustain life. That said, since you Shadow Lords can't hang out with others, do you organize social gatherings among yourselves?"

I nodded. "Yes, but not that often anymore. Most of the others have found their Ejayas, which allows them to mingle a lot more with the public."

"How many of you are there?" she asked.

"Only twenty-one, which makes each one of us precious," I explained. "Should we all die, this world would eventually collapse. At any given time, there must be at least five of us watching the gates while the others rest or recover from jokraz. It used to be quite difficult back when few among us had found their Ejayas. So many of my brothers had gone rabid from the toxins that there were only eight of us left to ensure the stability of the gates and rescue the lost. Thankfully, enough recovered by the time I fell to my most brutal case of jokraz."

"Wow. No wonder your Councilor was so adamant I come here. Then what do you do with your time?"

I scratched the scales at the side of my neck, suddenly feeling self-conscious. "I read a lot and watch plays... What you call movies."

Her eyes sparkled with a teasing glimmer. "Your romantic movies?"

I nodded. "Romantic and family plays."

"And are the books romance, too?"

This time, I shifted uneasily beneath her. From what I'd read of Kaida's people, human males didn't read or even like romance. Would she think me not virile enough if I spoke the truth to her?

A Shadow Lord and his Ejaya are always fully honest with each other.

Bracing for her reaction, I nodded again. "Yes. I love reading romance novels. They warm my hearts. I... enjoy experiencing love and a family life vicariously through the protagonists. You think that's bad?"

Her face softened in an affectionate smile. "No. I think that's super sweet. I wish more men learned to appreciate romance."

My hearts soared at her response, and especially at the fact she appeared to mean it. However, her expression changed, taking on a speculative edge while she studied my features.

"If you could have chosen, would you have become a Shadow Lord?"

That question took me aback. I hesitated, taking a moment to think about it. No Derakeen ever questioned something like this. Being a Shadow Lord was a supreme honor. But not one I had chosen. Knowing the type of life it had given me, would I have chosen this for myself?

"I never considered that. But now that you ask, I must say that, given a choice, I would still choose this life, despite its downsides," I said in all sincerity. "I love rescuing people. I like beating back the aqrats. It's not the thrill of killing, but the fact that my efforts make the world safe for others. It is knowing that my work, and that of my handful of brothers, is the only reason Dramnac continues to exist, and that both our people and our way of life can thrive. What other career would allow me to achieve so much for the greater good?"

Kaida smiled with so much affection and approval that I felt myself melting inside, while my hearts filled with the most pleasant warmth.

"I can totally relate. The desire to protect others, to make the world a safer place is the reason I joined the Enforcers. It's not always easy. It can be scary and lonely at times, but every completed mission is a huge reward in and of itself."

It was my turn to study her features with both wonder and disbelief. "I've seen you fight in the research lab, so I do not doubt your skills. But you look so incredibly fragile and defenseless."

She snorted and glanced with an amused expression at her soft, pale skin. "While humans do not possess all the natural defensive and offensive traits species like yours do, we're pretty good at coming up with badass armor and weapons. That said, in my six years as an Enforcer, you are the most dangerous being I have ever faced. In your battle form, you could have squashed me like a bug."

My arms tightened around her, and I gave her forehead a soft kiss. "And yet, I am the one thing you will never have to fear, my Ejaya. The Gods have blessed me with you. My life is bound to protect yours."

Kaida opened her mouth to answer, but a stunned gasp escaped her instead when a burst of colorful lights shot through the falling night sky, almost like a shock wave. With the sun now slowly vanishing between the horizon and the rift line where this phase of Oddran ended, the shimmering sky would dance in a symphony of colors until sundown.

"This is mesmerizing..." Kaida whispered, her voice filled with awe.

"This is your new world, my Kaida. Welcome home."

CHAPTER 8
KAIDA

I woke up with a mountain of muscles and scales wrapped all around me… and a massive hand resting squarely on my butt. I glanced up at Cedros, taking my time to really examine him. As alien and draconic as his features were, and as intimidating as the almost permanent scowl his scaly brow gave him was, I found Cedros pretty dang gorgeous. His body was banging. His muscular chest and chiseled abs were mouthwatering. And those incredibly human lips? Even now, I was fighting the urge to lean towards them and suck on that plump bottom lip.

Technically, he's my husband. It would be perfectly legit for me to enjoy him.

I clamped down on that thought really quickly. Cedros was a huge romantic, and a virgin one at that. If sex between us was any good, he'd likely convince himself he was in love with me. Considering their whole take on a Shadow Lord marrying his Ejaya, he'd further believe this to be proof we were destined. As much as I liked him—and I genuinely did—I didn't want to lead him on.

And yet, here I am getting all hot and bothered just lying in his arms.

What I needed was a cold shower to get my mind out of the gutter and to get ready to learn how to navigate the black gate. To my relief, Cedros didn't resist when I carefully wiggled out of his embrace to make my way to the hygiene room.

I had only been here twenty-four hours, more than half of which I had spent half-naked, snuggling with Cedros. And yet, I couldn't deny the effects of our contact. He no longer twitched and trembled. His speech was no longer slurred or slowed like when we'd first met. It hadn't been as noticeable then, but as the day and evening went by, the difference became glaringly obvious. Even his face looked more relaxed, almost younger.

To think my mere presence was doing this for him still boggled my mind. I resisted the temptation of caressing his silky, purplish-blue hair and quietly made my way to the hygiene room.

I gingerly sat on the toilet to relieve myself. Although Cedros had fixed the strength of the bidet for me last night, and despite me testing it before bed, I still braced for another potential fire hose strength assault. It would probably be a while before I got over that first traumatic experience.

All went well, and I quickly undressed to step under the shower. Once again, the beauty of the view from here took my breath away. I wondered how I would react if a Derakeen did a fly-by right outside. Even though they couldn't see inside, thanks to the reflective windows, I'd still likely feel paranoid that they could see everything.

I grabbed the soap, pleasantly surprised by its slightly sweet scent, neither fruity nor floral, but not what I would have expected for a male. As I had never perceived that scent on Cedros, I wondered if he'd acquired it specifically for me. I worked up a lather and began soaping my body. I didn't know what the heck it was made of, but it made my skin tingle in the most agreeable fashion.

Once done, I used my faithful back brush, my mind

wandering back to my mission. I needed to find the right moment to discuss it with Cedros. As if summoned by that thought, my husband suddenly opened the door and entered the hygiene room, startling me.

"What the fuck?! What are you doing in here?" I exclaimed, almost smashing the brush in my face in my hurry to cover my breasts with my right arm and my cooch with my left hand. "I thought we agreed you're not to enter when I'm in here?"

Although he didn't stop advancing, his steps faltered, as did his smile. "But you are showering, not using the waste seat," Cedros replied, sounding a little confused.

"It's the same thing!" I said, the pitch of my voice going up a notch.

He stopped, his brow creasing. "But we are married. Human couples shower together. It is a bonding ritual. Is it not?" Cedros argued.

"Real couples, yes! But *we* are not!"

A wave of guilt punched me in the gut when he flinched, the hurt look on his face quickly hidden. He rolled his shoulders, his wheels spinning as he seemed to battle with conflicting thoughts.

"Even if we aren't a 'real' couple, humans bathe together all the time in large bodies of water," he insisted.

"We *swim* together, with bathing suits. Not naked!" I countered, unable to believe we were seriously having this conversation with me trying to hide my naughty bits.

To my dismay, his gaze zeroed in on my partially hidden boobs, then on my hand trying to cover my pussy. Then his eyes widened as if in sudden understanding.

"I will not hug you naked, if that's what concerns you. I know you don't want that," Cedros said in a reassuring tone.

I rolled my eyes and huffed in discouragement. "It's not that, Cedros. You're simply not supposed to see me naked. Humans only undress in front of their lovers... or doctors, for medical treatment."

His jaw dropped, and he gave me the strangest look, as if he believed me beyond bizarre—which was likely the case. After a beat, he shrugged.

"Apologies. This human custom is quite incomprehensible to me," he said, looking sheepish. He scratched the scales below his right horn, glanced at the closed door behind him, as if wondering if he should leave, then back at me with an assessing expression. "Well, I have seen you naked now. So... can we shower together, since I already know what you look like?"

I gaped at him disbelievingly. "No! I mean, sure, you've seen me, but that's not a reason to continue ogling me!"

"But what's the problem? You see me and everyone else naked all the time," he argued, sounding a little annoyed.

"Women don't walk around with their boobs out. We—"

"That's not true," he interrupted forcefully. "On your beaches, human females often walk around with their breasts bare."

I groaned in exasperation. "Fine. *Some* women do. But not *me!*"

A million different expressions flitted over Cedros's face. The last one truly bothered me. I couldn't quite define it, but the underlying sadness screamed of a sense of rejection, disappointment, and crushed dreams. It dawned on me then that Cedros had likely fantasized for years about what having an Ejaya would be like. But I just kept bursting his bubble over things that made no sense to him.

In truth, what was the big deal about him seeing my boobs? Cedros and his people didn't look at nudity the way humans did. I wasn't self-conscious about my body, and I trusted him not to randomly assault me from a lack of self-control. So why was I making such a fuss?

"I'm sorry I've upset you. I thought it was a normal human ritual that would help our bonding. I will leave."

Another wave of guilt surged through me at the sight of his defeated and dejected expression as he turned to exit the room.

"Cedros, wait!" I called out.

He looked at me questioningly over his shoulder. I took in a deep breath and dropped my arms, baring it all.

"Like you said, you've already seen what I look like. You might as well stay," I said with a stiff smile.

I didn't know what response I had expected, but not for him to stare at me with a face devoid of any expression, his fiery gaze intense.

"No. You do not mean it. I can see that you don't really want me here. I will leave you alone."

With that, he walked out and closed the door behind him.

"Well, shit," I muttered under my breath.

I hated that I'd caused him any kind of distress. This culture clash business was turning out to be even more complicated than I expected. Then again, it had been naïve of me to hope it would all be smooth sailing, as long as I let him hug me for a few minutes every day. I quickly rinsed and dried myself.

Once again, I found the bedroom empty when I came out of the hygiene room. As I went to pick what to wear, my gaze landed on Kayog's wedding gift. First, the oddest Derakeen compass that, according to Cedros, Kayog had gotten adapted specifically for me. Second, the sleekest, fanciest, most advanced jetpack in the galaxy. And last, a ridiculously cool-looking visor. While I knew what to do with the jetpack, the other two gifts left me perplexed. Cedros was supposed to show me how to use them in the void later this morning.

And that only increased my guilt about this situation.

I took my sweet time getting dressed while trying to figure out my next move. For the next six months, Cedros and I would have to live together. Beyond the entire political bullshit that had semi-coerced me into coming here, I had committed to be the best Ejaya I could reasonably be for him. Cedros was bending over backwards to please me. Granted, he *needed* me, but that didn't mean I couldn't meet him halfway.

After coming to several decisions, I walked out of the bedroom wearing a braless tube top and a bohemian skirt with a thigh-high slit. All black, obviously…

I found Cedros sitting in the living area, a deep air of concentration while he read intensely on his tablet, a frown creasing his brow. On the kitchen's island, food sat ready to be cooked for me. As soon as he perceived my presence, Cedros all but jumped to his feet, a contrite expression on his face.

"Please, accept my apologies again," he said in a repentant tone. "I didn't think coming into the room for showers was wrong. I have to remember that you are not a Derakeen Ejaya. With them, there aren't so many boundaries and limits. I *am* trying very hard to learn your ways. Just please be patient with me. I will do better."

I walked up to him, and he seemed taken aback when I took his hands in mine. "Please don't apologize. You've done nothing wrong. I should be the one apologizing to you."

"What?"

"We are different species, with very different cultures and customs. You're going out of your way reading about humans to try and please me, and I just keep complaining about this and that because it's not the way of *my* people," I said, feeling embarrassed. "You and I may not be a traditional couple, but we're still in an exclusive form of relationship and living together. It cannot work if only one person is making concessions and trying to meet the other person halfway, which you have been doing. I need to do my share, too."

"I do not mind making the concessions, my Kaida. I want you to be happy," he argued.

"But then you will lose yourself and your own identity in the process. It will inevitably make you miserable, and me as well in the long run," I countered gently while giving his hands a squeeze. "We have a saying on Earth: When in Rome, do as the Romans do."

He tilted his head to the side with a curious expression. "Meaning?"

"Meaning that it's illogical for me to come settle on your world and expect to continue living my life according to my human ways," I explained. "Which means, when on Dramnac, I need to do as the Derakeens do instead of berating you to make you act like a human. And it starts with this."

I released Cedros's hands, reached for the bottom edge of my tube top, and began lifting it.

"No!" Cedros exclaimed, his large hands closing around my wrists, stopping me. "You do not have to do this."

"Derakeens walk around naked," I replied calmly. "I may not be ready to bare it all just yet, but I can at least meet you halfway on this."

His hold tightened around my wrists, and he shook his head with an almost sad expression. "No, my Kaida. I do not want you doing anything against your will, or that makes you uncomfortable, just to please me."

I smiled and gently forced him to release my arms. "See? You saying this only makes me want to do it even more. Many things are uncomfortable the first time, but once you've done it, you realize it's no big deal and get over it. You hugging me the first time felt super awkward because you were a stranger to me. Now, I don't mind. In fact, I rather enjoy it since you no longer smother me. You're a great cuddler."

The way Cedros's golden scales suddenly darkened, taking on an almost bronze color, made me burst out laughing. He was so adorably cute as he looked at me with both a pleased and embarrassed expression. His throat glowed, and some of that soothing heat I loved so much radiated from it.

"It pleases me tremendously to hear that you like cuddling with me, my Ejaya."

"I do," I said in all sincerity. "So being naked around you is going to be uncomfortable at first, but eventually, I'll get over it, too. Nudity is harmless and natural on Dramnac. Whatever the circumstances that brought me here, I committed to be a proper Ejaya to you. I'm supposed to be the person you can be yourself with, and with whom you can speak and interact freely, without worry, shame, or restraint. I don't want you not speaking or acting the way that comes naturally to you out of fear I might be offended or upset. If I don't like something, I will tell you. Okay?"

A powerful emotion crossed his features. The way his throat worked, I suspected he was trying to swallow down the overwhelming emotions coursing through him.

"Yes, my Kaida."

"So here goes," I said in a cheerful voice, yanking off my top in one swift move. "Here are female human boobs. No big deal…"

And it really wasn't. Even with him blatantly ogling my bare breasts, the expected embarrassment and self-consciousness never came. I didn't know if my mental preparation before coming out of the bedroom or his fascinated expression devoid of lust explained it.

He tilted his head this way and that as he examined them with a smile filled with wonder. "They are quite big. Are they heavy?" he asked matter-of-factly.

I snorted. "Big? That's a first," I said, more to myself. I liked saying I was a C cup, but depending on the model of the bra, B sometimes fit better. "By human standards, mine are average. And no, they're not heavy. But for women with much bigger breasts, their weight can actually cause severe back pain."

"I see. I understand human females feed their young with them. Do yours contain milk right now?"

My eyes nearly popped out of my head, then I chuckled as I recovered from the shock. "Oh, God, no! Definitely no milk here. I haven't given birth. Human females only start producing milk when they are close to giving birth to a baby, and will continue to lactate for as long as they breastfeed their child. Technically, you can induce lactation even without pregnancy, but that requires some committed effort."

"Oh," Cedros said, his face falling with disappointment.

I blinked, surprised by his unexpected reaction. "That's not what you wanted to hear."

He gave me a sheepish grin. "Well, I was curious about what your milk tasted like."

My jaw dropped, and I stared at him in disbelief. "You wanted to taste my breast milk?!"

This time, he was the one surprised by my reaction. "Yes, of course. Why wouldn't I? I was also quite curious how effective your fermented milk could be in replenishing our hydrogen sacs."

Robbed of words, I just continued staring at him. But he was still too focused on my boobs to even notice.

"I'm surprised they are not functional because of their size," Cedros mused out loud. "I assumed women's breasts were big because of all the milk they contained. Yours look so firm and perky, I would have expected them to be hard. But they always feel soft against me when I hug you."

"Wow! Firm and perky! Thanks! That's the nicest compliment you can give a woman about her boobs," I said with a giggle.

He smiled and raised a hand towards my right breast, but caught himself before touching it. "Sorry!" he said, giving me a worried look.

I smiled again. "It's okay, you can touch."

A major 'What the fuck?!' went off in my head even as the words left my lips. I couldn't believe I'd just told him to go ahead and grope my boob.

"Are you sure?" he asked hesitantly.

I should have jumped on that opportunity to recant, but the hopefulness in his voice and his gaze made me nod.

"Yes, you can. Go ahead."

I've had my boobs touched in the past, but having Cedros squeeze the left one like one would a clown horn nearly had me bursting out laughing.

"So soft and squishy," he said wistfully, making me chuckle.

I couldn't recall anyone ever touching me in a less sexy fashion. Even a doctor giving me a breast exam hadn't felt so awkward… but in a funny way. Although there was definitely nothing childish about Cedros, the innocent way in which he explored me was endearing. As he pawed at me, I felt like a stress ball in his hand.

Then, although his expression remained curious, his touch changed. He covered my breast with his palm, giving it a little squeeze before gently rubbing over it. His second hand settled on my other breast, cupping it while his thumb circled my areola. What had started as a playful exploration took on a different edge as an unexpected flame sparked low in my belly.

To my dismay, the tip of my nipples pebbled. Cedros's vertical pupils widened as he leaned forward, noticing the change.

"They are hardening. What's happening?" Cedros asked.

Embarrassed, I caught his wrists and gently pulled his hands away from me. "It's nothing. It happens sometimes when you fiddle with our nipples."

"But why?" he insisted, genuinely curious. "Is it—"

He abruptly stopped talking, his nostrils flaring, and his eyes widening. When his head jerked down, and he stared at my crotch before taking a deep whiff, no word could have described the extent of the mortification I felt.

He looked at me with shock and disbelief. "Are you aroused? Did my touch arouse you?"

My stupid face turning beet-red was all the answer he

needed. The most incredible air of wonder descended over his features. He looked in turn at his hand, at my boob, and then back at my face, his nostrils flaring the whole time. In that instant, I wished I could summon a portal and vanish right out of here.

"Okay, enough grabbing boobies for today," I said, looking at the food on the counter, eager to change the subject.

But Cedros was nowhere near done with this one.

"You *are* aroused, correct?" he insisted.

I crossed my arms over my chest, now feeling self-conscious about my partial nudity. "You're not supposed to ask questions like that."

"Why not? And why are you embarrassed?"

"Because it's just not the type of thing we openly discuss," I said.

"So you won't answer? Is that another human rule? One that I should leave alone?"

I made a face at him, both impressed and annoyed by the less-than-subtle fashion he was reminding me I'd committed to allowing him to openly express himself with me as he would with a Derakeen Ejaya.

I heaved a sigh and balefully looked at him. "Yes, breasts are erogenous. When touched gently in the right way, it may arouse a woman."

An awed smile stretched his lips. "I can't believe my touch aroused you."

That comment took me aback. I frowned and looked at him questioningly. "Why can't you believe it?"

It was his turn to appear taken aback. "I have scales, horns, a tail, digitigrade legs, and draconic features. I don't exactly fit the attractiveness criteria of the human aesthetic," he said matter-of-factly.

My frown deepened. "True, but that doesn't make you unattractive, either. Every species has their own form of beauty."

He nodded, but still didn't seem satisfied. "Is touching them the right way the only thing required to trigger that response? I mean, would you respond the same way, no matter how repulsive you may find the person touching you?"

"Oh, no! Arousal isn't just a physical thing. A lot of it is emotional. Someone I don't find attractive wouldn't arouse me. You may not be human, but I still think you're a very attractive male."

For a split second, as I spoke those words, I wondered if Cedros was fishing for compliments. But his genuine shock erased any doubt he truly thought I couldn't be drawn to him.

He beamed at me and puffed out his chest. "Your words please me very much, my Ejaya. I find you very attractive, too, which I didn't think possible with a human. I like how my body responds to you. And now, I understand why human males like breasts. They are wonderful, even when they're not functional, like yours."

Oh, brother!

I barely repressed the urge to facepalm. How the heck was I supposed to respond to that anyway? Thankfully, Cedros spared me from further embarrassment by taking my hand.

"Come, my Kaida. Let's feed you."

Relieved beyond words, I let him lead me to the counter where he began cooking my meal.

CHAPTER 9
CEDROS

Kaida found me attractive. My touch had aroused her. Even now, the aroma of her need lingered in my snout. It had smelled even more divine than her Ejaya scent. Never before had I felt such a powerful urge for my length to extrude. Kaida had aroused me… truly aroused.

And Kayog said we are compatible…

When he'd confirmed that Kaida would come and settle on Dramnac with me, I had expected nothing other than a platonic Ejaya-Shadow Lord relationship between us. I never pictured myself being sexually drawn to a human. But that had changed. Now, I wanted more… I wanted everything with my Kaida. I would need to find more opportunities and ways to make her aroused again. I needed to read up on human courtship rituals to make her attraction to me grow further.

However, I couldn't allow my mind to wander as I flew us down into the black gate. Despite her undeniable courage, Kaida slightly tensed in my arms when we entered what resembled a dark, swirling pool of smoke in the center of the city. The familiar coolness and tingling sensation ran over my scales as we landed inside the void.

"Wow!" Kaida exclaimed in a hushed voice when she took in the main hub of the black gate.

The vast—somewhat circular—space had multiple large portals lining its shadowy walls. And in-between them, long corridors led to even more doorways.

"This is the main hub of the black gate," I explained. "Each of these portals leads to a specific destination. Unlike the rift you got trapped in yesterday, these portals and pathways never change. We Shadow Lords make sure of it."

"They do look stable compared to where I was, but how do you know where they lead?" she asked, sounding concerned. "All I see are black vortices lining the wall. At least, in that rift, I could see what was on the other side."

I nodded. "You could see the other side because the destination was a very short distance away. These portals take you very far. Only a Shadow Lord is powerful enough to see to the other side. But there are markings all around the portals that we've woven in. Your human eyes simply cannot see them. Put on the visor Kayog gifted you."

Kaida complied, sticking the two small magnetic disks on each side of her temples. She then simultaneously pressed their centers to activate them. A bluish, translucent beam shot out of each disk, curving in front of her eyes and connecting in the middle, forming a sort of holographic goggles. Kaida gasped, her face brightening with awe.

"This is so badass! I can see it now. It looks like glowing runes made of shadow flames," she said in an excited voice. "But I can't read what they say."

"Right. The visor only enhances your vision so that you can perceive things we can. There was no time to upgrade it enough to integrate a translator that could fit it and not interfere with its other functions. But the compass will fix that," I explained. "Rub your thumb over the central interface to activate it, then point the compass at the gate."

Kaida did as I instructed.

"Oh, my God! That's awesome! The runes changed into normal letters. It says 'Plains of Kolvar' on this one!"

I grinned, pleased to see it work flawlessly. "That's correct. Any other portal you point at will display its name on your visor. But you want to look at the gate you are targeting with the compass or you may get overlapping text."

"Okay, that makes sense," Kaida said, pivoting to look at each of the portals while pointing the compass at them. "Why does the text turn yellow on some of them?"

"Good observation, my Ejaya," I said proudly. "This means that the portal's destination either isn't on solid ground or has very little landing surface. Therefore, you want to fly through that portal or be ready to do so as soon as you exit on the other side."

"Oh shit. Well, good to know. They should have made it red."

I shook my head. "No, red is for dangerous or restricted destinations. Derakeens only enter such portals if they're ready for battle or with a hunting party. You should *never* enter one of them. There is no reason for you to do that. You do not want to face off against aqrats alone."

"Fair enough," she said in a chastised tone.

I smiled, relieved she didn't argue. "The main hub has the principal destinations in the Oddran region, as well as direct gateways to the other major cities and regions of Dramnac. But for more specific locations within those regions, just follow the pathway next to that portal, and you will find much smaller portals along that corridor."

"Oh, that's super cool!" she said excitedly. "But it also sounds like I could traipse around for a while looking for a specific one."

I chuckled. "You could traipse around for days without having seen them all. You might even end up exploring the same one repeatedly because some names can be quite similar."

I laughed at her horrified expression.

She glared at me before giving the compass an assessing look. "Surely this little guy can help?"

I nodded. "Yes, my Ejaya, it can. If you know the name of the destination you want to go to, you can either speak it to the interface, type it, or select it on the holographic map. I would avoid the map for now since you do not know the regions well enough. It can get very confusing. Go ahead and try it. Take us to Mehuro's portal. The command is 'set destination' followed by the name of the place where you want to go."

Eyes sparkling, Kaida smiled at me and raised the compass to her lips. "Set destination: Mehuro," she said in a firm voice.

The compass flashed, and the luminous needle pointed to our right. Buzzing with excitement, Kaida immediately started walking in that direction, leading us into one of the large pathways between two portals. We walked about fifty meters before reaching the smaller portal.

"Right here!" she said proudly, pointing at the gate. "And it's a safe destination. The text is blue."

"Well done, my Kaida," I said approvingly. "Now, how would you go back home?"

Her face fell. She chewed her bottom lip while pondering, then resolutely backtracked to the main hub. She looked at the various portals around us before casting a glance upward at the swirling black mist above our heads.

"Don't we need to fly out through that 'shadow ceiling' up there, just like we flew in when we arrived?" she asked.

I nodded. "That is indeed what most of us do. But should you find yourself stranded without a jetpack, or for those of us who cannot fly—be it because of a wound or any other impairment—there is an alternative way. Every city has a permanent gateway you can walk out of and that will take you to its marketplace. You only have to ask your compass for Oddran Market here. But in any other city main hub, you could simply say 'market' to yield the same result for that city if you do not know its name."

She followed those instructions, leading us to the market portal, and we walked through it.

"Oh, I recognize this place," she exclaimed, relieved. "I can see the fruit stands we were looking at over there to our left. But I hadn't seen the portal from there."

"The kiosks hide it. Now you know how to get back to the city on your own." I explained, while leading her to the rental stand right next to the portal. "Here, you can rent a hover platform to transport goods or yourself up to our lair."

"Oh! In case I don't have my jetpack with me, right?" Kaida asked.

"Correct. They are very safe. You can use the smallest one. It has a protective railing all around to prevent you from falling off the sides, not that it should be a problem. We do not have strong winds here. Once you have reached your destination and disembarked, it will automatically return here on its own. For that too, you do not need to worry about credits. They will charge my account."

Kaida pursed her lips again. It amused me that she seemed bothered about me paying for her. That was another thing I would need to cure her of. I had more credits than I knew what to do with, as I hardly ever spent my very generous Shadow Lord compensation. On what? I had everything I needed at home. I hunted for my food and had no one to spoil.

Or rather, I 'used' to have no one to spoil.

My hearts swelled just thinking about all the ways I wanted to spoil my Ejaya. But first, we needed to pursue her training.

"Let's go back inside the gate. I want to take you to some of our more unstable areas so that you can practice detecting and avoiding rifts," I said.

"Yes, please! I'd rather avoid a repeat of yesterday," Kaida said, scrunching her face.

We reentered the black gate through the portal, and I instructed Kaida to take us to the Storm Lands in the southern continent. With impressive confidence, she correctly headed towards its portal by following her compass. Halfway there, we ran into Rovain, one of my Shadow Lord brothers, working on stabilizing the Jaeliant Valley portal with his shadow flames.

"Wicked!" Kaida whispered as she admired my brother.

My chest swelled with pride as I observed my elder. In his late fifties, Rovain was among the oldest living Shadow Lords. Thanks to Trinit—his Ejaya—he would likely live to a Derakeen average lifespan of 175 years.

As would I now!

His shadow horns were glowing from the ethereal energy they were gathering and that he was channeling through shadow flames and through his hands. From his palms, it shot out like a purplish beam of energy, filling the gaps and weaknesses in the portal, as one would patch the fissures and cracks in the foundation of a building.

"You can do that?" Kaida asked in a hushed voice, as if afraid to disturb Rovain.

"Of course," I said, slightly offended she needed to ask.

Then again, her tone had sounded less like a doubtful question than a desire for confirmation.

Rovain finished stabilizing the section he'd been working on before turning to look at us. I felt the gentle nudge of his consciousness against mine as he gave me a telepathic greeting. As we closed the distance with him, he shifted out of his towering battle form. It was not only to be at a height with us but also so that Kaida wouldn't be excluded from the conversation we would have, as she had no telepathic abilities.

Yet...

She deactivated her visor so that he could clearly see her face.

"Brother," Rovain said with his deep, rumbling voice. "It is a pleasure to see you so well accompanied."

"It is a blessing from the Gods," I said, slipping a possessive arm around Kaida's waist while looking at her with pride.

To my delight, she leaned against my side, and I gently rubbed my cheek against the top of her head.

"Kaida, this is the Elder Shadow Lord Rovain, a veteran who I have the honor of calling a mentor and a friend. Rovain, this is my Ejaya, Kaida Daigo from Earth."

"Welcome to Dramnac, Kaida. It is a blessing to see I have a new sister. You couldn't have been created for a more deserving Shadow Lord than Cedros."

Kaida blushed and gave Rovain a friendly smile. "It's an honor to meet you as well. I didn't know what to expect when I came here, but Cedros has been beyond charming to me since my arrival."

"As he should be!" Rovain said forcefully before turning back to me. "My hearts soar for you, my brother. Your loss to jokraz would have been a tragedy. But I told you not to lose hope."

I nodded in concession. "You did. However, who would have thought my Ejaya would come to me from another world?"

"The Gods work in mysterious ways. It was fate." He eyed the compass in Kaida's hands. "I see you're teaching her how to navigate the void. Wise. Is this a new model?"

"It's been modified specifically to compensate for her human eyesight. She cannot see rifts, phase shifts, or the writings on the portals without it."

"I see. That would indeed be problematic."

"Which is why I'm taking her to the Storm Lands to practice avoiding unstable rifts," I explained.

"Good!" he exclaimed before turning to Kaida. "Do not get discouraged if you struggle to avoid them. It takes our younglings a long time, and they have phasing abilities. Every day, I recover a dozen of them who got lost in the void. Just keep practicing. If you need a partner, my mate will be more than happy to provide additional training once Cedros returns to work."

"Thank you," Kaida said with a genuine gratitude that reflected the one I felt towards my friend. "All of this is a little intimidating. But Cedros has been a brilliant teacher so far. Knowing it's normal to struggle with the rifts will make it easier on my overachiever ego when I fail. And I would love to meet your mate. Having another Ejaya to learn from will be great."

"I will arrange it," Rovain said. "Just be prepared that—now that Cedros has you to protect him from the unpleasantness of other people's proximity—my Trinit will insist on you both joining us in the countless social events she keeps dragging me to."

Kaida burst out laughing at the long-suffering way in which he said that last sentence. I couldn't help a smile, either. I had mixed feelings about that prospect. Some apprehension, but also a great deal of excitement to finally experience all that I had missed out on. I could only hope freeloaders wouldn't make it unpleasant.

"I look forward to it!" Kaida replied with a glowing smile.

"Well, I should get back to work," Rovain said. "Be warned that you should avoid the Vessant sector. The Lelvians are on a pilgrimage again, and aqrats have been roaming nearby. Elros has been quite busy dealing with them."

I nodded with a frown. "Sounds like I will have my hands full tomorrow when I relieve him."

"Fighting?" Kaida said, with a sliver of worry in her voice.

"Mm hmm. Fighting and looking for lost pilgrims. For void creatures, the Lelvians are quite terrible at navigating it," I said in a playful tone before sobering as Kaida continued to frown.

"Do not fret, my Ejaya. I will return. We fight aqrats all the time."

"But you've been very sick. You've gone into rage," she argued.

"True. But now I have you. You've brought me back from the brink in only a few hours instead of weeks or months," I said in a reassuring tone. "Plus, this will give me an excuse to cuddle with you more."

Rovain snorted while Kaida shook her head at me.

I gave Rovain an assessing look. "That said, you look strained, brother."

He nodded. "I am, but do not worry. I'm almost done here. Trinit will be by in the next thirty minutes. Then I'll be doing a great deal of hugging and cuddling myself."

This time, both Kaida and I chuckled.

"Very well, brother. We'll see you later," I said.

He nodded, smiled at my Kaida, then shifted back to his combat form to resume his work.

We reached the Storm Lands, named as such for the frequent lightning that ripped through the sky, and the electricity that charged the air all around us. No one lived here, but a number of companies with high needs in power leveraged this bounty in the more stable parts of that region. My Ejaya and I went straight to the most unstable area for her to practice avoiding rifts.

Saying she struggled was the understatement of a lifetime.

After two hours, she kept walking right inside them or freezing in place while debating which direction to go, until she got swallowed in the expanding rift. Her dejected expression every time I came to get her out was adorable. But for all that, my Kaida was a good sport and a great pupil. She'd taken to timing how long it took me to rescue her, making it a game of her trying to last the longest without getting sucked into a rift, and of me getting her out as fast as possible.

I couldn't recall ever feeling this happy and carefree. As I trained her, images of me teaching little human-Derakeen hybrids how to avoid or get out of rifts wouldn't stop flashing before my eyes. A powerful longing accompanied it as countless questions fired off in my mind. Could I get Kaida to share that desire?

"I've tortured you enough for one day, my Ejaya," I said in a gentle voice after one of countless rescues. "You deserve a break. And then I must take you home to feed you."

She chuckled, and looked at me as if I'd said something cute. "Normally, I would argue for one more round, but I believe I've gotten lost enough for one day."

"Give me a second to morph, my Kaida, and I will show you some more beauties of your new world."

CHAPTER 10
KAIDA

I would never cease to be amazed by Cedros's transformation into his dragon form. Besides the awesomeness of the visual itself, I always felt so tiny and vulnerable next to him—which I effectively was. Cedros was a stunning dragon, even though he mostly stood upright rather than on all fours.

Once again, he reached for me with his massive paw, then held me with both hands, my back pressed to his chest. As soon as he took flight, a huge portal opened before us in the air. The same queasy feeling I was beginning to get used to gave my stomach a whirl as we passed through it. We emerged a second later over a vast plain.

Unlike Oddran, it didn't have the plethora of floating plateaus. If not for the horizon fading into a darker shimmer where the region faded into the void, I would have believed myself in a normal world. A long rocky cliff framed one side of the valley, ending in a waterfall and a river. Along the valley, herds were running wild. Some appeared to have their refuges carved into the cliff face, while others disappeared inside the forest to the west.

However, despite the lack of floating islands, a series of large rings cluttered the sky in one area.

"Behold the Kairns of Alja," Cedros telepathically spoke to me. *"We use these rings for our national sport, Vayarka. We activate hovering platforms nearby for the audience to watch. But many people also just settle at the edge of the cliff."*

He flew down closer to the ground so that I could have a better look at the exotic flora and fauna. While the creatures bore some vague similarities with some of Earth's wildlife, there was no question we were no longer in Kansas.

"And this is Alja's Fair Grounds," Cedros said as we flew over what clearly resembled an amusement park a short distance from the river. *"There are foods, games, rides, musical and visual entertainments—what I believe humans call concerts and shows. It is a very popular place where most big events are held. Trinit loves coming here."*

I could totally see Cedros and I going on a double-date with Rovain and Trinit at the fair. The image of Cedros winning a giant teddy bear for me at one of the carnival games made me chuckle. I couldn't recall the last time I'd gone out on that kind of date with anyone. I'd promised Cedros I'd get him to experience all those social things he never did before, but now I feared getting caught in my own game.

"There are many sports games and competitions held in the Mogodan river and waterfall. The dumbest, yet most popular one, is to fly up the waterfall through the rushing water. It always results in many a torn wing or broken bone," Cedros continued, sounding unimpressed.

To my shame, I immediately added it to my 'must-see' list. I was a sucker for extreme sports—watching, not participating. There was something fascinating about observing people doing completely stupid things just because… It was especially great when they somehow pulled it off unscathed. Yeah, I had a healthy dose of morbid curiosity in me.

Cedros flew up to the plateau on top of the cliff and landed. Maybe fifty meters from the open area by the edge, a series of orchards and berry bushes spread almost as far as the eye could see. The sweet scent of various ripe fruits filled the air.

After putting me down on my feet, he switched back to his normal form.

"Every single fruit you see here is edible," he said, pointing at the orchards. "Most adults will mix their juice to their fermented drinks or with their raw meat for added flavor. But younglings eat them as dessert or treats."

"They certainly smell good," I said, my mouth watering.

"Good! I'm going to make you sample a few. When there are no sporting events happening, people will often come here simply to relax or have family picnics. And we're about to have ours. Hang on."

His shadow horns glimmered with a purplish inner glow and immense power appeared to emanate from his chest seconds before a large portal opened next to us.

"Wait here. I'll be right back."

He hopped inside the portal as soon as he spoke those words, not waiting for my response. Burning with curiosity, I eagerly awaited his return, which only took seconds. Cedros came back out carrying a large container that appeared to have two sections, one of them temperature-controlled. He dispelled the portal while putting the container on the grass.

Cedros opened the left side of the crate, removing a large, checkered, folded fabric.

"Normally, our picnic mats are a solid color, usually matching the color of the grass, sand, or rocks where we settle down. But I saw humans use red and white or blue and white checkered mats. Therefore, I had a blue one made for us, so you would feel more at home," Cedros explained while laying it out on the ground.

"Aww, that's so incredibly sweet of you," I said, deeply

touched. "You don't have to go out of your way like this for me."

"Of course, I do. I *love* taking care of you. I've waited my whole life for this pleasure. You will not deny me."

The mulish way in which he said it made me chuckle. "If you insist!"

"I do!" he said with a firm nod.

He pulled out a small dark-blue square that seemed made of foam. As soon as he placed it on the mat, it started unfolding and inflating into an impressive cushion. It could easily serve as either a seat or a large pillow.

"Sit, my Ejaya," he said, indicating the cushion.

I complied with a thank you, observing with great interest while he retrieved a series of small bowls from the same section of the container, laying them out on the mat in front of me.

"I will return shortly," he then said, rising to his feet.

With a powerful flap of his wings, he headed to the orchard, where he grabbed a series of fruits before returning to me. With impressive dexterity, he peeled and sliced some of them up with his claws, separating them neatly in the various bowls. Some he squeezed, a sweet-scented thick goop pouring out of the fruit into the small container.

"Now, you get to sample," he said with a toothy grin.

From the refrigerated section of the container, he took out a bunch of small vials filled with various liquids, some clear, some thick, others akin to yogurt or cream. He also had crispy breads and meats. For the next half-hour, he made me taste a mix of everything, pairing certain meats with certain fruits, diluting some of the goopy fruits into a vial, which I swallowed in one or two gulps. While the fruits with the crispy breads felt like eating various jams on toast, the little drinks were the hero for me. Some of them felt like fruity liquor shots, others like smoothies or yogurts. Although I wasn't big on alcohol, I could totally see myself getting hooked on some of those shots.

While I was savoring these treats—some of which he

consumed as well, mainly the fermented stuff—Cedros inquired about my past. The alcohol having loosened my tongue, I shared without restraint.

"I grew up in the refugee colony of Iliat," I said wistfully. "When I was three weeks old, a natural disaster destroyed nearly a third of my planet Loros. So many people died. And of those who survived, many were never reunited with their kin, as was my case."

"You were separated from your family?" he asked in a sympathetic tone.

I nodded. "I don't recall any of it, as I was much too young. According to my records, the rescuers heard me screaming from the third story of an apartment building. Half of the building had been torn off and collapsed into the ground. I'd apparently been fairly dehydrated, but safely tucked in my crib. They wondered if my parents had been in the half of the residence that collapsed, or if they'd simply been unable to climb up to rescue me."

"I'm sorry, my Kaida. I didn't mean to bring up a painful topic for you," Cedros said, looking guilty.

I smiled and patted the back of his hand reassuringly. "It's okay. It's not like I have any actual recollection of this. I was a newborn, literally days old, and too young to have been registered in the Galactic Archives. In theory, I didn't even exist," I said with a chuckle. "Since no one claimed a missing newborn with my description, and DNA matching with their database yielded nothing, they sent me to the colony."

"Have you tried looking for your parents since?" he asked in a soft voice.

I took a shot of something that made me think of a mix of mango, kiwi, and vodka. "I did. Sadly, I had little info to go off of, and found nothing that even remotely matched my situation. I believe my parents died during the disaster, but I'll never know for sure."

"Is that why you joined the Enforcers? To have more

resources to track your parents?"

I chuckled. "No, it's not. Although I initially thought of that. Colonies are many things but not a paradise anyone *wants* to live in. There are few prospects, a lot of poverty, and especially a lot of crime. I've always had an inquisitive mind, so school was a wonderful escape for me. I enjoyed reading and studying, which earned me good grades. That, in turn, gave me better living conditions through the scholarships that included a warm bed and three meals a day."

"I am relieved to hear it. But it is terrible that younglings should face the possibility of going cold and hungry," Cedros said with a frown.

I shrugged. "It is terrible, but it is a sad reality on far too many worlds still. I just knew I wanted to get out of Iliat. I refused to spend the rest of my days there, stagnating. Thankfully, the UPO offered a few training programs to those who qualified in the skill tests they ran annually."

"Skill test?" Cedros asked, tilting his head to the side.

I nodded. "They tested everything, including our I.Q., physical and psychic abilities. As a human, I had fewer options than some other species. Still, when I was sixteen, I qualified for both their scientific and peacekeeping programs."

"Why did you choose peacekeeping?" he asked, surprised.

"As much as I loved science, where that program would take me was far too uncertain. With the peacekeeping program, I knew exactly which curriculum to tackle to land in one of the roles I wanted. Beyond the fact that I was always athletic, I'd seen too much violence and crime in the colonies. I no longer wanted to be helpless in the face of that kind of shit. I wanted to help bring order and safety to other people like me."

"And yet, you left the colony," he stated matter-of-factly, his expression merely curious, devoid of any condemnation.

"Yes. The program eventually required me to leave Iliat, as I earned more scholarships and more advancement. When the opportunity to become an Enforcer presented itself, I couldn't pass it up. With the UPO's peacekeeping force, I would protect oppressed and endangered people throughout the galaxy."

"Did it live up to your expectations? Do you enjoy it?" Cedros asked.

I beamed at him. "Yes. I absolutely love it. It can sometimes be hard and gut-wrenching. But knowing that I make a difference, that I bring happiness, justice, and safety to those in need is the greatest reward I could ever ask for or want."

It was his turn to beam at me. Cedros leaned forward and caressed my cheek with an approving glimmer in his fiery eyes.

"I fully understand the flame that drives you. It is the same for me, although our duties are quite different," he said in a gentle voice. "We have law enforcement here as well, but nothing as perilous and grand scale as what you do. I'm assuming that once our 'honeymoon' is over, you will resume your Enforcer duties?"

I licked my lips nervously, grateful for this perfect opening he was giving me to come clean.

"You are correct, although I'm technically already back to work," I said carefully.

His scaly eyebrows shot up. "Already? How so?"

I shifted on my cushion and lifted my chin. "There were two reasons for me to come to Dramnac. First and foremost was to heal you and act as your Ejaya." He nodded, his attentive gaze boring into me. "But I also came here on a mission for the UPO."

This time, he stiffened and frowned, a sliver of suspicion entering his eyes. "You have a mission on Dramnac for the UPO? Is the Council aware of it?"

I nervously tucked my hair behind my ear and shrugged my ignorance. "I don't know if they are. But I've not been sworn to secrecy, so I'm assuming they are aware. I cannot complete this mission without the collaboration of the local people. And they certainly won't answer my questions without me explaining my purpose."

Some tension bled out of Cedros's shoulders. "I see. What is your mission?"

"The UPO wants me to find out a few things to prevent further incidents like the one at Veladeem Research. Who are the mercenaries acquiring shadow obsidian stones? How are they acquiring those stones? Do they have a contact or seller here? Do they already have stockpiles we must confiscate? And how do we stop them from acquiring more stones?"

His brow creased deeper with each of my words. To my relief, no anger animated him. Instead, Cedros was pursing his lips while slowly nodding.

"All excellent questions, and both a very valid and important mission. It actually troubled my Shadow Lord brothers and me that our Council hadn't requested such an investigation," Cedros said pensively.

"Really? They have brought it up?" I asked, instantly falling into detective mode.

He nodded. "Yes. In the past year, we've had to clean several similar incidents to the one where you and I met in the research lab. Most were minor inconveniences where a portal was just left open, leading to a random location, from a vacant building to an open field. In some instances, there were aqrats or other shadow beasts roaming that we had to eliminate."

"Any victims?"

"Sadly, on a few occasions, yes," he said in an apologetic voice.

"Derakeens?" I insisted.

"No. In some cases, the victims were humans. But we also found species unknown to us and animals."

"Where are their remains?" I asked, perking up.

"We left them there," he said, looking surprised by the question.

"You left them?!"

"Of course. Why would we bring them here? Their people should find them and give them whatever afterlife ritual they deem fit."

"But didn't you want to investigate?" I countered.

Baffled, he tilted his head to the side, giving me a strange look. "What could we possibly investigate that required us to take their remains? The cause of their deaths was self-evident. All we could do was to eradicate the beasts and close the portal so no more would threaten the local people."

"Okay, fine, I get that. But didn't you want to find out who had opened that portal, and why that had occurred?"

He hesitated before shaking his head. "No. Initially, we did not. Accidental portals are a sad reality on Dramnac. A variety of reasons can create one. Usually, the summoner will dispel it. If they are unable to do so, they are required by law to call upon a Shadow Lord or Gate Master to handle it."

My shoulders slumped. "Oh. So you know who opened those gates."

Once more, he hesitated before shaking his head again. "Not all of them. Like I said, people are required by law to ask for help. But not everyone does. Often, accidental portals occur because they did something they shouldn't have. Depending on the nature of the offense, the punishment can be quite severe, especially if it causes the death of innocents."

"Well, that sounds like solid grounds for you guys to have started an investigation!" I exclaimed.

He gave me an indulgent smile that, under different circumstances, might have come across as patronizing. "Yes. Normally, it would have been grounds for an investigation. Unfortunately, a Derakeen had not summoned the portals that caused those lethal incidents. At least, we have no reason to believe so."

"What do you mean?" I asked, taken aback.

"Remember how I told you that if you get caught in a rift, do not move because I can track the origin and destination of a phase shift?" Cedros asked.

I nodded.

"Well, the same applies to a portal. I can say where it originated and where it leads, just by looking at it. If I'm close enough to an active portal, I can get a sense of how many people went through it, and in which direction they traveled."

"Oh wow! That's badass!"

I chuckled, still finding that expression silly. "The main reason the Councilors gave us for not investigating is that we do not have galactic law enforcers to tackle such an endeavor, and we wouldn't even know where to start. Anyway, by the time we reached the origin, everyone was already gone."

"Right, but that's why having the remains of the victims would have helped. Their identity might have given us a trail to follow, assuming they were the summoners," I argued.

"Fair point. But we didn't think of that then. But the escalation of incidents is becoming a problem for us," Cedros said. "Beyond the fact that those portals are stretching us thin fighting aqrats roaming other worlds, they present a serious local threat. Right now, void beasts are going off-world. But what if the summoners start sending off-world beasts onto Dramnac?"

"Shit, I didn't think of that," I said, kicking myself for it.

"I will assist you in whatever capacity I can in achieving your mission, my Kaida," Cedros said in a solemn voice. "It is of great importance to your organization and my people that this be resolved."

"Really? You'll help?"

"Of course," he replied, as if that was self-evident.

"You're freaking awesome!" I exclaimed, throwing myself into his arms.

He burst out laughing and drew me onto his lap, immediately rubbing his face in my neck. His scales tickled me again, making me giggle.

"I will list all the incidents that took me to battle off-world, and will ask my brothers to do the same," Cedros offered.

"That would be fantastic! Any chance they could include the times, dates, origin and destination of the portals? Well, to the best of their recollection, of course."

"Yes, my Kaida. We will provide as much detail as we can recall."

"Oh!" I exclaimed, struck by a sudden idea. "Have any of the portals led to the shadow obsidian mines, or originated from them?"

He shook his head. "Not for any incident we've had to deal with. But there are a lot of accidental portals opened during the mining process. That's why there is always a Shadow Lord nearby, and at least a couple of Gate Masters on site at all times."

"Okay, that sounds like a good place to start. Any chance I can go check it out?" I asked, hopeful.

"Access to the shadow obsidian mine is strictly regulated. But I will be able to take you on my next day off," Cedros offered. "However, I must tell you that no Derakeen would *choose* to give away shadow obsidian stones, let alone to an off-worlder. They are far too valuable and much too dangerous in the wrong hands."

"I do not challenge your words, but off-worlders are somehow getting their hands on them. That needs to be stopped. And that means looking at every possibility, even the most improbable ones," I countered in a gentle tone.

"Agreed. I have faith in you, my Ejaya. I will do all in my power to see that you succeed in this endeavor."

I smiled and playfully tapped the rounded, little bone spikes that protruded from his chin. "If you're trying to make me like you, Cedros Qhelian, you're doing a great job of it!"

"Good! My mission to conquer you is working."

I chuckled and snuggled against him as he tightened his embrace and kissed my forehead.

CHAPTER 11
KAIDA

Waking up in Cedros's arms, naked but for my panties, was proving to be a herculean exercise in willpower. Notwithstanding his ridiculously hot body—alien though it was—the gentle but possessive way he always held me seriously messed with my girly bits. I'd spent the entire night having naughty dreams about him. And now, his stirring had awakened me right in the middle of a pretty torrid moment, leaving me every shade of horny.

Cedros rolled me onto my back. Lying on his side, his large palm resting possessively on my side, he stared at me with an unsettling intensity. My mouth went dry, and my stomach flip-flopped as I waited with great anticipation for what he would do. His fiery eyes appeared to glow as they studied my features. The complete silence only made his stance both more ominous and more thrilling. I almost expected him to bare his teeth at me and savagely sink his fangs into my throat.

He did not bare his teeth but leaned forward. With a will of their own, my lips parted, hoping for the kiss I craved with mind-boggling violence. I lifted my face towards his. To my dismay,

Cedros tilted his head to the side, kissing the artery pulsing in my neck instead. He then proceeded to rub his face there and along the curve of my shoulder before following a path down to my chest.

My fingers sank into his soft mane, my breath catching in my throat as his face hovered over my left breast. Just imagining how the rough texture of his tongue would feel on my already hardening nipples had me throbbing with need. With a very slow movement, his thumb caressed the side of my stomach. His throat began to glow, the soft heat emanating from it making my skin erupt in goosebumps. Still staring at my nipple, his face so close I could feel his breath fanning over it, Cedros smiled.

He slightly turned his head to give me a sideways glance, his smile taking on a smug edge that instantly had my cheeks burning.

"You are aroused again, my Kaida. And I haven't even touched your breasts."

I flinched, feeling both mortified and annoyed.

Yes, genius! I'm so fucking horny I could ride your tail if not your cock. Rather than pointing out the obvious, why the hell aren't you doing something about it?

Naturally, I said none of that out loud and reverted to a dumb human defense mechanism.

"You're not supposed to point that out," I said, frowning at him.

"Why not? It fills me with pride that I should arouse you," he said matter-of-factly.

"I was just having a wet dream," I said, hating the defensive tone of my voice. "It happens."

His scaly eyebrows rose as his smile broadened. "Wet dreams? Does that mean erotic dreams?"

My face further reddening was all the answer he needed. He chuckled, looking overly pleased with himself.

"Were those dreams about me? About us?"

"Cedros!"

His playfulness faded, and a serious, almost stern expression settled on his features. The sudden change in his demeanor took me aback.

"What, Kaida? It is a simple question. One we both know the answer to. Why do you insist on making such a big deal out of something so simple? I aroused you. Your body and your scent aren't so skittish about the facts. Why is it so hard for you to simply admit that you fantasized about us? I fantasize about you day and night. It flatters and honors me to know that I ignite your fire. Why do you deny me its acknowledgement? I want you, and I hope one day to make you burn for me. See? I said it, and the world didn't end."

I remained speechless, feeling both shamed and aroused by this assertive side of Cedros I'd never fully experienced before. As much as I hated getting called out, in this instance, I couldn't even counter any of his statements. I *was* being ridiculously prudish. But you didn't shed a lifetime of habits overnight.

"Your arousal woke me. You moaned my name. Do you have any idea what that did to me?"

I could have tried to imagine if his words, and the almost growling way in which he had spoken them hadn't increased the throbbing between my thighs. As if sensing their effect on me, Cedros turned to look at my crotch, his nostrils flaring. His teeth clenched, almost with anger. To my shock, he leaned down and licked my left nipple. The scratchy feel of his tongue on my hard nub had a bolt of fire exploding in the pit of my stomach. A strangled moan escaped me, and my toes curled while a shiver ran through me.

Cedros lifted his head to glower at me. "I am your Shadow Lord, and you are my Ejaya. There is nothing we can't say to each other or do together. Shed your irrational human constraints. They have no place between us. If you want something, just say it."

Before I could come up with an appropriate response, Cedros flapped his wings, just enough to fly out of the bed and to the entrance of the hygiene room. He cast a glance at me over his shoulder.

"I must prepare and head out to the black gate. You should find all the sustenance you require in the cooling unit. Trinit will come by in a couple of hours. Let her know if you need anything."

With that, he entered the hygiene room. The sound of the shower reached my ears moments later. But all I could think about was how wet he'd gotten me. My hand found its way inside my panties. I rubbed my clit while listening to the raining water in the other room. I could see how it was caressing his scales, trickling between the deep grooves of his muscular body, imagining it was my hands and tongue on him instead.

I bit on my tongue to silence the moans that wanted to rise from my throat as pleasure steadily built within me. My free hand pinched and caressed the nipple he had licked, trying to rekindle the intense sensation he had provoked with that single swipe of his tongue. Imagining how it would feel between my thighs had me toppling over the edge. I barely managed to bury my face in my pillow to muffle the sound of my shout of ecstasy.

I continued riding my hand until the tidal wave of pleasure began receding. The whole time, I hoped Cedros would walk back inside the room, find me in this compromising position, and ravage me. But as was his wont, as soon as he finished showering, he flew out of the house through the opening ceiling of the hygiene room, and vanished inside the portal he summoned mid-air.

Dejected, and annoyed with myself and this misery of my own making, I forced myself out of bed. After a quick shower, I got dressed. While I was working my way up to baring it all in front of Cedros, I wasn't there yet with complete strangers, female or otherwise.

I settled at the kitchen table to eat breakfast while sending a detailed request to Tedrick. Those other incidents Cedros had spoken of would give me a place to start. Many of these files were likely classified, and well above my pay grade. But there was no way the UPO hadn't documented each one of them. If they wanted me to solve this mess, they had better loosen their tongues and release a few files my way.

While waiting for a response, I tapped into the Dramnac knowledge network and read up everything I could about shadow obsidian, both in stone and dust form. The mines also held a particular fascination for me. I couldn't wait to take a gander there in person. I silently thanked the powers above that I should be a Shadow Lord's Ejaya. That alone opened countless doors for me. As a regular civilian, I would have needed to request a time slot to be allowed inside the premises and to be able to mine.

Every citizen of Dramnac could mine for four hours, once every two weeks. As this only applied to the legal bloodlines of the planet, I doubted I would even qualify for a slot. I considered submitting a request to the Oddran municipal authorities, but decided against it. I didn't want to risk an overzealous bureaucrat barring me entry until things could get sorted out.

These restrictions aimed at controlling the shadow obsidian market, and to prevent people from trying to raise their plateau level too quickly. From what I could read, carving shadow obsidian was a slow and painstaking process to avoid burning its energy by triggering accidental portals. With great care and patience, the miner excised small stones that could fit in the palm of a child's hand.

A professional miner could extract an average of ten stones in their four-hour window along with a small pouch of shadow obsidian dust. A regular civilian doing the work himself would get about half. Therefore, the wealthy usually hired a professional miner to work the mines in their stead during their slot. But like Cedros had explained, considering how much more obsidian was required to make their plateaus float even higher, it made sense they would try to maximize their extraction potential in the mines.

A shadow at the edge of my vision drew my attention. My lips parted in surprise at the sight of a beautiful emerald-green Derakeen landing on the terrace outside. She looked rather petite —by Derakeen standards—which put her at a height with me. Her golden eyes sparkled with warmth when I went to welcome her.

"Greetings, my sister," the female said, extending both of her hands towards me.

"Hello! You must be Trinit?" I said, instantly liking her.

I took her hands and, although surprised, didn't resist when she drew me in for a hug. Apparently, Cedros had done a good job of training me on that front. Thankfully, she didn't rub her face all over me. That would have been extremely awkward. However, her throat glowed, sending the most amazing warmth through my chest while she gave me a sisterly hug. It was insane how soothing and affectionate that felt.

"I am indeed Trinit," she said in a singsong voice as she released me. "My Rovain couldn't stop speaking about you. He said you seemed very sweet and that you were pretty, despite your strange appearance."

My jaw dropped. I blinked, stunned by such brutal honesty. "Strange appearance?" I echoed.

She nodded. "I'd never seen a human before. Rovain told me about your flat face, scaleless body, and the missing segment in your legs. I thought you would walk very stiffly with those straight legs. But your gait is incredibly fluid and elegant. I'm impressed. And your skin is so soft. I bet Cedros is constantly rubbing all over you. You must be wonderful to cuddle with at night."

"Wow, you guys truly have no problem just speaking your mind," I said, unable to decide if I was more amused than flabbergasted.

Her eyes widened, and she tilted her head to the side, giving me a curious look. "Of course we do. We're always honest among ourselves."

"Jeez… Do come in," I said, gesturing for her to follow me inside. "Are all Derakeens this forward?"

She shook her head. "No. Only Shadow Lords and Ejayas… or rather, only we are this fully open with each other."

As she settled on the couch, she gave me an assessing look while pursing her lips. I braced for what would follow.

"Why are you wearing these coverings?" she asked with genuine curiosity. "Aren't you hot or uncomfortable with them?"

"No," I said, while settling next to her. "As a human, it's a lifelong habit for me. Plus, we don't have scales like Derakeens to protect our soft skin."

"I see. That's unfortunate. I feel sorry for Cedros."

My back stiffened, liking less and less that brutal honesty. "Why sorry?"

"Your human customs are depriving him of the full contact he needs. That's rather unfair to him."

My face lost all warmth, and I lifted my chin defiantly. "I do not deprive him. That I'm not traipsing around the house naked all day doesn't mean that I don't strip out of my clothes for him when he needs contact."

She tilted her head again, this time looking at me like I was some oddity. "You are offended," she said, sounding surprised.

"Yes, a little. You've only just met me and are already passing harsh judgments about my interactions with Cedros," I said, annoyed by the defensiveness in my voice.

She smiled at me in an oddly maternal fashion, her face softening. "It is not harsh judgment, Kaida, and I certainly do not intend to offend you. Words are only mean-spirited if spoken untruthfully or out of malice. Your defensive reaction tells me Cedros has brought up the issue already."

"Yes, he has. And I'm working on it."

"Which is all anyone can ask. I do not pretend to understand how overwhelming it must be for you to be plucked from your world and dropped in this one. You've inherited the important role of an Ejaya, and so much of it clashes with everything your culture ever taught you."

I clasped my hands on my lap, trying to calm down. "It does feel rather overwhelming. I want to be a good Ejaya to Cedros, but I don't even fully understand the role. And the culture shock is a lot to assimilate."

Trinit gave me a sympathetic look and nodded slowly. She opened her mouth to say something, then appeared to change her mind, going with something else instead.

"Do you know why Shadow Lords and Ejayas are so fully honest with each other?" she asked.

I shook my head, majorly curious about that.

"It's because, in many ways, Shadow Lords are like younglings. As they raised themselves, they didn't develop the filters we normally do as we grow among others. They have the candor and forwardness of the little ones. They openly speak of what they think and feel, and ask the questions that pop up in their minds the minute they do. But do not mistake that for naivety or immaturity. They are responsible adults. They merely never developed the artifices and deception one acquires when immersed in social interactions."

"I see," I said, pensively.

"Do you?" Trinit asked without condemnation or provocation. "Like every unpaired Shadow Lord, Cedros has lived most of his life isolated. Your arrival has finally allowed him to break out of his shell. Through you, and thanks to you, his true personality can finally emerge. His interactions with you will play a huge role in defining just how much he will open up. Do not stunt him with your human customs."

I once more bristled at that. "I do not stunt him!"

"Not voluntarily, I'm sure. But your discomfort with straightforwardness tells me you've likely done it more than once already. For example, have you told him that he shouldn't say or ask certain things because it's unbecoming?"

My cheeks all but burst into flames. "What are you saying?" I asked, the defensiveness seeping back into my voice. "Should I just let him have his way with whatever he asks or wants?"

"Yes," she said, as if it was self-evident. "You should only refuse him if you believe it is bad for him or if it strongly makes you uncomfortable. Your purpose as an Ejaya is to keep him healthy and make him happy by whatever means necessary."

"Well, walking around naked makes me uncomfortable," I countered.

She gave me an indulgent smile. "Yes, it does, because it is your human way. I do not dismiss the reality of your discomfort. However, my sister, answer me this. So what if you're naked? It means nothing to us Derakeens. It will not cause you harm while inside your lair, and it will give Cedros what he sorely needs. Providing him full contact with you should be your number one priority, to keep him physically and mentally healthy and strong. What do you lose by granting him this? And what do you gain by denying him?"

I hated how stupid it made me feel to have it put it this way. "Nothing. I gain and lose nothing," I conceded. "But like I said, I'm working on it."

"Good. But then I will ask you the same thing about open communications with him."

I glared at her.

She chuckled. "Do not give me the evil eye, Kaida. I am not attacking you. I merely want to give you a different perspective, from an experienced, Dramnac-born Ejaya to a fledgling one. Some questions can be uncomfortable, and some topics embarrassing. But the sooner you shed your inhibitions, the sooner you will develop a strong bond with your Shadow Lord. You will never have a closer, more loyal friend in the universe than Cedros, like Rovain is mine."

I tucked my hair behind my right ear before tapping a finger on my bottom lip while I pondered her words.

"May I ask what kind of conversations or questions Rovain asked you that you deemed uncomfortable?"

"When he asked me to become his mate," Trinit answered without hesitation.

I recoiled, stunned by the unexpected answer. "Why? Did you already have someone else?"

She shook her head. "No. I was single when Rovain and I met. He was forty-one, and I was twenty-eight. It was already quite late for a Shadow Lord to find his Ejaya. We became lovers after a week, and he asked me to become his mate six months later. As I wasn't in love with him, I declined. It was quite difficult to reject his request, as I knew how much he wanted a family. But in this, I had to be true to myself."

"Ugh, that must have been very awkward. Were things tense between the two of you afterward?" I asked.

"Oh no! Not at all. He knew there was a good chance I would refuse. But he wanted me to know that, should I ever consider it, he would love for us to be mated."

"Did your affair stop then?" I asked, slightly stunned.

"Not at all. We continued as before for a little over eight years. And then he turned fifty."

"Why do I sense a big twist coming?" I said, burning with curiosity.

Trinit chuckled. "I wouldn't call it a big twist. But something forced me to make a decision. You see, when an unmated Shadow Lord turns fifty, he is expected to try to reproduce with any willing female whose presence is tolerable to him. However, for those who, like Rovain, have an Ejaya, there is no restriction as to who they can couple with."

She let the words hang between us for a moment, leaving me to sort it out.

And then it hit me.

"Oh, hell no! Please don't tell me you're expected to sit in the room with them while they're going at it so that your presence can dampen the discomfort for him?!" I exclaimed, horrified.

She nodded. "That is *exactly* the expectation... Although, it's usually flying alongside them since most of the couplings occur in flight. But the thought of bearing witness to him attempting to impregnate however many females while making it easier for him drove me insane. Therefore, I told him that if he still wanted me, I would marry him."

"It made you realize you were in love with him, after all," I said with a smile.

Trinit laughed. "No. I'm still not *in love* with him. Rovain isn't my soulmate. But I do love him, and I never met anyone else that I loved equally or more. Rovain is my best friend, a wonderful lover, an amazing father to our offspring, and he makes me very happy."

"Oh. Hmm… Does he know?"

She laughed again. "Of course he does. I told you, there are no secrets between an Ejaya and her Shadow Lord. He knows that I'm not in love with him, but he loves me, and the love I bear him is enough. He is happy. It's all that matters."

"Wow," I said, shifting uneasily in my seat. "It is common for Ejayas and Shadow Lords to be lovers?"

"Yes, very common. But it's not compulsory. This is one of the things that you should refuse him if you're not comfortable with it."

"But… Aren't they all virgins before meeting an Ejaya?" I asked, heat creeping back up my cheeks.

"Yes, they all are."

"Well, isn't it pretty much guaranteeing that they will fall in love with their Ejaya? It seems a little cruel, like leading them on, if you're not in love with them," I said, choosing my words carefully.

By the knowing smile she gave me, Trinit wasn't fooled at all by my underlying meaning. "Oh, my dear sister, a Shadow Lord *always* falls in love with his Ejaya. No other female in the universe can make him feel what we do. Whether you couple with Cedros or not, he is already in love with you. Sex will not increase or diminish his feelings for you. If you desire him, then enjoy yourself. Denying him—and yourself—is merely punishment for both of you. Do not overthink or overcomplicate things. Approach your life on Dramnac with Cedros with the same candor and boldness of a youngling. Be there for Cedros, and let him be there for you."

"Sheesh. You've certainly given me a lot to think about. But it's great to finally talk with someone who understands what my role is meant to be," I said sheepishly. "Speaking of which, I do have a question for you. How much say do I have when it comes to the way others interact with Cedros?"

Her eyes widened in surprise upon hearing my question. "I'm not quite sure what you mean."

I recounted the market incident with the freeloaders asking for portals.

"Oh Gods! Tell those stingy leeches to get lost. When it comes to the welfare of her Shadow Lord, the word of an Ejaya is the law. Be as viciously protective of him as you deem appropriate. No one will challenge you. It is your right *and* your duty."

"I'm loving the sound of that," I said with an evil grin.

Trinit chuckled in approval.

"Tell me, do you have a career, or is being an Ejaya a full-time role?" I asked.

"I do have a career. I'm an educator for younglings, which makes me the perfect mentor for you. One of my specialties is preparing them for the Shadow Trail. Speaking of which, I came here to give you some rift training. On your feet, my dear. It's time to get you lost in the void."

CHAPTER 12
CEDROS

My head spun as I opened the portal home. The most virulent toxin coursed through my veins from fighting the aqrats and other fiendish void creatures. The roots of my scales burned like a thousand fires. I wanted to claw them off my flesh. After only a few days of bliss with my Kaida, I had forgotten just how excruciating the aqrat toxin was.

Rovain had been right in warning me of just how dangerous the Vessant sector had become. The pilgrims had lured an absurd number of beasts, many of them getting grievously injured. It would take at least a couple more days to track down and eradicate all the roaming threats in the area. But now wasn't the time for me to dwell on it. Anyway, I couldn't focus enough for it.

I emerged from the portal on the terrace of my lair. The large glass doors lay wide open. The scent of sizzling meat wafted to me, but my brain only registered Kaida's divine aroma. Through the fog of my pain, it struck me like a boulder to the head. My knees wobbled, and an almost vicious growl rose from my throat as a rabid hunger surged through me.

Flapping my wings, I dashed forward to capture my salvation. I barely processed the presence of the green Derakeen female sitting on a stool.

"Oh, shit!" Kaida whispered, her eyes wide with shock and a sliver of fear as I swooped down on her.

She took two steps away from the cooking plate where she was preparing her meal before I grabbed her. In my debilitating need, I nearly crushed her in my arms, my protective instincts reining me in at the last minute. The oddest sound trickled out of my throat, part whimper, part purr, and part growl as I rubbed my face all over hers.

The feel and scent of her immediately sent my glands into overdrive. My nezarone hormones began running through my veins, dampening some of the pain. But it was too little, a mere trickle. I needed more… much more.

Through the painful haze, I realized those wretched coverings she wore were the cause. With a will of their own, my claws shot out, and with a savage roar, I tore the obnoxious fabric to shreds. I vaguely heard a distant gasp, but my own strangled moan of ecstasy at the contact of her bare flesh against mine buried it. My knees wobbled again, and I fought to keep my eyes from rolling to the back of my head.

With the floodgates now fully open, my nezarone rushed through me, making me dizzy. My skin tingled, and my head swam. Feeling drunk, I started stumbling out of the kitchen.

A familiar feminine voice chuckled behind us. "By the Gods! Someone is in serious need!" the female said with amusement. "I will leave you both to it, then. See you in the morning for your next training, Kaida!"

At the same time she flapped her wings to leave, Kaida's voice calling my name pierced through my daze.

"Cedros! The food will burn! Let me at least take it off the cooking plate! Cedros!"

I waved a hand towards the cooking plate, my kinetic powers

tossing aside whatever had been cooking on top of it onto the counter.

"But… it… ugh…"

Whatever Kaida had meant to say, she apparently gave up. Anyway, I wouldn't have been in any state to respond. I carried her to my nest, half-running, half-flying. As soon as we landed on the cushion, I wrapped myself around my Ejaya, rubbing my body and my face all over her. I couldn't seem to get close enough to her. I ended up resting my face between her breasts, where her divine scent was strong. Feeling groggy, I fell asleep to the sound of her single heart beating and the gentle caress of her delicate fingers in my hair.

~

A fluttering sensation brought me back to awareness. I almost opened my eyes, but remained still when I realized Kaida's fingers were gently tracing the grooves of my abdominal muscles. It slightly tickled, eventually drawing a smile from me.

"You're awake," Kaida whispered, without stopping the motion of her hand on me.

I opened my eyes to look at her. "I am now. I'm sorry I so brutally grabbed you and damaged your coverings," I whispered back, sheepishly.

She smiled. "It was quite the dramatic entrance, one that my poor clothes will sadly not recover from. But it's okay. I could see that you were in pain."

"I was. And you made it all better," I said, my gaze locked on her fingers still drawing lines between my muscles. "I like when you touch me. I wish I could touch you, too."

Kaida frowned at my words. "You touch me all the time," she argued.

I shook my head. "I hug you and cuddle with you, but I do

not touch you. I would like to explore you, all of you, like when you let me touch your breasts," I said wistfully.

Instead of the expected explanation as to why it would be improper for me to do so according to human standards, Kaida held my gaze with an unreadable expression.

"I'm not stopping you," she said in a soft voice.

I stiffened, my gaze boring into hers to make sure I had correctly understood her meaning. "But... won't that bother you? Won't it make you uncomfortable?"

"If it does, I'll tell you."

I hesitated for a second longer, my fingers twitching with anticipation. I lifted my hand and carefully began tracing her features, from her delicate eyebrows, to the bridge of her dainty nose, to her full lips, and the gentle curve of her cheeks. She remained still, her body relaxed as she observed me while I explored her.

By the Gods! Her skin was so incredibly soft under my hand. I never thought I could become so addicted to this. To me, a sensuous touch always involved the supple hardness of scales and their gentle scraping against my palm. The sensation of my scales was likely odd to her. Did she enjoy it, or did it irritate her?

I was readying to ask her the question when my hand gliding over her breast elicited a completely different urge. Unable to resist, I leaned down and licked her nipple. Kaida shivered. I glanced up at her, my hand cupping her breast while my thumb flicked the hardening little numb.

"Did you like when I licked it? We can tell each other anything, my Ejaya," I added, when her cheeks turned pink, and she appeared to hesitate.

She took a deep breath, then nodded. "Yes, it feels very nice."

I smiled, pleased by Kaida's response and proud of her for letting go more and more of her illogical human inhibitions. I lowered my head to lick her nipple once more, loving its odd texture against my tongue.

"Is my tongue too rough?" I asked.

She shook her head. "No. It's actually wonderful," my Ejaya said with a nervous laugh.

I grinned smugly, before returning my attention to her breasts, licking, pinching, and fondling them until Kaida's breathing accelerated. The growing scent of her arousal had my abdominal muscles constricting and my length straining to extrude. The delectable aroma lured me downward, my mouth watering as I kissed and caressed my way down to her pelvic area.

A rumbling purr rose from my throat when I deeply inhaled her musk. Kaida emitted a strange sound that had me looking up at her. I shook my head at the embarrassment on her face.

"Let me guess… By human standards, you're not supposed to inhale another person's arousal," I said tauntingly.

Kaida's face turned crimson red, making me chuckle. "I would assume this would apply to pretty much any civilized culture," she replied defensively. "I mean, I didn't see anyone walking around the black gate sniffing random people's crotches."

"But you are not a random person. You are my Ejaya," I said with a possessive growl in my voice. "Every single one of your scents, in all their shades, are mine to enjoy. And the exquisite aroma of the arousal *I* stirred within you is *my* prize, *my reward*. You *will not* deny it to me."

I had expected her to argue or to mumble something in response to my claim. Instead, Kaida bit her bottom lip, her eyes darkening while the scent of her need grew even more potent, filling my nostrils.

A violent desire surged through me. On instinct, I spread her legs wide open and buried my face between her thighs. Kaida gasped, one of her hands closing around one of my shadow horns. I rubbed my face all over her sex while taking another deep breath. A hungry growl rumbled in my chest as I slowly licked her from bottom to top. The taste of her natural lubricant dampening the aggravating thin fabric that covered her core nearly drove me insane with need.

A bolt of lust exploded in my loins, and I parted my pelvic scales, freeing my length. I hissed in pleasure-pain from finally being released from my confines, my shaft standing proudly erect. With that pressure alleviated, I returned my attention to my prize. Before I could stop myself, I sliced the thin string of fabric holding the bottom undies on Kaida.

My Ejaya gasped again, this time with a hint of protest that turned into a moan when my tongue once more swiped over her core, this time unimpeded. Dear Gods! The taste of her nearly had me spilling my seed. I had wanted to take my time admiring the unusual appearance of a human female's sex, but my need to taste and devour her was too great.

I lapped at her with greed, reveling in the sound of her moans in my ears, their intensity growing each time I focused my attention on the engorged little nub above her slit. I sucked on it, like my readings on humans had suggested. Kaida's immediate response, her hands tightening around my horns while her pelvis lifted towards my face, had another wave of lust rush to my loins.

Retracting my claws, I slipped two fingers inside my female's opening. It was warm, slick with arousal as her inner walls constricted around them. Without slowing down my attention to her clitoris, I began making love to Kaida with my hand, my fingertips soon finding the sensitive bundle of nerves inside her.

My Ejaya suddenly crying out and her body seizing took me by surprise. My head jerked up, my fingers still moving in and out of her while I admired the expression of pure bliss on her face. Gods, she was breathtaking in all her otherworldliness. Her skin flushed, eyes tightly closed, lips parted, Kaida was shaking from the last tremors of ecstasy. And it was I, Cedros Qhelian, who had given so much pleasure to this female.

As she came back down to reality, I climbed on top of her, holding my weight with one arm. I cupped her face with my free hand, my thumb caressed her lips. To my shock, she took it inside her mouth and gently sucked on it. The unexpected gesture resonated directly in my groin. My shaft jerked in response.

Kaida stiffened, her eyes widening as she realized my extruded length was pressing against her stomach. Although I ached to couple with her, and despite my need to find my own release, I would not pressure her into anything.

"Calm, my Kaida. I will not try to couple with you," I said in a soft voice, while pulling my thumb from her mouth to caress her cheek in a soothing gesture. "Your scent, your taste, and your pleasure aroused me. Keeping my shaft confined was painful. Give me a few moments, and I will soften."

A strange expression flitted over her features. I leaned down and pressed my lips to hers. To my delight, Kaida immediately responded, her arms closing around me. When her mouth opened and her tongue teased mine for entry, I complied, feeling both curious and nervous. I had never kissed anyone like that.

Gods! Even her tongue was soft as it swirled around mine, teasing, tasting, exploring. I didn't need Kaida to tell me that my performance was clumsy. That she didn't seem to mind, and that it didn't dampen her enthusiasm, put me at ease and even emboldened me. However, too soon, Kaida ended the kiss. Her hands caressing my back slipped to my chest to gently push me away.

At first, I thought she wanted me to simply get off her, but she guided me onto my back instead. To my shock, my Ejaya did what I'd been doing to her ever since we'd first met. She rubbed her face all over mine, brushing her lips over my cheeks, eyes, nose, and lips before burying her face in my neck. I purred with pleasure as Kaida's hands roamed over my body while she continued to rub herself against me.

A powerful shiver coursed through me when her soft, wet tongue began tracing the lines of my chest muscles in a downward path towards my stomach. When her hand glided towards my shaft, I caught her wrist, startling her.

"What are you doing, my Kaida?" I asked in a breathy tone.

She lifted her head to look me straight in the eye. "Reciprocating," she said, as if it was self-evident.

A burning need erupted in my pelvic area, liquid fire burning deep in my belly at the thought of Kaida's mouth on my sex. I swallowed hard as I tried to silence my instinctive urge to tell her to proceed.

"You don't have to do that, Kaida. No debt is owed. The pleasure I gave you was freely granted while sating my own curiosity," I whispered.

"I know I don't have to. I just *want* to," she said matter-of-factly. "I am as curious about you as you were about me."

My throat heated, the warm glow radiating as my hearts filled with delight at her response. "I love that you are openly speaking your mind and your desires. I love that you are beginning to see that there should be no embarrassment, secrets, or restrictions between us."

She once again gave me a strange look while she reflected on my words. "You know, you're right. It *is* nice to be able to just say what I think and want without worrying about propriety or being judged."

"*Never*, my Kaida. Never between us. I want to know all of you, the real you, and for you to know all of me, no barriers."

She smiled in that wonderful way that made her eyes spark. "I'm really starting to like you, Cedros Qhelian."

"You had better, Kaida Daigo. I intend to make you crazy about me," I said with a boldness I never realized I possessed.

She chuckled and rubbed her hand over my stomach like one would ruffle the hair of a bratty youngling. The gesture drew her gaze to my shaft, still half erect. All amusement faded from her expression, and she stared at my length in shock, not to say horror. A sense of dread descended over me, and I held my breath, waiting to hear what thoughts were crossing her mind. I'd read enough about human males to know we shared many similarities but also significant differences. Were my ridges and spikes frightening her?

"Damn, Cedros… You're huge!" Kaida whispered.

I blinked, having expected a completely different type of comment. "Huge? As in too huge for a human? For you?" I asked carefully.

Kaida glanced my way, looking borderline traumatized, before returning her attention towards my shaft. She swallowed hard, then shrugged, looking uncertain.

"Well, we stretch, so that would eventually fit. But damn…" she muttered, sounding as if she was talking more to herself than answering me.

She extended a hand towards my shaft, tentatively brushing her fingertips against its side. An inferno erupted low in my belly, and I barely silenced a moan.

"Oh, my God! You're pre-lubricated?!" Kaida exclaimed, her head jerking towards me.

"Yes." I nodded while eyeing her warily, unable to decide if she thought it was a good or a bad thing.

"Well, that's going to be helpful," she mumbled, once more sounding like she was talking to herself.

My abdominal muscles contracted again when her hand wrapped more decisively around my shaft, my girth too great for her fingers to fully close around me. Although her hand moved up and around my length, she wasn't stroking me, but rather examining and studying it with great fascination. Despite my burning arousal, her reactions fascinated me, too. A multitude of expressions flitted over her face, from curiosity to a mix of awe and confusion.

My shaft had many ridges, mirrored on each side, two big ones at the bottom, and four medium ones around the middle, and a series of smaller ones framing my dormant spikes, which she would merely assume to be a row of circular bumps on the transversal side. But they were so much more.

I took in a whistling breath as Kaida finally began to stroke me. No one had ever touched that most intimate part of me before. Sure, I'd pleasured myself in the past, but this… this was unlike anything I'd ever experienced before. Her hand moved up and down, her thumb giving my ridges a wondrous extra rub. But it was the way she twisted her wrist when she reached the head, her grip tightening in an exquisite fashion, before she stroked me back down that had me panting in no time.

I'd just closed my eyes to surrender myself to the pleasure my Ejaya was giving me when she gasped and yanked her hand away from me. My eyes jerked open, and I stared at her in confusion. But Kaida was staring at my length in shock.

"What's that? What's happening?" she asked.

"It's just my ridges. The median ones swell during intercourse to enhance the female's sensations, and to expose their more sensitive inner edges to enhance my own sensations," I explained, my voice gravelly from having my building pleasure so brutally interrupted. "The smaller ridges will start undulating after."

"Ooh wow! Okay, that's wicked," Kaida said.

To my relief, she didn't prolong my torture and wrapped her hand around me once more, resuming her ministrations. I closed my eyes again and moaned in delight as liquid flames swirled in my nether region. As pleasure built, my heating chamber warmed, and my tongue itched with the urge to strike a spark so that I could breathe fire. But then an unexpected wet warmth settled on the tip of my shaft, forcing my eyes open again.

Before I could fully grasp what had been the cause, Kaida looked up at me with a flabbergasted expression.

"Oh, my God! You taste like mango!" she exclaimed.

"I taste like…?"

I never finished my sentence. Kaida bowed down her head, engulfing the upper half of my shaft into her mouth as if she'd been starving for days. I sat up with a shout, this pleasure almost too much to bear as her head greedily bobbed over me. One hand fisting the blanket covering our nest, my free one found its way into Kaida's hair. It took every bit of my willpower not to direct the movement of her head, nor to fist her soft locks with painful strength.

Gods! I could die with pleasure in that instant. Heated hydrogen filled my chamber, clamoring to be burned. My muscles contracted, and my body tensed as I neared completion. Simultaneously, the spikes along the upper sides of my shaft extruded, the inferno of Kaida's mouth on their overly sensitive surface, making me cry out.

I felt Kaida pulling away from me the moment my spikes began undulating. "No!" I shouted, my hand closing over hers to keep it from moving away. "Please, don't stop. It's just my spikes. They won't hurt you. Please… don't stop!"

I threw my head back with a hiss of pleasure when my Kaida complied, accelerating the movement of her hand on me. An uninterrupted flow of growly moans were pouring out of me, my hips moving up in counterpoint to her hand stroking me as I readied to topple over. Her mouth closing over my shaft, and her teeth grazing my undulating spikes did me in.

My spine seized violently, and a volcano erupted in my loins, its searing fire rushing through me. My powerful roar died in a stream of shadow flames as liquid bliss shot out of me. My eyes rolled to the back of my head while my Kaida continued to frantically bob over me, her hand still working me, drawing out every last drop of my seed. I collapsed on the cushion the minute I'd used up the warm hydrogen in my heating chamber.

Dazed, I remained boneless, my body shaking while I waited for the room to stop spinning. As I regained my bearings, I refocused on Kaida, who had settled on top of me. I embraced her, one arm wrapped around her back, and the hand of the other resting on the bare mound of her behind. She was looking at me with the strangest but softest expression, laced with something akin to amusement.

"Now we know," she said softly.

I blinked, unsure what she meant. "What do we know, my Kaida?"

"You breathe shadow flames when you climax," she responded teasingly. "Good thing your house is flame-proof. That was an impressive eruption."

I chuckled, my scales darkening with embarrassment. By the way she'd wiggled her eyebrows when she said the word "eruption" I could guess she wasn't merely referring to my shadow flames.

"I clearly do. Better shadow flames than fire, though. They don't leave dark smudges on the walls," I said, before rubbing my snout against her nose. "Thank you for this unexpected gift, my Kaida. There aren't enough words for me to tell you just how happy you make me."

She opened her mouth to respond. By the tenderness on her face, I suspected she had been about to reciprocate, but then closed her mouth. I didn't think she was holding back. My Kaida didn't quite know yet how to word what she was feeling. I didn't mind. We had plenty of time. She was mine, and before our six months were over, Kaida would be my true mate.

I smiled and claimed her lips in a possessive kiss. Her passionate response confirmed what I knew in my hearts. She was mine.

CHAPTER 13
KAIDA

Sitting at the kitchen table in my oversized t-shirt and bikini bottom, I pored over the files Tedrick had sent me regarding various shadow portal incidents. It boggled my mind that the UPO had managed to keep a lid on some of the gruesomely tragic instances that had occurred. While I understood why they would want to keep this hush-hush, it made me wonder what other terrible secrets they were keeping from the galactic community.

As much as I wished our leaders could show more transparency, I'd been an Enforcer long enough to know how too much knowledge led to panic and unrest. If tomorrow people found out that a random portal could open out of the blue in their backyard, and that nightmarish creatures could pour out of it to decimate their loved ones, things would get messy very quickly. Those who would take an angel dive into the paranoia rabbit hole would prove problematic. But it was the opportunists that worried me the most. If the news spread, shady individuals would come out of the woodwork to join the race to conquer portals.

As if summoned by that thought, the muted thunderclap of a

portal opening had me jerking my head up from my laptop. Through the large patio doors, I saw Cedros emerge from the black vortex. My heart fluttered, and a smile immediately settled on my face. It still baffled me how quickly I'd developed a major crush on the alien that I got to call my husband.

Cedros was sweet, funny, and so easy to be around. No one had ever gone so much out of their way to please me. And it wasn't even forced. My dragon genuinely loved taking care of me and making me happy. Every time I smiled, whatever the reason, he smiled too—glowed even—as if this simple display of my joyful state echoed into him. Cedros wasn't an Empath, yet you'd think he was merely by the way he responded to my emotions.

I jumped out of my chair, quickly ridding myself of my over-sized t-shirt to go greet him. Aside from the fact that I no longer minded strutting about naked in his presence, I'd grown quite addicted to the feel of his scales and hard body against my bare skin. I could already hear the rumbling purr he would make, and how his scales would gently scrape my neck and shoulder line. My toes curled in anticipation as I hurried to the patio doors.

They parted before him, and he opened his arms wide for me. His glowing smile, the tenderness filled with happiness in his eyes, as he gazed upon me, turned me upside down. Cedros always looked at me as if I were the most wonderful treasure in the universe. I had never felt so wanted and loved—not to say adored—ever before in my life. Trinit's words about how Cedros would fall in love with me replayed in my head as I threw myself into his arms. I didn't doubt for a minute that he was indeed well on his way there.

"My Kaida," he whispered, picking me up before rubbing his face all over mine.

I wrapped my legs around his waist, my hands sinking into his hair, while his settled on my bum to hold me up. Right on cue, he started purring while his scales tickled my neck. I giggled, which made him chuckle, too. He lifted his head to look at me, a world of affection brimming in his fiery eyes. He leaned forward and claimed my mouth. I gladly responded to his kiss, my lips parting in order to deepen it.

I would never tire of the roughness of his tongue as it tangled with mine. Every time, it reminded me how it had felt between my thighs four days ago. Things had definitely changed between us since that moment. Although we hadn't repeated that, we now showered together, regularly kissed like lovers, and indulged in the occasional heavy petting. It was only a matter of days before we took things to the next level.

One thing was certain: Cedros would wait for me to give a clear signal to push things further. Like most males, I could tell that he was constantly horny. And yet, he never made a move unless I gave him an undisputable sign that I was in the mood, or if the undeniable scent of my arousal tipped him off I was itching for a little something.

It had troubled me at first, considering Cedros had constantly been on my ass about openly expressing my desires. However, further talks with Trinit during our morning trainings had enlightened me. As Ejayas were sworn to do everything in their power to please their Shadow Lords, the latter avoided putting them on the spot with certain things, such as sex. Unless they clearly believed she might be interested, they wouldn't put her in a position where she would feel obligated to consent, or feel horrible for refusing.

I already knew that there was a definite consent from me coming his way. However, I liked this slow building of the sexual tension between us. It would make it even more enjoyable once we went the whole nine yards.

Assuming that massive cock of his doesn't split me in half.

His hand roaming over my back had a few shivers coursing through me. I softly moaned, wanting more. To my chagrin, instead of growing bolder, Cedros broke the kiss.

"Why do you insist on wearing that tiny piece of fabric?" he asked softly, his voice devoid of condemnation but filled with confusion as he pulled on the small string of my bikini.

I glanced between us at the black bikini bottom I hadn't removed after ditching my t-shirt, then looked back up at Cedros.

"Because I'm not comfortable sitting my bare butt and cooch down on every surface in this house," I said in a mocking tone.

"Why not?" he asked with genuine curiosity.

"In case you have forgotten, my nether region isn't like your people's. The Derakeens' private parts are protected inside your bodies, not mine. I'd rather not worry about what bacteria I might sit on, or if some freaky Dramnac critter is trying to crawl inside my cooch to take a nap while I'm working."

Cedros burst out laughing. "Fair point," he conceded. "I cannot deny the appeal of wanting to crawl into the welcoming warmth of your... *cooch.*"

He silenced my shocked gasp with a kiss and rubbed his snout against my nose. I loved a naughty sense of humor. And my Cedros was beautifully coming out of his timid and awkward shell with each passing day. As Trinit had so accurately predicted, now that he had an Ejaya, his true personality was finally emerging—and I was loving every bit of it.

"I have presents for you, my Kaida," Cedros said proudly, changing the subject. He gestured with his head at something behind him. "Sadly, I cannot stay too long. I asked Elros to cover for me for an hour, but things are still a little heated in the Vessant sector."

"A present?" I asked, stretching my neck to look over his shoulder.

I'd been so busy sucking face with my man that I hadn't noticed the hover platform ladened with massive wrapped goods that had followed him out of the portal.

"Presentsss," he rectified, emphasizing the plural. He kissed the tip of my nose before setting me back down on my feet. "You were overdue for a proper work desk, vidscreen, holographic projector, and your personal gym."

I squealed and clapped my hands like a schoolgirl before running to the platform to take a closer look.

Cedros chuckled. "Take the platform to your room. I have another to fetch. Then I can set everything up for you."

"Sir, yes, sir!" I said with a salute before ordering the hover platform to follow me.

Cedros shook his head at me and reentered the portal. I'd barely reached the large room he'd put at my disposal when I heard him return. For the next half-hour, I buzzed around him like an overly excited kid, making him laugh as he deftly set up everything for me, since he wouldn't let me help. Apparently, you didn't work on setting up your own presents.

The badass desk's height could be adjusted with vocal commands, including configurable presets. The high-res, large-scale vidscreen would have even the highest-ranking execs at the Enforcers HQ drooling with envy. Although impressively big, my desk chair was plush and comfy. Figuring out I could easily do three-sixty spins on it had Cedros both laughing and facepalming when I made myself drunkenly dizzy from spinning too much.

When he went on to put together a complete home gym with both resistance and cardio equipment, I couldn't help being impressed.

"You're fantastic at setting this stuff up. I'd be pulling my hair out, trying to figure out the instructions and making a complete mess of things," I said.

Cedros's scales darken as he gave me a sheepish, almost guilty grin. "Well, I actually practiced first," he confessed. "I didn't want to embarrass myself in front of you by being utterly clueless."

I burst out laughing and went to kiss his cheek. "You are

freaking adorable," I said, melting before such sweet honesty. "No human male would have ever admitted that."

He gave me an inquisitive look. "Why? Is that another thing humans shouldn't say?"

I shook my head. "Nope, it's just human men being silly. They have this misplaced ego and the need to show they're 'the competent manly-man in charge' even when they don't know what the fuck they are doing. In fact, that trait tends to show *especially* when they're clueless about something. And the more they fumble, the more they'll double down on pretending they got it."

Cedros scrunched his face. "That sounds terribly unproductive."

"That, my dear, is quite the understatement. Annoying as fuck is a lot more accurate. Especially when you're lost in the middle of bumfuck nowhere, and you're hungry, and terribly need to pee, and Mister Manly-Man refuses to ask for directions because, for some dumb reason, he thinks asking for help undermines his manhood and virility," I said, rolling my eyes.

Cedros chuckled. "Sounds to me like you would be better off with a Derakeen male then. We... *I*... have no such issues."

I laughed at the shameless way in which he batted his eyes at me as he said that, a behavior he'd started copying from me.

"I would tend to agree," I said with a wink.

He beamed at me, then resumed his work. In no time, he had everything up and running.

"I have one last present for you," he said, his eyes sparkling. "I hope you'll love it!"

"I'm sure I will," I said, dying with curiosity.

This time, he opened the portal directly inside my room instead of going back to the terrace, although he did so near the door. Shifting restlessly on my feet, I waited impatiently for his return, my imagination running wild as to the nature of the present.

I wasn't a material girl. I needed nothing fancy and wasn't high maintenance. But I loved surprises and gifts in general. It could be something as simple as a bag of gummy bears. Growing up an orphan in a poor colony, I hadn't gotten spoiled often. Therefore, the merest gesture touched me deeply. It told me that another person had thought of me, that they had held me in high enough esteem to want to do something nice for me, simply because they cared.

And Cedros was the master at showing me just how much he cared.

My heart leapt when he emerged from the portal. However, my enthusiasm instantly faded when I saw the apologetic expression on his face.

"I'm sorry, my Kaida. But the surprise will have to wait. A fresh wave of aqrats is swarming the Vessant sector. I am needed."

"Of course!" I exclaimed, walking up to him. "Do what you must to keep people safe. I can wait. You be careful and come back to me in one piece."

"Always, my Ejaya."

He kissed my lips, then reentered the portal. Heaving a sigh of worry, I turned towards my new desk. However, halfway through the motion, movement at the edge of my vision had me jerking my head back towards the collapsing portal. As the dark vortex vanished, I glanced around the door, especially the upper left corner of the wall, near the ceiling. I could have sworn something had come out of the portal and flown upward in a blur.

Seeing and hearing nothing, I shrugged it off and returned my attention to connecting all of my new gear to the network. But a solid ten-minutes into it, the growing impression of being observed unsettled me. I kept looking around the room and out of the large windows, but saw nothing. I even stopped moving a couple of times, keeping my breathing shallow to see if I could catch any sound… in vain. At some point, a powerful shiver ran down my spine.

No wonder I'm chilled, sitting here with my boobs hanging out.

I headed to the kitchen, where I'd discarded my t-shirt when Cedros had arrived. Just as I was about to put it on, I saw the blur again, this time fading by the wall next to the table. On instinct, I swiped my t-shirt in that direction. My heart nearly jumped out of my chest when, for a split second, I saw a large, purplish pair of glowing eyes and a wide, toothy mouth. I screamed, stumbling backwards before running towards the bedroom.

Something had entered the house through the portal. Not an aqrat, but something else. Something stealthy and with a mouth big enough to chop my head off clean with one bite of its dagger teeth.

I needed to get to my blaster if I was to survive the beast.

Another blur shot past me overhead before the vision of horror materialized before me. Floating almost two meters above the floor, the shadowy creature appeared to simply be a round head with glowing purple eyes and a Cheshire Cat mouth. Countless shadow tentacles surrounded it with glowing tips from whence emanated what resembled electric tendrils.

I screamed again. Carried by my momentum, and knowing I couldn't turn around and hope to escape it, I dove into a roll under it and right back onto my feet to keep running towards the bedroom. As I did so, it stretched one of its tentacles at me at dizzying speed. I felt the electric shock right below my shoulder blades before the creature vanished again. However, the debilitating, Taser-like pain I had expected never came. It slightly pinched at the most, but nowhere near enough to hurt or cause discomfort. I could only assume I'd gotten lucky and that the beast's tentacle hadn't managed to get proper contact with me.

And I will not give it a chance to.

I dashed inside our bedroom and made a beeline for the closet. The creature zapped me a couple more times in the process. Like the first time, neither inflicted actual pain. It qualified as a strong tingle at best. Instead of reassuring me, my overactive imagination went into overdrive. Maybe the creature's lightning wasn't meant to electrocute but was instead infecting me with God only knew what. Was it some kind of slow acting paralytic? Was it some toxin similar to the one from the aqrats that made Cedros go rabid?

Heart pounding, I shoved the dreadful thoughts at the back of my mind as I fumbled with the crate containing my weapons. I shouted when the length of a shadowy tentacle slipped along my back. A powerful tingling lingered for a moment while my head jerked in every direction in my vain attempt to locate my stalker.

The wretched thing was toying with me. While a part of me rejoiced that it hadn't already bitten half of my face off, the paranoid side of me was coming up with explanations for this odd behavior that I didn't like one bit. Plenty of fiendish creatures played with their prey before feasting. Some did it because fear kicked their target's hormonal system into overdrive, flooding their system with what their predator craved. Others did it to allow whatever venom or toxin they were tactically injecting their victim with to act in a way that would make digesting them easier later. I suspected my stalker fell into the latter category. It was fast enough that it could have killed me a long time ago, if that had been its intention.

I finally got a hold of my blaster, setting it to lethal, then yanking my combat uniform out of the crate. My eyes still scanning the room for any blur that could reveal the creature's location, I quickly moved towards the glass wall of the room, all but pressing my back to it to make sure it couldn't attack me from behind. Weapon raised, I battled with my suit, trying to slip it on. If I was going to be found dead, mangled by some shadow beast, it sure as hell wouldn't be with my tits hanging out and my ass mostly exposed in my barely there excuse of a bikini bottom.

At last, I caught the blur closing in on me. Without hesitation, I took multiple shots at it, but missed as it swerved, its shadowy form appearing briefly before it disappeared again. Still struggling to put on my suit, I decided to make a dash for the hygiene room and lock myself inside. Randomly shooting at the ceiling, grateful that the stone walls appeared as impervious to blaster fire as to dragon flames, I made a run for it.

I all but dove inside the room, slamming the door behind me. Without pause, I slipped my feet inside the legs of my pants, yanking the waist up to close the magnetic clasp. Thankfully, years of practice made it easy, despite the blaster still clutched in my right hand. I was stuffing my left arm into the vest of my combat suit when the creature materialized less than a meter in front of me. Two of its tentacles wrapped around the dangling part of my vest, yanking it, and tossing it halfway across the room.

I screeched, thinking my heart would give in from fright, yet managed to shoot the nightmarish thing straight in the face. It turned into vaporous shadows. For a split second, I almost shouted in victory, expecting the dark smoke to fade and dissipate like it had with the aqrats when we shot them in the research lab. But the shadowy vapor once more coalesced, regaining its shape. This time, the beast looked mighty angry.

Yanking the door open, I bolted out of there, praying to all the powers that be not to let me die this way. If I could get to my jetpack in the closet by the terrace, I might have a chance. It was a hail Mary as the creature was much too fast, but I wouldn't go down without a fight.

And yet, seconds after I emerged from the hygiene room back into the bedroom, down I went when a tentacle wrapped around my ankle, lifting it up. The massive mattress eating up two-thirds of the room rushed towards me. I landed face first on the soft cushion, absorbing the impact of my fall. Despite my panic, I immediately rolled onto my back, blaster raised to shoot at the beast, even though it seemed ineffective.

I never got a chance to fire.

Two of the creature's tentacles wrapped around my wrists, pinning them to the mattress, while a third yanked the weapon from my hand, tossing it away. More tentacles restrained my legs and my midsection, leaving me helpless. I screamed Cedros's name in terror as the beast crawled towards my face, the strident sound of my voice almost burying the clanking of my weapon landing on the floor. The creature's purple, glowing eyes all but hypnotized me as it opened its massive, toothy mouth inches from my face.

I shouted Cedros's name again, his beautiful face flashing before my mind's eye, while regret and loss flooded through me. A crazy number of thoughts and memories rushed through my head. Two thoughts dominated. First, I had failed Cedros as an Ejaya. Because I had let myself get killed, he would suffer and die and at an early age. And second, I had wasted our much too short time together by hanging on to silly and repressive human customs. If only I could go back. If only…

Just when I thought the creature would chomp my face off with its dagger teeth, it pulled out the biggest, purplish-black tongue I had ever seen and licked my face. I froze, as did my brain, as the creature bared its teeth at me before releasing me and flying back up to the ceiling.

I remained lying there, staring at the creature, who hadn't vanished from view, unable to process what had just happened. The bedroom door, all but smashing open, snapped me out of my daze. I shouted in surprise, my fright turning to joy when I saw Cedros.

"KAIDA! I heard your scream. What is—?"

He stopped talking, his head jerking up, and his eyes widening in shock.

"A monster came in through your last portal and attacked me," I exclaimed, both pointing at the creature and trying to crawl out of the bed towards him.

To my dismay, the creature had gone invisible again. And yet Cedros was staring intently at something, displeasure giving way to the almost enraged stance he had when he first arrived.

"Nero! What are you doing here?" he asked in a severe tone at what looked like an empty space near the ceiling. "Didn't I tell you to wait?"

My jaw dropped as the creature came out of stealth, its terrifying face taking on a… Was it a guilty expression?

"Get down here," Cedros ordered, pointing at his feet.

The creature he'd called Nero complied, casting a brief look my way before coming to hover by Cedros's feet. It extended a couple of tentacles towards his scaly legs, gently caressing them. Cedros pulled his leg away, still glaring severely at the creature. I was in too much shock to even find words.

"It's not me you have to apologize to. It's to Kaida. You frightened her because you couldn't wait," he added, pointing at me.

Nero looked up at him, then peered at me. The glowing of his eyes—which had dimmed when Cedros had begun chastising him—grew in intensity again. He started floating towards me. I screamed and scrambled back.

"Get away from me!" I shouted.

Nero stopped, his tentacles sparkling with electricity as he cast a glance at Cedros.

"It's okay, my Kaida. Nero isn't a monster. He's a shadow dweller. He can be unbearably mischievous, but he's not a threat. Shadow dwellers are loyal friends and powerful protectors in the void."

"He chased me around the house and zapped me with his tentacles," I argued weakly, understanding what had happened.

"He was just playing with you. That's how he tickles people," Cedros said.

"Tickles…" I echoed, struggling to come to terms with the slew of emotions raging inside me.

Never more than in this instance had I wished for Cedros to hug me. But Nero was hovering between us, looking mightily eager to come my way. He looked terrifying with his big, round eyes, and the razor teeth filling his Cheshire Cat mouth. His efforts to take on a cute, harmless, and needy expression only made him appear even more predatory.

"Why did he come here?" I asked at last. "Was he the surprise?"

Cedros nodded, puffing out his chest proudly. "Nero agreed to be your companion. A shadow dweller is the closest thing we have on Dramnac that could compare to a pet. I read that humans love pets, sometimes even more than other humans or their own relatives."

I blinked. "You got me a shadow dweller as a pet?" I asked disbelievingly, although it was more of a statement. I held back the 'terrifying and nightmarish' part out of the question.

"Yes! You're going to love him. Nero is so much better than those strange cat creatures humans adopt all the time. Frankly, that confuses me. Sure, they look pretty and fluffy. However, from everything I've read, they're pretty obnoxious, expect you to serve them and cater to their needs. They're stingy with their affection, only offering it when they're in the mood, demanding when they want your attention, and quite rude once they decide they want to be left alone. Some humans even implied that cats are plotting the demise of the human race. Why would you ever adopt such creatures?"

I couldn't help but chuckle about his rather accurate description. "Cats are not plotting our demise. They just look like they are. Despite their many flaws, cats *are* cute and fluffy. When they're in a playful and affectionate mood, they are the best thing in the world."

Cedros waved a dismissive hand. "But it always depends on their mood of the moment, *and* they won't protect you from danger. Nero here is *always* in the mood to play and give you a cuddle. More importantly, he is an extremely fierce fighter. Remember that lightning he was tickling you with? When used in combat, it is powerful enough to shatter rocks. He can tear an aqrat limb from limb in under ten seconds. His venom is three times more potent than theirs. If anyone ever threatens you, they will not live long enough to realize the terrible mistake they made."

"Whoa, okay. He does sound badass," I said, giving Nero a new assessing look. "Does he understand everything you're saying? Because he appears to be listening very intently."

Cedros shook his head. "He doesn't speak or have an advanced language like we do. But he understands a great deal of commands, can communicate things such as danger or tell us to follow so that he can show us something of interest, whether because it's pretty, important, or requires our immediate attention —like rescuing someone in distress. Right now, he knows I'm trying to appease you about him. He doesn't know what I'm saying, but he's waiting for a sign that you have forgiven his mischief."

I narrowed my eyes at him. "What kind of sign?"

Cedros grinned in a taunting fashion. "He wants a hug."

He burst out laughing at my horrified expression. I considered myself a pretty tough chick, but hugging that shadowy, toothy ball of tentacles was a tall order.

"Let me show you," Cedros said with an air of amused sympathy. "To me, Nero."

He spoke the words in a gentle voice, while extending a hand towards the shadow dweller. The creature's face lit up, his eyes glowing, and his frightening mouth stretching further in a nightmarish fashion that I guessed to be a smile. He dashed towards Cedros, his tentacles wrapping all over his chest, arms, and horns while Nero rubbed his face against his cheek. As much as that tableau freaked me out, it also moved me.

Cedros chuckled in a low, affectionate rumble while caressing the sphere that served as both Nero's head and body. He smiled at me in a wistful fashion.

"Nero's father, Gola, watched over me when I was a youngling, during my three years in the void," he said. "He was a little older than Nero currently is. He kept me from going to dangerous areas when my ability to see what lay beyond a portal hadn't developed enough yet. While I provided for myself, whenever he went hunting, Gola always brought me part of his catch."

"That was sweet of him. Did he…?"

"Die? No. Gola is still around. Like me, he's become an adult and has responsibilities. We see each other from time to time, but he has a mate and offspring to look after and a lair to protect from predators."

"Right, that makes sense," I said, eyeing Nero warily.

"Nero can do for you what his father did for me. I do not want to hold back your mission, but I also cannot let you walk the void alone. With Nero, I'll be at ease. He will protect you."

That was extremely good news. The shadow dweller still freaked the hell out of me, but I wasn't a wimp. Cedros had told me he was safe. Continuing to resist would basically be me rejecting Nero merely because of his appearance. I took a deep breath and went for it.

"Nero, to me."

His big purple eyes nearly doubled in size as did their glow, testifying to his surprise—which I believed to be a pleasant one. He untangled himself from Cedros and darted towards me at such speed I thought he'd knock me onto my back from my sitting position on the mattress. To my relief, he came nearly to a halt in a split second and wrapped himself around me the same way he'd done with Cedros.

Nero rubbed his cheek against mine, his tentacles giving me gentle squeezes. The electric tips tapped my skin, multiple times, in what felt like little kisses, most of which tickled. Within seconds, I was giggling and melting for the odd creature.

Cedros beamed at us. "You two will soon become best friends. But for now, off you go, Nero. I need my Ejaya to hug me to get rid of the toxin eating me from within."

Nero released me as Cedros helped me out of the bed and drew me into his embrace. The shadow dweller zapped our cheeks in what I believe to be a kiss goodbye, then I felt a cool draft, like with a shift phase, and he disappeared.

CHAPTER 14
KAIDA

Standing next to Cedros, I finally noticed the new scratches he'd earned himself fighting the latest aqrat invasion. Although he wasn't showing it, I knew him enough now to recognize the tension in his body that betrayed his pain as he went to pick up my discarded blaster.

"So, should I worry about Nero playing pranks on us in the middle of the night?" I asked as I got rid of the pants of my combat suit.

Cedros laughed. "No. Nero has gone back to the void."

"That cold draft we felt before he vanished?" I asked for confirmation.

"Yes. He can easily phase back into the void. Leaving it is a bit more demanding for him on his own, especially if going to an unknown destination," Cedros explained while bringing my weapon back to its container. "He's gone hunting and feeding. He will be back in the morning."

"Good! I don't need a heart attack in the middle of the night."

He snorted, his eyes darkening as he looked at me. The heat in his gaze made my stomach flutter.

"Hang on, I'll be right back," I said, rushing into the hygiene room to recover my vest that Nero had yanked away from me earlier.

When I returned to the bedroom, Cedros's gaze was still weighing heavily on me. I placed my uniform back in its place before turning back towards him, my mouth going dry under his intensity. He frowned at my bikini bottom. I usually only removed it now when we went to bed for the night. Technically, he only needed a cuddle to help him heal, but it could take until well into the night.

Not making a fuss, I removed it, feeling almost intimidated by Cedros's expression.

"You're staring," I said at last.

"Your body is surprisingly pleasing to the eye," he said matter-of-factly.

My brows shot up. "Surprisingly?"

He nodded. "I didn't think I'd ever find a human attractive."

"Sheesh. Really?" I asked, unsure how to take that.

"You have straight legs, a swollen chest, a flat face, no horns, no tail, and no scales. And yet…"

I chuckled in disbelief. Had he not openly shown his attraction to me previously, I might have been offended, despite the factual truth of his critical assessment.

"Damn, you sure know how to flatter a woman," I said teasingly, while approaching him.

He smiled. "I mean it, and not maliciously. Your appearance is odd to a Derakeen. And yet, everything about you is so harmonious, so soft, and delicate. You are a work of art. I can't stop looking at you, my Kaida. You are a feast for the eyes," he said, drawing me into his embrace.

I melted against him, my heart filling to bursting while he purred with delight as contact with me kicked his hormones into overdrive to mend him.

"Wow, you have the best comebacks. Nobody has ever said anything so sweet to me. Nobody sees me like you do."

"Because they're blind," he said softly, flapping his wings to take us to the center of the immense bed.

Instead of cuddling and rubbing all over me, as was his wont after a battle, Cedros started kissing and caressing me. Although his palm roamed over my breast, his touch wasn't bold. It was tender, respectful, and loving. I would never tire of kissing him. I loved that despite being forked, his tongue wasn't narrow like that of a snake, but almost similar in shape and size to a human's. Its rougher texture against mine gave me extra sensation that always had me wet in seconds.

Cedros broke the kiss and finally buried his face in my neck. I bent my head back, giving him better access while he nipped and licked the spots he knew to be sensitive, making me shiver. He emitted a purring growl, and his hands became a bit more possessive on me.

He inhaled deeply and lifted his head to look at me. "I love how aroused you become for me. The smell of your desire drives me insane. I want you, too, my Kaida."

My stomach flip-flopped, and I licked my lips nervously. His still absentmindedly caressing my body made it hard to focus.

"What are you saying?" I whispered. "What are you asking me?"

He smiled and shook his head. "I'm not asking you for anything, my Ejaya. But I can offer to relieve your need, if you wish me to."

"You never have to wait for my permission on that. Unless we're in public, if you've got me aroused, then I want you to do something about it," I said, shocked how liberating it felt to be able to speak openly about my desires without feeling embarrassed.

The slit of his pupils widened for a split second before narrowing again as he looked at me with uncertainty.

"Are you certain, my Kaida? I do not want to presume and—"

"If you get frisky, and I'm actually not in the mood, despite my arousal, I promise I will tell you," I said, interrupting him. "But the chances of that happening are pretty slim, unless I'm PMSing."

"PMSing?" he asked, confused.

"It's part of a human female's reproductive cycle. For a few days every month, we bleed."

"Oh, your menstrual cycle! Yes, I read about it. Why would you not want me to soothe your arousal during your cycle? Is it because you'll be in a foul mood?"

I burst out laughing and shook my head. Good God, he was unbearably cute. "No. It's just because it's a little messy, and men usually are rather stupid and grossed out by it."

He frowned, looking baffled. "But why? It's only a bit of blood for a few days. I read that human females get extremely aroused during that time, that sex is even more enjoyable for them, and that the hormones you release during orgasm can help reduce menstrual cramps and headaches. If you couple in the water or in the cleansing room, there will be no mess. I see nothing but benefits for the females. Why wouldn't your males want that?"

"You know, if you're trying to make me like you, you're really doing a hell of a good job," I said, once more impressed with how simple everything always was with him.

"My goal is to please you, my Kaida. Your pleasure is mine."

I nodded, sobering. "But your pleasure should be mine, too. You can smell my arousal. I can't smell or see yours. I can only guess by the way you look at me. You talk about all the ways you want to please me, but what about you? What do *you* want? What can *I* do to please you?"

"What I want is simple, my Ejaya. I want you, all of you, forever. I want you to be the first and hopefully the only female I ever couple with. I don't want it to be with some strangers for breeding purposes when I reach fifty. I want to fill this lair with younglings that you would give me. They would have the best features from both our species, and would allow me to actually be a father and have the family I always dreamed of. I want to fall asleep every night holding you and awaken in your arms every morning for the rest of my days. Not watch you go to some other male and family every day. Even though I know it's a long shot, I want you to fall in love with me as much as I am already in love with you. You are everything to me."

My throat constricted, words failing me as a slew of emotions overwhelmed me. I caressed his cheek. He closed his eyes with a smile, his much larger hand covering mine, pressing it against his face before slowly reopening his eyes. They burned with an infinite love and tenderness that turned me upside down.

"I may not be in love with you right now, but do not doubt that I love you. No male has ever been as wonderful to me as you have," I said in all sincerity. "I do not know what the future holds for us, but I hope to fall in love with you and give you the family you wish for. As for being your first, there couldn't be a greater honor for me. It would shock you to know how much I've been fantasizing about us together since my arrival here, and even more so since we pleasured each other. But I'm afraid it will only hurt you more if I end up going with someone else."

He shook his head, then kissed the inside of my palm before looking back at me. "No, my Kaida. That will not make me hurt more. Either way, I will hurt. But fear of the future shouldn't stop us from enjoying the present. You're not in love with me, and yet you've made me happier since your arrival than I have been in the past three decades. Even if you end up choosing another male, it will not erase the joy we've shared. I will cherish forever the memories I am currently making with you. And I intend to make as many more as I can, while I can."

My eyes flicked between his, wanting to assess the honesty of his words. "Is that truly how you feel?"

"Yes," he said, his voice firm and his gaze unwavering.

I ran my hand down his muscular chest and around his back before pressing myself further against him. "Then let's stop wasting time and build more memories. Let me be your first."

Cedros stiffened, his eyes widening. "You don't have to do this, Kaida."

"I *want* to do this, silly male. Have you already forgotten how often you get me aroused? Make love to me, Cedros. I want you."

The pure joy, desire, and love on his face turned me upside down. He didn't jump me with brutal impatience. As always with Cedros, his touch was careful and reverent as he paid homage to every inch of my body with his hands, lips, and tongue. When his mouth settled on my achy nipple, I tried to slip my fingers through his hair, but he grabbed my wrists and pinned them to the mattress next to my face, startling me.

"Stay!" he ordered, his commanding voice and stern expression resonating directly in my girly bits.

Behind the sweet, sometimes clumsy, and often shy Cedros lurked a dominant male who made my toes curl and my knees wobble. I licked my lips nervously, my inner walls throbbing as I complied. Satisfied, he released my wrists and returned his attention to my breast. Each flick of his rough tongue fanned the flame growing in the pit of my stomach.

I gave myself over to him as he shifted his attention to my other nipple, his hands caressing my body, and his claws gently scraping the flesh around my pelvis. He'd discovered how sensitive the entire area right below my navel was, especially on the sides.

My stomach fluttered, and I fisted the blanket when his head finally slipped lower. A soft moan escaped me when his breath fanned over my sex, the warmth of his heating chamber radiating over my nether region. He inhaled deeply, and a powerful rumbling purr emanated from him. Once more, my stomach flip-flopped when Cedros slid his hands behind my calves. I held my breath in anticipation of him parting my legs open before blessing me with the divine feel of his tongue on my clit.

To my dismay, Cedros flipped me onto my stomach instead. I gasped in surprise, only to moan in delight when his weight settled on top of me. The heat radiating from his throat seeped into my back, deep inside my muscles, all the way down to the bones. I instantly felt relaxed, almost groggy from an over-whelming sense of well-being as Cedros kissed and caressed my back.

One shiver after the other coursed through me under the magical heat of his throat and chest as he pursued a path down-ward, kissing my back. Cedros licked then bit my butt cheek, making my legs jerk while a bolt of fire went off between my thighs. He loved my behind—whose roundness I was rather proud of. With their big tails largely covering the rear of his Derakeen peers, he'd never really paid attention to other people's behinds. That mine was 'soft and cushiony' as he so eloquently liked to put it, only made it even more irresistible to him.

But he didn't linger there much, resuming his journey down my legs and to my feet before flipping me back around. This time, as he licked his way back up, I knew the moment I was craving loomed near. The light scraping of his scales against my inner thighs as he parted me open to settle between them had every single one of my nerve endings on high alert.

And then his mouth finally closed over my sex. I cried out, my back arching over the bed at the explosion of pleasure a single lick on my engorged clit had triggered. His gentle explo-ration of my body and the soothing effect of his heating cham-ber's warmth had lulled me into a sea of well-being where I'd not realized just how achy and needy I'd become.

In only a few flicks of his tongue, Cedros already had me

nearing the edge. Sensing my impending climax, the wretch shifted his attention away from my little nub. His fingers dove inside me, scissoring in and out, stretching me while he kissed and nipped at my pelvis. My hips moved in response to his touch as I chased the completion he was denying me. I knew he was delaying it to further prepare me to receive him. However, in my desperate need, I shamelessly started begging him. I never fully vocalized what I wanted, content to whisper a litany of 'please' in-between two moans.

Legs trembling, my stomach contracting with need as I teetered at the edge, I was about to disobey his command to stay still and rub my clit to get me just over the line when his mouth finally closed once more over it. I went off like a rocket. The powerful orgasm that rocked me felt like a bomb had just detonated inside me.

Cedros continued to lick and suck on my little nub while inserting a third finger. His hand moved in a frenzy, further stretching me. He never gave me a chance to fully recover. Even as I was coming down, another orgasm was building up with Cedros crooking his fingers inside me. With deadly accuracy, he rubbed my G-spot with each stroking motion of his hand, making me see stars again.

Shaking from head to toe from the tremors of bliss, I only realized Cedros had climbed on top of me when his weight settled on my chest. Still half dazed, I spread my legs wide for him. A shiver of fear and anticipation ran down my spine when I felt the wetness of his pre-lubricated shaft extrude against my thigh.

Cedros didn't push himself in right away. He claimed my lips first in a deep and passionate kiss. This time, he didn't rebel when I began caressing him. As our tongues mingled, he gently rubbed his length against my slit, making me throb with the need to be filled. When he broke the kiss, and his fiery gaze bore into mine, I smiled and nodded, knowing he was seeking my ultimate consent.

He smiled back with infinite tenderness and reclaimed my mouth in another deep kiss as his head started pressing against my opening. Good God! Cedros was massive. I had known it would be a tight fit, but not this much. Considering he'd barely gotten a centimeter in before my body rebelled, I was beginning to wonder if he could get in at all.

Despite his natural lubrication, how wet he'd gotten me, and the careful and shallow thrusts with which Cedros was attempting to penetrate me, we were hardly making any progress worth mentioning. Aside from it getting increasingly uncomfortable for me, it was becoming visibly harder for him to restrain himself.

Cedros had made me climax twice. He still hadn't found his release. As a virgin, I expected him to have even less control. That he hadn't given in to what had to be a burning hunger for him and rammed himself home was all but a miracle. But if he did, he'd likely damage me. Discomfort gave way to worry as Cedros clenched his teeth and started trembling in my arms from the visible effort he was making to control himself.

Just when I was going to suggest I suck him off instead to release the pressure, Cedros's shadow horns glowed. His scales suddenly grew cold against my feverish skin, and the golden glow of his throat took on a darker, purplish hue as shadowy tendrils swirled all around him.

"What is—?"

My baffled question ended in a stunned gasp when my hands on his back fell through him, and his weight on me vanished as he became vaporous. I yanked my hands away, wondering what the hell was going on. But before the thought could fully form, Cedros materialized again.

I threw my head back against the pillows and cried out at the impossible fullness of Cedros's cock fully sheathed inside me.

He also threw his head back, hissing, his eyes closed and teeth clenched. I felt stretched to the limit, my body uncertain how to handle the sudden invasion. Cedros buried his face in my neck, trembling even more than before. I couldn't tell if pain or an excruciating need to start moving inside me was the cause. Either way, I was grateful for his current immobility that gave me a chance to adjust to his insane girth.

"I'm sorry for the pain, my Kaida," Cedros whispered in the crook of my neck, his voice strained.

"It's okay. It was clever," I whispered back, caressing his hair.

While that method had indeed been creative, I would have welcomed a heads up first. Still, it was thankfully done. The normal way, it would probably have taken us hours, and we'd likely have given up long before that.

As the initial pain of that brutal stretch faded, my inner walls contracted around him, coaxing him into action. Displaying mind-boggling control for a virgin, Cedros started moving in and out of me in a measured fashion, with slow thrusts at first. With each stroke, he emitted a pained moan, his eyes shut, his face constricted, and his hand fisting the blanket. But I knew unbearable pleasure prompted this reaction… The same insane pleasure the countless ridges of his alien cock were giving me.

Each motion rubbed my sensitive spot, sending electric tendrils of pleasure through me. When his middle ridges distended inside me, creating even greater friction, I shouted Cedros's name, my nails digging into his back. He emitted a growling shout that sent a searing bolt of lust in my core.

He lifted his head and shot out a brief stream of shadow flames at the ceiling before picking up the pace. Fear and the thrill of the unknown mingled with the waves of pleasure crashing over me as Cedros began shifting. He wasn't going into his full battle form, but his body gained more mass, his face took on more draconic features, and his already impossibly gigantic cock seemed to grow thicker. His eyes and shadow horns glowed while he emitted almost animalistic grunts.

It terrified me, liquified my insides with lust, and had me begging him for more. And more he gave.

Opening my legs wider to accommodate his enhanced size, Cedros spread his wings as he started pounding into me, taking me harder, deeper. Despite the brutality with which he was now claiming my body, I writhed beneath him, my pelvis lifting to meet him thrust for thrust. My moans of ecstasy blended with his feral growls as he destroyed me with savage abandon. When the transversal spikes of his cock burst into action, undulating against my G-spot, a bright light exploded before my eyes.

I felt as if I'd gotten knocked right out of my body under the violence of my climax. My inner walls clamped down on Cedros's cock. He roared, his throat and horns glowing, before he threw his head back and fired a long stream of shadow flames. At the same time, I felt his burning seed shoot powerfully inside me. Instead of calming his passion, that first release appeared to whip him into a frenzy.

Without ever pulling out of me, Cedros collected me into his arms and sat on his haunches. Holding me in an almost bruising embrace, he pumped into me with reckless fury while speaking unintelligible words in Derakeen, interspersed with throaty growls. In between bouts of breathing fire, he would crush my lips in hungry, possessive kisses. By the way his wings spread and closed, I suspected he was battling the instinctive urge to take flight during our coupling. But another brutal orgasm sweeping me away ended any attempt at rational thought.

By the time Cedros relented, I had lost count of how many orgasms he had wrested from me, or how many times he'd shot out his hot seed on my battered insides. I remained boneless in his arms as he turned us around and settled me on top of him. I vaguely realized he hadn't pulled out of me. As he wrapped his wings around me, I felt one pair of the lower ridges of his cock swelling inside of me, locking us together.

Head resting on his broad chest, surrendering to the sweet call of oblivion, the last thing I heard over the thunderous beating of his twin hearts were these soft words.

"I love you, my mate."

Saying Cedros was a sex machine would be the understatement of the century. I got little sleep that night, and I woke up to an encore this morning. If he didn't have to go to work today, I likely would have spent the day on my back or impaled on his cock while he pounded into me from below.

That he could knot took me by surprise, and even more so that he only used it before we fell asleep. But then I realized he'd only done it for the binding intimacy it created, not for its reproductive benefits. Anyway, my contraceptive implant made it all pointless. But I rather enjoyed being bound to him that way.

Even as we finished showering together, I braced for another round when Cedros drew me into his embrace. I wrapped my arms around his neck and my legs around his waist while he gave me a deep, toe-curling kiss. To both my relief and disappointment, my man didn't extrude. After the grueling sex marathon we'd just had, my poor cooch was beyond sore and could use a reprieve... even as it throbbed with anticipation.

The little ho!

But Cedros carried me out of the shower's recessed ring, then proceeded to dry me. He never bothered doing it for himself, leaving his scales to dry during flight.

"I hate having to leave you. I'm afraid I've grown addicted to you, my Kaida," Cedros said sheepishly, while gently rubbing the towel over my legs.

"Absence makes the heart grow fonder," I said affectionately. "It's only for a few hours."

"I have two hearts, my mate. It makes it more excruciating."

I chuckled and patted his chest in an encouraging fashion. "You're a strong male. You'll survive."

"Only because I must," he said with a long-suffering sigh.

I smiled and rubbed my nose against his snout before kissing him. But even as I did, his words replayed in my mind.

It was the third time Cedros had referred to me as his mate. The first time had been before I fell asleep last night. The second time was this morning while we made love again, and the third time now. I didn't know what to do about it or if I should even bring it up. There was no doubt in my mind that those were unintentional slips of the tongue. But they also reflected his avowed deeper desire, and likely the way he already considered me.

It was a dangerous thing. And yet, it didn't actually bother me. Quite the opposite, in fact. I was falling hard for my dragon. As ridiculously massive as his cock was, it had made my pussy sing arias all night long. I didn't doubt for a second that Cedros had ruined me for any other male. That he wanted me to be his first and only was playing a crazy game with my mind. I wasn't in love with Cedros—at least not yet—but the thought of some Derakeen bitch rubbing all over him, writhing beneath him in the hopes of bearing him a child, had me seeing red.

No freaking wonder Trinit decided to marry Rovain instead.

If I had to play babysitter to allow Cedros to fuck some other chick, I'd commit murder. We were still way too early in this relationship for me to make any type of commitment about the future, but I could already see the writing on the wall.

Kayog said I'd never want to leave him.

Damn Temerns and their accurate assessments…

"I will return soon, my Kaida. Don't be frightened when Nero shows up. He will probably just spend some time with you during your training with Trinit so that you can get to know each other better."

"Okay, sounds good. I'll see you later."

He gave me one last passionate kiss before taking flight, the glass dome of the hygiene room opening to let him out. I gazed wistfully at him while he circled around the shimmering, opalescent sky, no doubt drying his body, before summoning a portal and vanishing through it.

With a sigh, I went into the bedroom to put on some basic clothes for my training with Trinit and ate a quick breakfast. I then settled at my computer desk to continue cross-referencing the incidents Tedrick had sent me against the events Cedros and his Shadow Lord brothers had provided me with reports on.

It didn't take long to realize that every incident matched one from Dramnac. But the UPO had not detected all of Dramnac's events. Based on the destinations of the undetected random portals reported by the Shadow Lords, the anomaly opened in the middle of bumfuck nowhere, which explained why no one in the galactic alliance had noticed it—or at least mentioned it.

In half the incidents recorded by the UPO, they found absolutely nothing. All of them corresponded to those isolated places or areas where the Shadow Lords had cleaned out the roaming beasts before they could make any victims. In a quarter of the other incidents, they found mangled corpses of the poor sods that happened to be at the wrong place, at the wrong time. They belonged to random people of various species, with nothing in their history or known connections that could hint at any type of shady involvement or activity.

The last segment of incidents led to locations that presented visible signs of battle, from scorched spots where blaster shots had hit, to vicious claw marks on the walls and floor, clearly belonging to aqrats. Those scenes implied an undeniable level of military preparedness. Even a thorough forensic examination of those areas failed to provide any type of DNA or fiber that could have given us a trail to track down those who had fought there.

Whoever was behind this was no low-level mercenary trying to make a quick buck. We were dealing with a very organized and professional group of individuals. Sadly, I could think of quite a few galactic criminal cartels with the capability and desire to pursue such an 'opportunity.'

The most frustrating part was that the origins of the portals on the galactic side and their destinations into the void were completely random. But why? Were the summoners chasing something which led them to these varied locations before they opened their portal? Were they deliberately moving around to hide their trail and send people like me who were tracking them on a wild goose chase? Could it be that their portals were unstable and, therefore leading to the oddest places?

I shook my head, annoyed. Cedros had said the shadow obsidian stones opened safe and stable portals. Could the off-worlder summoners be using them the wrong way? One thing was certain, they weren't accidental. Proof of combat indicated those people came prepared. It just sucked I had so little to work with.

A cool draft and a tingling sensation startled me out of my deep thoughts. I jerked my head towards the door, to see a now familiar blur. This time, instead of messing with my head and stalking me, Nero came right out of stealth—although I suspected it was merely him materializing into the real world from crossing the veil.

With his mouth closed into a barely visible line and his big, glowing purple eyes, he could have almost passed for cute— Chibi face kind of cute. That is, assuming you didn't have a tentacle phobia. But the minute he saw me, Nero's mouth split into that massively toothy grin that took up half of his face. My survival instincts were screaming for me to haul ass, but I kept my butt on my chair and smiled.

"Hello, Nero," I said in a gentle voice.

Deeming that an invitation, his creepy smile broadened as he flew towards me. I braced for impact, but once more he gently wrapped his tentacles all around my neck, shoulders, and waist, but not in a restraining fashion. He rubbed his cheek against mine, and I found myself melting for the odd creature.

Despite his obvious love of cuddles, Nero couldn't have been more different than Cedros. Instead of the gentle scraping of scales against my skin, rubbing against Nero felt like hugging a cloud or a very soft foam pillow. He gave me those zapping 'kisses' with the electric tips of his tentacles before slinking all over my desk.

The next forty-five minutes proved mostly unproductive. Nero might not be a cat, but he sure shared some of their most obnoxiously entitled traits. As I tried to work, he would park his beach ball-sized self either right on top of my keyboard, or smack in front of my monitor, blocking my view. Whenever he would feel playful or restless, he would settle on top of my head or on my shoulder and flick one or more of his tentacles at my face, like a cat would its tail. Thankfully, he weighed next to nothing. Naturally, he tried to tickle me countless times in between.

I couldn't even be mad about it. You couldn't hate on someone freely giving you their affection. He was growing on me, tentacles and all.

CHAPTER 15
CEDROS

Over the next three days, I took Kaida to visit the various locations on Dramnac where the incidents had occurred. Because of my work, I could only devote a few hours a day to this endeavor. But today was my day off, and I had planned a few things for my Ejaya.

I no longer wanted to call her that. Keeping myself from calling her my mate was almost torture. I constantly had to remind myself not to. It had slipped from my lips a few times, and Kaida hadn't seemed to mind. Was the idea growing on her, or was she merely pretending not to hear to avoid having to deal with it?

I wanted to keep her. I *needed* to keep her. This no longer was merely a Shadow Lord depending on his Ejaya. I loved her. I was madly in love with her. Coupling with her had only confirmed and strengthened what I had been feeling. Kaida had feared such a response from me, if we went all the way. But this didn't compare to other Shadow Lords and their Ejayas.

Many who got married loved each other but weren't in love, like Rovain and Trinit. They were happy couples, but the Shadow Lord wouldn't have been crushed had his Ejaya found a different mate. Kaida was my soulmate. Of that, I had no doubt. There couldn't be another male for her, and especially not another female for me. The mere thought of coupling with anyone else for breeding purposes made me nauseous.

If Kaida left me for another, I would be the first Shadow Lord to defy the custom of reproducing with random females at the age of fifty.

But that will not be necessary.

Kaida was mine, and I was hers. By the way she responded to me—both when we coupled and during our normal interactions—I could see that she was falling in love with me. Kayog had said we were a perfect match. I wouldn't worry about it and let nature follow its course. This was destiny.

Which didn't mean I couldn't give fate a nudge in the right direction.

Holding my Kaida by the hand, I led her past my Shadow Lord brother Elros, who was on duty today at the shadow obsidian mine. He nodded at us in greeting and winked at Kaida. She gave him a friendly, almost affectionate smile as I led her inside.

I loved that my Ejaya was establishing instant chemistry with my brothers. Shadow Lords and their Ejayas formed one big family. They were the siblings and relatives we'd been deprived of growing up. I had worried that her being an off-worlder would have made it harder to form a connection with us, considering how much our mentalities differed on so many things.

But my Kaida was perfect.

"Whoa!" Kaida exclaimed, as she took in the giant cave. "This feels like we just walked inside a giant obsidian geode!"

"That's an accurate comparison, if geodes had many hallways and nooks to get lost in, as well as shadows slithering over their minerals," I said teasingly.

She scrunched her face, looking at the deep drop over the

edge where we stood. "Looks like I should have brought my jetpack. You never let me play with it."

I chuckled. "There will be time for it," I promised. Leaning down, I pressed my lips to her ear. "After all, we haven't coupled in flight yet." I burst out laughing when she gasped right on cue. Not giving her a chance to chastise me for my boldness, I picked her up like a bride. "Come, my Ejaya. Let's give you a closer look."

I flew us around the cave filled with various people extremely focused on their mining task. Every minute, every second was precious if they wanted to mine as much obsidian as possible before their time was up. I remained at a respectable distance from them to avoid unwelcome distractions.

"That's one impressive stalactite," Kaida said, as I circled around a massive chunk of mineral dangling from the ceiling like a giant icicle.

"Indeed. It is a major headache that the Council is trying to solve," I explained. "Poor planning caused it, with people chipping away at the obsidian wherever they thought they'd have better success. The faces of this stalactite are too mangled. You'd have to shave a lot of it off before you could get to the smooth surfaces needed to carve a proper shadow obsidian stone."

"Oh! And because people have a limited amount of time here, they don't want to waste it on smoothing it out for the next person," she said, her eyes widening with understanding.

"Exactly. But also, the ground all around and below it has been carved away. You would need to fly to work on it, which would make your movements too unstable, thus damaging the stone."

"Couldn't they stand on a hover platform or something?" Kaida argued.

I smiled. "Yes. Specific hover platform models have recently been authorized for use here. The type of tools people can bring here are strictly monitored to avoid abuse and unfortunate accidents."

"But it looks like that still didn't convince people to give the stalactite a go," she said teasingly.

"It certainly hasn't. You'd still waste your time getting nothing but dust. While it has its purpose, you mainly want good stones. The Council is considering allocating an extra hour to whoever consents to mine exclusively from the stalactite."

"Oooh, now that sounds like a nice incentive," Kaida exclaimed.

"Indeed. Once they do, people will fight for those spots. And I can already tell you that miners will charge a premium for working there."

"Seriously? I guess price gougers exist in every world," she mumbled.

I chuckled. "Yes, but it will also be to discourage their clients so that they can use their own time carving for themselves with that extra hour."

I landed on an obsidian outcropping a few meters away from Hezin, one of the top Master Miners of Dramnac currently working for a noble. His focus was legendary. As long as we remained discreet, our presence wouldn't disturb him.

"See how fine the cut is?" I whispered to Kaida, pointing at Hezin's laser, slicing a tiny piece of obsidian off the face of the mine.

"Why so small?" she whispered back.

"You can only cut the size of an actual portal stone at a time. First, to control the quantity people harvest, but also because smaller pieces have less risk of triggering an accidental rift, and especially a bad one."

"A bad one?" she asked.

"One that would open a portal into an area infested by void beasts," I explained. "That's why there's always a Shadow Lord nearby. This female over here, and that male down there are both

Gate Masters. Their job is to close any accidental rift the minute they open."

"Does it happen often?" Kaida asked while openly eyeing the female who was slowly roaming around the cave, ready to intervene at the first sign of trouble.

"Bad portals are rare. They require someone to attempt to cut a huge chunk. Or something very heavy would have to fall on an already frayed piece of shadow obsidian. But small rifts—basically phase shifts—are frequent," I said. "Considering people have to report every rift they accidentally open here, they are quite careful. If it happens too often, they could lose their mining privileges, and either be forced to take a rather costly mining training course, or hire a Master Miner to work in their stead."

"Ugh, brutal," Kaida said, before chewing her bottom lip, her wheels spinning. "This place seems pretty much under control. There are too many eyes here and supervision for anyone to be conducting their shady business right from the mine. Who else is likely to open accidental portals? And I don't mean to create a phase shift, but an actual portal that an off-worlder could see and enter?"

"Aside from Shadow Lords, the only other people capable of opening portals without stones are Gate Masters, as well as Elder Scribe," I said.

"Do they mess up often?" Kaida asked, perking up.

I snorted and gave her an apologetic look. "No, my Kaida. They are masters and elders for a reason. However, their apprentices mess up all the time. It takes years to earn their professional title. But…!" I added quickly when she grew far too excited. "Like here, the apprentices are under strict supervision when training. There is always a Gate Master nearby."

Kaida glared at me as if I was conspiring against her, which made me laugh.

"I'd still like to have a talk with those masters," she mumbled, her face taking on a mulish expression.

"As you humans say, your wish is my command," I said with a flourishing curtsy.

Kaida gave me a playful tap and let me fly her back out of the mine. While I could have safely cast a portal to the Scribes Conclave from inside the mine, it was standard procedure never to open a portal from there, not only to avoid random people from sneaking in outside of their allocated times, but also to avoid any confusion as to whether another incident had occurred.

I opened it right outside the Scribes Conclave located on its own massive plateau on the twelfth level—prime real estate that many considered wasted on such an institution instead of residences. Kaida feasted her eyes on the massive fortress-like building, made of beige stones similar to those in my lair, but with far fewer windows. Statues of a male and a female Derakeens, carved directly into the stone, framed the imposing doorway of the academy.

Its heavy metal doors always sat open during the day. A few apprentices, standing on the lawn outside, stared with surprise at the sight of a Shadow Lord here, but also with envy at the ease with which I dismissed my portal. Their curiosity then shifted to my mate when I set her back down on her feet before taking her hand possessively to lead her inside. I wanted to slip my arm around her waist instead, but it felt too bold in this setting.

Only a few steps in, Headmaster Aldyr came rushing out of his office. His welcoming and deferent expression did nothing to hide his curiosity as to what could bring a Shadow Lord and a human to his establishment.

"Welcome to you, Shadow Lord Cedros, and to your lovely companion. I am Headmaster Aldyr Semyer. How can I be of assistance?"

"Greetings, Headmaster Aldyr. This is my Ejaya, Kaida Daigo. She works as an Enforcer with the United Planets Organization and is investigating the surge in 'accidental' portals summoned by off-worlders. She has a few questions for you and your apprentices."

His eyes widened in shock, and he cast an intrigued look at my Ejaya. "It's a pleasure to meet you, Miss Daigo!"

"The pleasure is all mine, Headmaster," she said with a polite smile.

"Please, let me take you to my office where we can discuss this more at ease," he said, his glowing silver eyes contrasting sharply with his midnight-blue scales.

At one-hundred-and-three years of age, Aldyr was fairly young to be holding such a prestigious position. But he had a stellar reputation, not only as a Gate Master but also as a mentor to young aspiring minds. Many of said minds were lurking around, trying to glean some information as to what had brought us here.

The sizable Headmaster's office spoke volumes about his status. A wide bookshelf lined the back wall behind his desk. Along the left wall, three pedestals respectively displayed a statue representing a jagged section of shadow obsidian from the mines, a giant version of a marked shadow obsidian stone hovering a few centimeters in the air, and a holographic display of an animated portal, occasionally folding in on itself. On the opposite side, large glass doors led to a balcony overlooking a yard where apprentices were training with their masters.

Kaida stared with curiosity at what the pedestals displayed.

"They represent the three disciplines taught here at the Conclave," Headmaster Aldyr said in response to her unspoken question. "We train the Master Miners that people hire at the mines, although many citizens come for some occasional personal training to improve their own techniques. We also teach young Scribes how to perfectly mark obsidian stones so that the consumers always arrive safely at the intended destination etched on the stone. And then, we mentor the future Gate Masters, both to open and close portals for rescue and emergency services, as well as to alleviate the burden on Shadow Lords in keeping us all safe."

"I didn't realize you trained the miners as well. Can anyone become an apprentice in any of these fields?" Kaida asked, as Aldyr gestured for us to take a seat on the stools facing his desk.

With our tails and wings, it was common for very few seats to have backrests. Kaida settled in the one on the left—the stool much too wide for her—and I sat beside her. Under different circumstances, I would have been jealous of the way she studied the older male's admittedly handsome face. But she was focusing on his horns. She opened her mouth, hesitated, and gave me an uncertain sideways glance.

I smiled and turned my attention to the Headmaster. "My Ejaya is curious about your horns."

Aldyr chuckled as Kaida blushed while glaring sideways at me, which only made me chuckle as well.

"I didn't mean to be rude. I couldn't help but notice that you and the other apprentices have six horns," she said carefully. "Aside from the Shadow Lords who have eight, I believe everyone else only has four."

Aldyr beamed at her. "That is correct. And it is not rude at all to inquire about things you don't know or don't understand. The answer to that also answers your previous question. No, we do not accept just anyone who applies for our programs. Candidates *must* have six horns or at least a burgeoning crest," he said, pointing at the dark shape in the middle of his forehead between his horns.

His was much smaller than mine but was also obsidian, whereas 'regular' citizens only had an empty area there. His fifth and sixth horns matched the smaller shadow horns that Shadow Lords like me possessed right above our ears.

"I'm guessing it grants you some additional powers?" Kaida asked.

Aldyr nodded, a glimmer of approval in his silver eyes. "Yes. We are Kwesars, the polite way of saying failed Shadow Lords."

I frowned and gave the Headmaster a stern look. We always found it offensive when people would demean the Kwesars with such insensitive comments.

He chuckled and gave me an amused look. "It's okay, Shadow Lord Cedros. If we cannot laugh at ourselves, then we take life much too seriously."

While I understood his meaning and intention, his words didn't mollify me. "You shouldn't make light of what mean-spirited people say. And least of all, normalize it through humor. Those words never should have been spoken or the thought even crossed anyone's mind in the first place. You are what the Gods intended you to be—a gift to our people. The services only you can provide are essential to the good functioning of our society. You are not 'failed' anything."

A strange expression settled on Aldyr's face. "I stand corrected, Shadow Lord Cedros. Your words honor me and every other Kwesar."

"They are merely the truth, Headmaster," I said in a gentler voice.

"Which is why they honor us so much," he countered, then turned to my Kaida, who was looking at us slightly confused. "Are you familiar with the Shadow Trail that young Derakeens must travel when they reach the age of five?"

"Yes. Cedros told me about his journey," Kaida replied.

"Good. Kwesars like me are the children who didn't leave the void within ten days because we began to embrace the shadows. But our transformation stalled at some point. As you can see, I have both of my lesser shadow horns and a third of my crest. It took thirteen months before I knew they would grow no further, and that it was time for me to leave the void," Aldyr explained in a gentle voice.

"So you had developed enough to have greater power than

the rest of the population, but not enough to be a Shadow Lord," Kaida concluded.

"Exactly. First, only golden-scaled Derakeens have the potential to become a Shadow Lord. The rest of us can only hope to become Kwesars. About ten percent of all the younglings who enter the Shadow Trail will linger past a couple of weeks," Aldyr continued. "Each day spent in the void increases their affinity with the shadows and their control over their phasing abilities. However, unless they remain for at least six months, their skills will not be strong enough to become a Miner. You need a minimum of nine months for a Scribe, and more than a year for a Gate Master."

"Wow, that's fascinating!" Kaida said. "Do you take in the children the minute they come out of the void?"

I smiled, loving how fascinated my Ejaya was about the ways of my people. Although it would help her investigation, I could also tell that she was genuinely curious by the way she was leaning forward in her chair, eating up every single one of his words.

"No. Kwesars return to their parents and are raised normally. However, they will have qualification tests at specific age mile-stones to assess their suitability for their chosen role and take classes from the general curriculum that support that choice."

"Chosen role? I thought the time spent in the void deter-mined that?" Kaida argued.

I smiled at my mate. "We still have free choice, my Kaida. Although I emerged from the void with the crown of a Shadow Lord, I technically could have chosen to become a Scribe, a merchant, an artist, or whatever other profession appealed to me. Has that ever happened? Not based on any history that I've read. But it would still be our choice."

"That's correct," Aldyr said. "Considering how few Shadow Lords exist at any given time and how essential their roles are, should one ever choose *not* to pursue that vocation, there would certainly be some pressure to try and change his or her mind, but no coercion. With Kwesars, while they cannot choose a profession above their shadow affinity, they could opt for a career with lesser requirements, but which they could accomplish with a much higher degree of success."

Kaida nodded in understanding. "Because they are more powerful than if they had just met the minimum requirement."

"Exactly. Most Kwesars who barely passed twelve months in the void become Scribes instead, even though they have sufficient power to be Gate Masters. Since they have the strict minimum, they often struggle to open stable portals or with the precision of their destination, and they take a lot more time to close greater portals to distant destinations."

"Oh okay," Kaida said, perking up. I could almost hear the thoughts firing off in her mind now that she thought she had a possible trail. "You say it's their choice, but could a Kwesar be forced to specialize in a field with lower requirements? Are there Gate Masters who insist on summoning portals even though they occasionally land in random, and sometimes dangerous places?"

Aldyr chuckled and shook his head. "No, Miss Daigo. While the opposite has happened where we had to convince someone to go for a higher tiered profession, the other way around never happens. Your reputation directly impacts your employability and the rates you can charge for your services. People want instant gratification. They will not stand around for ten minutes while you're fumbling in failed attempts to summon a portal. And they won't hire you to mark stones for them if you are too slow or if the marked destinations are off."

Kaida's shoulders slumped, and my hearts broke for my female. "Right. That makes sense."

Aldyr tilted his head to the side with an air of sympathy. "I'm sorry that I'm not giving you the type of answers you sought. But I'm confused about how this line of questioning would help your specific case." He cast a slightly confused glance my way before turning back towards her. "I thought your Shadow Lord said you were trying to find out more about the off-worlders casting portals into our world. I assumed you wanted to question me about portal summoning using obsidian stones."

"Yes, but first I need to know how they got their hands on shadow obsidian to begin with," Kaida explained. "No off-worlder travels to Dramnac anymore since the Shattering. The phase shifting all around your planet would basically send any approaching vessel into the equivalent of a wormhole, and they'd end up only God knows where. The Shattering occurred many decades ago. These incidents only started occurring a year ago. That means whoever the off-worlder summoners are, they likely got their hands on the stones in the past twelve to twenty-four months. But how? How did they come in contact with Derakeens or Dramnac?"

Aldyr rubbed the bone spikes on his chin with a pensive expression. The same question had plagued me, and there could only be one way for it to have occurred.

"So you understand the issue, Headmaster?" I asked. "A Derakeen unequivocally opened the first portal that gave them access. The mines are too closely watched and much too busy at all times for a human to have entered an accidental portal and no one noticing or reporting it. Aside from Shadow Lords, the only people able to open portals are your colleagues and students."

His brow creased. "True. However, we also keep a very close eye on them. No summoning, scribing, or mining is allowed unless a Master is present to handle any accident. And they happen *a lot*, especially at the beginning of a novice's training. But none ever led off-world. We do not have that kind of shadow power. And you *know* we would have warned both the Shadow Lords and the Council if an accidental portal had brought off-worlders onto Dramnac."

I sighed and nodded in concession. "Yes, you would."

"Which brings us right back to square one. We're missing

something," Kaida said, sounding dejected. She cast a glance out the glass doors where the apprentices were summoning, then gave Aldyr an assessing look. "How do novices train exactly? Right now, these apprentices appear to be using shadow obsidian."

Aldyr perked up. "Ah yes! Miner and Scribe Novices start on onyx. For the Miners, it is merely to first develop their cutting technique and precision without wasting the very precious and expensive shadow obsidian. For Scribes, it is to allow them to hone their skill at gathering the shadows and channeling it precisely into a finicky stone before moving on to the real thing."

"Right, shadow obsidian is expensive. The Conclave would want to avoid wasting them on beginners," Kaida said pensively.

"By the Gods! We do not provide the shadow obsidian to our pupils," the Headmaster exclaimed, as if my Ejaya had said something outrageous—which she had. "We'd be bankrupt within a month or only able to train one person of each profession at a time. Students have to provide their own stones. The minute younglings return from the void as Kwesars, their parents start stockpiling stones for when they will enter the Conclave."

"Oh wow! But what if they don't have enough stones to continue their training?" Kaida argued.

"Then they will buy more or pause their education until they have acquired more during their respective turns at the mines," I answered softly.

Kaida frowned, her displeasure taking both Aldyr and I aback. "Basically, what you're saying is that the rich kids get a fast-track to a career, but commoners and poorer people could drag on indefinitely before they can finish?"

"Not necessarily," I said in an appeasing tone. "Granted, nobles can buy more stones and hire highly skilled Miners to maximize their harvest during their time in the mines. But they also consume far more of them for their leisure travels and to raise the level of their plateaus. More importantly, how many stones you need to master your profession comes down to individual skills. Someone with greater shadow power who becomes a Scribe or Miner instead will likely require a lot fewer stones."

"That is correct," Aldyr chimed in. "Your shadow power will play a huge part in the speed at which you learn, but also your natural talents—neither of which has anything to do with the apprentice's family wealth. Some people are simply more gifted than others. In fact, this cohort has a handful of superstars of humble means. Their progress quite literally leaves the nobles behind to eat their shadow dust."

"That's good to hear it doesn't disadvantage them," Kaida said, although not fully mollified. "Well, I guess we've taken up enough of your time, Headmaster. Thank you so much for taking the time to enlighten me."

"It was my pleasure, Miss Daigo. Do not hesitate to come back at any point if you have further questions. I will be glad to assist you in any way I can," Aldyr said warmly.

After exchanging our goodbyes, I led my Ejaya out of the Conclave. She tried to put on a brave front, but her disappointment was palpable. Aldyr had indeed been her best hope of some kind of trail. Even I couldn't think of where to go next to move her mission forward.

"Let's take a break from all these serious things, my Kaida," I said in a soft voice, cupping her face between my hands. "I would like to take you to a place I haven't visited in a very long time and for you to meet someone special."

"Sure," Kaida said, perking up with curiosity. "Who is it?"

"That's a surprise," I said, beaming at her.

I picked her up in my arms, kissed her lips, and took flight. I opened my portal in the air. I usually did this when in a public area to avoid random people nearby walking into it, whether or not accidentally. This was especially true when my destination was a special location or someone's private residence.

I flew through the portal, collapsing it behind me as soon as we emerged on the other side. My hearts leapt, and an overwhelming flow of emotions surged within me at the sight of the three adult Derakeens on the plateau below. Sitting at the table on the terrace while sipping fermented drinks, they were engaged in an animated conversation. After all these years, they still observed the gathering ritual on the eleventh and twenty-second days of every month.

"Cedros, who are these people?" Kaida whispered as I began my descent.

"My mother and my siblings," I said, my throat almost too constricted to speak.

As if she'd heard my words, my mother suddenly looked up. Her shocked expression drew my siblings' attention. Their jaws dropped as they all rose from their seats to watch me land a few meters away from them, as was standard for Shadow Lords.

"Cedros!" my mother exclaimed, her voice shaking as she stared at me in disbelief.

"Greetings, Mother," I said while carefully putting Kaida on her feet. "It's been too long. You are even more beautiful than in my souvenirs."

Her lips quivered, and her eyes filled with tears as she hugged her midsection. My brother and sister slipped an arm around her while looking at me with affection.

"I wanted to present to you my Ejaya, Kaida Daigo, a human Enforcer of the UPO," I said, my voice still unsteady. "Kaida, this is my mother Oshtara Kendriz, my younger sister Caldri, and my baby brother Roldren."

"It's an honor to meet all of you," Kaida said, looking as overwhelmed with emotion as my family was.

I caressed her cheek, then took a couple of hesitant steps towards my family. They stiffened, shocked by this unusual behavior.

"Will you not embrace me, Mother? I have an Ejaya now. It's okay to touch me," I reminded her softly.

A stunned expression descended on her features before giving way to wonder as understanding dawned on her. A slow smile stretched her lips and then something seemed to snap inside her. She broke into a run and threw herself into my arms.

Having inherited my father's height, I towered by a good head over my mother. I easily picked her up and buried my face in her neck. A tsunami of emotions crashed into me as I deeply inhaled the beloved maternal scent I had been denied for decades.

"My baby! My beautiful baby! I thought I'd never hold you again. My Cedros!"

Tears rolled down my cheeks as she covered my face with kisses and held me in a bone crushing hug that belied her otherwise delicate stature. Gods, how I had missed her... missed them... missed this. Coming to see them in the past and being forced to stay at a distance had become too much of a torture for all of us. Therefore, we'd resorted to only speaking through vidcoms. But this...

My sister complaining for her turn finally convinced my mother and I to reluctantly let go of each other. I embraced Caldri and Roldren in turn, each of them giving me just as powerful and emotionally charged hugs.

But seeing my mother pull my Kaida into her arms completely turned me upside down. My Ejaya, my perfect mate... She had given me everything: love, happiness, and my family back.

CHAPTER 16
KAIDA

Stunned at first by his mother's unexpected hug, I melted in her arms and returned it. My already constricted throat, from watching the moving reunion between Cedros and his mother, tightened further. I'd never known what a maternal embrace felt like. Oshtara didn't just hug me with her arms, but with her tail as well.

Unlike Cedros, she didn't rub her face all over mine—which would have been awkward—but only her temple against mine, marking me with her scent. While her tail still held me close against her, Oshtara cupped my face with both hands and examined my features like I was a marvel that filled her with awe.

"Thank you, Kaida. Thank you, my daughter. You have given me my son back and filled the gaping hole in my mother's hearts. With each passing year without him having an Ejaya, I mentally prepared for the fact I'd lose my firstborn to a premature death. But the Gods answered my prayers. They reached across the stars and brought you to my Cedros. You are a blessing to my son, to our family, and to the people of Dramnac. Welcome home, my daughter."

I blinked rapidly to stem the tears threatening to gush out of my eyes. I'd never been claimed like this. Growing up, I'd just been one of many orphans adding to the burden of the struggling colony.

"Thank you for the warm welcome, Ms. Kendriz. Being Cedros's Ejaya is a great honor. He's been wonderful to me," I said, my voice shaking with emotion.

"Tut, tut! No such formalities between us. You can call me Mother or Oshtara," she said with false severity.

I chuckled and gave her a sheepish look. I licked my lips nervously, wondering if I would be so bold as to give her the name I wanted to.

She did offer…

"Thank you… Mother," I said with a nervous laugh.

The way she beamed at me, as well as the approving glances her children gave me, confirmed I had made the right choice. Each of Cedros's siblings gave me a bruising hug, making me feel unbelievably welcome and at ease.

For the next little while, we sat at their patio table, having a spirited conversation. We sipped on some alcohol and fruit mixes similar to those Cedros had made me try during our picnic. The whole time, Oshtara was constantly touching Cedros as if to reassure herself that he was truly here. And his siblings were having a field day recounting embarrassing anecdotes about him growing up.

"Cedros used to hold me by one leg and dangle me over the edge of the plateau because I'd eaten his treats," Roldren said with a shit-eating grin. "Since my flight was still iffy back then, I'd cry out to Mother to come save me."

Cedros scrunched his face, playfully glaring at his brother while his scales darkened with a sliver of embarrassment. "He was doing it on purpose. He never stole Caldri's food or things, always mine. I often caught him spying on Mother when she was preparing our snacks, so that he could snatch mine."

I chuckled. "So he ate both his and yours?"

"No," Roldren said, unrepentant, proud even. "I specifically wanted his and would leave my own behind."

I gasped. "Oh, my God, but why?!"

"Because he was my big brother. I wanted to be like him. Eating his treats and taking his stuff made me more like him… in my head," Roldren said with a shrug.

Cedros's face melted, and he leaned over the table to kiss his brother's forehead before sitting back. Roldren gave him an affectionate smile. Then his expression took on a mischievous edge.

"But it was also just for the fun of pissing him off," Roldren added tauntingly. "It is a younger sibling's duty to annoy his elders."

We all burst out laughing, and Cedros playfully breathed out a tiny stream of shadow flames at his brother, who made a face at him.

"Cedros always had a prodigious appetite as a youngling," Oshtara said with a wistful smile. "It's not surprising seeing how big and tall he has grown to be. His father was just as massive… on all fronts. And with quite the healthy appetite… also on all fronts."

I nearly choked on my drink upon hearing those words. Cedros snorted while his family stared at me with surprise. Oshtara suddenly spun her head towards Cedros, and her eyes slightly widened before she gave me a speculative look. An odd expression flitted over her noble features, then an even odder smile settled on her lips.

"Have you coupled with my Cedros? Your human body is so small. If my firstborn shares his sire's girth, I fear you might not match," Oshtara said with an air of sympathetic concern.

I wanted the ground to open beneath me and swallow me whole while Roldren and Caldri also looked at me with that same compassionate expression.

"Yes, Mother. My Kaida and I are perfectly compatible. Humans are quite adaptable," Cedros said matter-of-factly.

"CEDROS!" I exclaimed, staring at him disbelievingly.

He looked back at me with the most innocent expression. "What? It is a valid concern. I'm merely reassuring them of your welfare."

Before I could come up with a politically correct answer, Roldren chimed in.

"It is indeed reassuring," Roldren said, looking relieved. "From all accounts, Shadow Lords are rumored to be relentless in their attention and to have phenomenal stamina."

Caldri nodded. "It's quite understandable," she concurred in a reasonable tone. "After all, they have decades of forced abstinence to catch up on."

That was it. I needed to get the hell out of there to put an end to this conversation. I hopped down from my bench and flicked my hair over my shoulder.

"If you'll excuse me for a second, this delicious drink is playing a number on my bladder. I need to use the hygiene room for a moment."

Before I could take a single step, Cedros wrapped his tail around my waist and drew me to him. He then picked me up and plopped me onto his lap.

"No, you don't. You're just trying to run away," Cedros said with a laugh in his voice. He rubbed his face in my neck, then kissed me. "We're teasing you because your prudish human ways are just too delightful."

The others burst out laughing while I gaped at all of them in disbelief.

"The redness of your face is quite wondrous, my daughter," Oshtara said with a chuckle.

I blinked, and then it hit me. I jerked my head towards Cedros over my shoulder to glare at him. "Oh my God, you put them up to this! You told them telepathically!"

"I did," he confessed without any shame. "They never would have believed me otherwise."

I made a face at him. "I thought you said only Shadow Lords and their Ejayas were this crude and open with each other?"

"Crude?" Caldri echoed, slightly recoiling in surprise. "This doesn't qualify as crude for us. Shadow Lords and Ejayas are supposed to be open with each other about everything, especially their personal feelings in all of their interactions, as harmony and unity between them is primordial to the success of their relationship. But coupling is a natural function for everyone."

"Right, but nobody wants to hear about their parents coupling," I exclaimed, expecting them to concur with me.

To my dismay, they all looked at me like *I* was the weird one.

"Why wouldn't we?" Roldren asked. "Them coupling is the reason we're here. Who better than our parents to teach us about it? Don't human parents explain mating rituals to their younglings to make sure they have a healthy sex life?"

I mumbled something about how the birds and the bees talk was every parent's nightmare.

By the look they gave me, they clearly found humans strange, if not illogical. They were right, but old habits die hard.

I glared at Cedros again. "I'm so sleeping in my own room tonight with ten layers of clothes on."

He burst out laughing and once more shook his head. "No, my Kaida, you're not. Or I'll scratch on your door while making whiny sounds throughout the night. And I'll tell Nero to come tickle you."

His family laughed some more.

"All right, enough teasing Kaida for today," Caldri said, taking pity on me. "Let's see how rusty you've gotten at Vayarka, big brother."

"Yes! I can't wait to brag about how I defeated a Shadow Lord at Vayarka!" Roldren exclaimed.

A predatory smile settled on Cedros's face. "I'm about to

show you why the oldest is always the best, Shadow Lord or not!" He gave me a passionate kiss before standing up and sitting me on his stool next to his mom. "Prepare to be amazed, my m… Ejaya."

I smiled, pretending I hadn't noticed he'd almost called me his mate again. Roldren went to fetch something while his brother and sister took flight. Moments later, a series of rings appeared in the sky a short distance above our plateau. The three siblings entered into some kind of aerial acrobatics dance that appeared to involve flying through the rings when their center filled with a colored energy field while the others tried to stop you, or avoiding it when it turned to a different color while your rivals tried to force you through it. I didn't quite get it, but they seemed to be having a blast.

The heavy weight of Oshtara's stare on me drew my attention away from her children. She was studying my features with a soft expression. In that instant, I knew beyond a doubt Caldri had deliberately lured her brothers away to leave me with her mother so that we could talk. I swallowed nervously, wondering what that talk would entail.

"When I first learned that my Cedros had finally found his Ejaya, my hearts rejoiced. But then dread filled me when I heard you were human," she said matter-of-factly. "I didn't know what that would mean for him. Would you understand your role? Would you be able and especially willing to fulfill it? Would you be able to adapt to our ways and our world? That worry gnawed at me until the moment the two of you came through that portal."

"You're no longer worried?" I asked, feeling irrationally nervous about her answer.

She smiled and shook her head. "No, I'm not. My Cedros is madly in love with you. I don't know if you are in love with him, but I can see that you have genuine love for him. Cedros was always a good-spirited and playful youngling. But I've never seen him this happy. And it's all because of you."

My face heated with embarrassment. "I really don't deserve that much merit. I just let him hug me, and he gets that happy buzz from the hormones," I said with a nervous laugh.

"It's more than that, and you know it," Oshtara said factually. "The merit for all this is yours. Own your achievements, my daughter. There is no need to be humble with the truth. But I have to ask you something. Is there a chance you might consider my Cedros as your mate?"

I shifted uneasily in my chair and tucked my hair behind my ear as I chose my words carefully. "Anything is possible. Like you said, I love Cedros dearly. We've only met recently and are getting to know each other. But in time, I might consider it, yes."

"But?" Oshtara insisted. "I can sense something is troubling you. Maybe I could alleviate some concerns for you? I know we've also just met, but you are a daughter to me now. I hope you can grow comfortable to discuss anything that troubles you with me, as you would if I'd given birth to you myself."

I gave her a trembling smile, emotions overwhelming me again at this maternal attention she was granting me. "This world differs greatly from what I'm used to. I'll certainly have many questions about it. But there is one topic that I believe you, better than anyone, can shed some light on for me."

"Ask away, my daughter. I'll gladly provide whatever insight I can," she said with an encouraging smile.

"I worry about children, if Cedros and I ever were to become mates," I confessed sheepishly.

Oshtara frowned slightly, a sliver of worry flashing through her light green eyes. "Why? You do not wish to have any?"

"Oh no! Not at all! I grew up an orphan. I always dreamt of a family of my own with many children running around, surrounded by the love of both their parents," I said passionately. "But Cedros is a Shadow Lord. That means there is a good chance at least one of our children would be one as well. How do you handle letting your five-year-old child fend for himself in the void for months or even years? What if he's scared, cold, or hungry? What if something bad happens, and he's screaming for his mom and dad, but there is no one around to save him? What if—?"

"Stop, Kaida. It is not like that. Yes, sending your offspring into the void for the Shadow Trail is always a monumental challenge for both them and the parents," Oshtara said in a soft but firm voice, interrupting me. "When two weeks went by and my firstborn didn't return, I knew. One of my hearts rejoiced while the other broke. I missed him terribly, his hugs, his laughter, his mischief, his scent… He was my first baby and had always been so affectionate. It simply was his destiny."

"But how do you cope? How do you not go insane and go chasing after him to make sure he's fine?" I insisted.

"As scary as it may seem to you, the Shadow Trail is extremely safe. No youngling has *ever* been lost or died during his journey. This trial is not a cultural choice that we impose on our young. It is a natural physiological and spiritual step in the growth of a Derakeen. We *need* to immerse ourselves in the void. It's what cements our phasing abilities. The same way the caterpillar feels the irresistible need to form a chrysalis for its transformation, so do we Derakeens feel the call of the void."

I nodded, some—but very little—tension draining from my shoulders upon hearing her words. "I understand what you are saying, and it is a major relief to know that no child has ever died from this. However, I still don't understand how a parent, especially a mother, can endure that kind of separation."

Oshtara smiled and caressed my cheek. "That's because you are thinking like a human. Do your people not leave their parents' nest at some point?"

"Sure, but not at five!" I exclaimed, slightly outraged. "They're just babies!"

"*Humans* are just babies at five. Not Derakeens. By the time they are five, our younglings can stalk and hunt prey, fight and escape predators, fly at speeds exceeding two-hundred-and-fifty kilometers per hour, and phase shift to get out of a dangerous situation. They are not helpless."

"Wow, okay. Our little ones definitely can't do that," I conceded, chastised.

She gave me a sympathetic look. "It doesn't make it any easier. I kept my youngest throughout their youth, but when they left my lair at twenty-four for Roldren and twenty-six for Caldri, it was just as difficult. During the Shadow Trail, we get monthly check-ins from the younglings. We embed a tracker in their arm should something happen. Shadow Lords also regularly scout through the Trail and the deeper void to keep a distant watch over them. And then there are shadow dwellers who roam around the different realms where future Kwesars and Shadow Lords spend their evolution years. They are extremely protective of them."

"Sounds like you have quite the safeguards put in place to keep the children safe," I admitted, rather impressed.

"We do. We love our little ones and do what we must to protect them during their journey," Oshtara said proudly. "It is undeniable that when one of them returns a Shadow Lord, it is difficult to no longer be able to hold them and kiss them like our mother's hearts demand. But you learn to cope. There are many established ways now to still keep them part of the family and show them love."

"That's the other part I would really struggle with," I confessed. "Cedros told me how he was in a separate house from you and watching his siblings play together while he had to remain at a distance."

"That's true, but *you* would not have that problem," Oshtara said eagerly.

"What? Why?" I asked, taken aback.

"Because, unlike me, you are an Ejaya. Thenzi, Cedros's father, couldn't be around me because he didn't have an Ejaya.

You are Cedros's Ejaya. Meaning that he will be able to raise his own offspring because he will have you as his mate to silence the discomfort from the little ones."

"Right, but that won't fix the problem of our Shadow Lord children. Once they come back from the void, they won't be able to stand us," I argued.

"A Shadow Lord's primary function is to stabilize phase shifts," Oshtara said smugly. "With you giving him peace, Cedros will have the focus to balance the phasing your other offspring could generate around your little Shadows. Ask Rovain and Trinit. Their second-born is a Shadow and lives happily in their lair with her other siblings."

"Jeez! I didn't realize that was a possibility. It certainly puts things in a different light," I said, stunned.

"And a good one at that, I hope. I am quite looking forward to you and Cedros making me a grandmother for the first time," she deadpanned.

I burst out laughing at her less-than-subtle statement. I genuinely liked Oshtara, and her obvious ploy to bind me to her son had given me some serious food for thought.

Three weeks after introducing me to his family, Cedros and I had fallen into a very comfortable routine. Although he hadn't brought up his desire for us to be mates again, we technically, unofficially were. Aside from sharing his bed—and making love like rabbits on every surface of our home—we multiplied the romantic outings, from more picnics and going to the fair to attending plays, sports events, and concerts. Spending an evening at Rovain's and Trinit's house with their four kids had been eye-opening.

With a little over four months to go before I had to decide whether to stay or leave, there was no rush. But I already had a good idea where my head was leaning. Cedros embodied everything I could have ever wanted in a man, and the way his family welcomed me made it an even more perfect package. To think I'd always worried I would end up with the mother-in-law from hell!

However, if my deepening bond with Cedros exceeded all of my wildest hopes and dreams, my mission was proving to be a total and complete disaster. I had nothing. No actual trail to follow and only a slew of wild speculations. In my desperation, I'd taken to walking around the void with Nero as my search dog and bodyguard.

I'd concluded that I wouldn't find anything in the stable void through the black gate. Too many people traipsed through the various main pathways. Crooks up to shady business always did so in the most unlikely places and away from prying eyes. The primary places I could think of were phase shifts. Everyone dodged them or got the fuck out of them quickly if they ever got caught by one.

That theory was the first solid trail I got with some common link between multiple incidents. It hadn't been obvious at first because many of the "accidental portals" created on Dramnac had originated from completely random locations scattered around various cities and continents. Or rather, they had *appeared* random before I had the phase shift key as a common denominator. When I cross-referenced them with that factor, suddenly, I realized every location was in the most unstable hotspots of each of those areas.

Okay, that didn't qualify as a massive discovery. The greater instability and thinness of the veil in those sectors could have been the cause that someone doing something totally innocent triggered the accidental rift. However, further investigation also demonstrated that those incidents matched the timing of *calendar* instability peaks of that specific area, but not necessarily the real peak in terms of actual instability that day.

Just like Earth's meteorologist would more or less accurately predict snow, thunderstorms, or tornadoes, Derakeen scientists gave daily, weekly, and monthly warnings about the least safe areas and expected highest shift fluctuations. The recorded incidents perfectly matched the annual calendar marking which regions averaged the greatest number of rifts for a given month.

It seemed far too calculated and deliberate to be a coincidence, especially since on a few occasions the accidental portal opened on a day where the fluctuations were quite weak in comparison to the severe instability a couple of days later where nothing happened. If these were truly fluke occurrences, then something didn't add up.

For this reason, Nero and I took to chasing phase shifts in the area where I suspected the culprit would be lurking. That didn't yield much results, aside from me getting a chill from all the cool drafts announcing a nearby rift, and spending an ungodly amount of time traipsing in the darkness. At least, I got my minimum daily steps in.

We'd been at this exercise in futility for the past couple of hours, wandering around the ever-changing pathways of an unstable rift when Nero suddenly stiffened. He turned abruptly towards his left, looking at one of the larger corridors in our current rift. His eyes and the tips of his tentacles glowed a brighter purple, which I'd come to realize meant he was infusing himself with a greater amount of the shadows and probing the void.

To my shock, Nero began swelling, almost doubling his size, before wrapping four of his tentacles around me. My surprised gasp turned into a yelp when he hovered a little higher, and my feet stopped touching the ground. He then dashed forward, carrying me at dizzying speed. Our surroundings blurred, and I felt the familiar tingle on my skin of crossing into a different phase.

Nero covered my mouth with one of his tentacles as he

slowed to a stop. Heart pounding, I nodded, understanding he wanted me to remain silent. Although my surroundings became clear again, it had a strange, dream-like glow. It took me a second to understand that Nero had both of us hidden in his stealth aura.

Flabbergasted, I stared in disbelief at the three Derakeens—two males and one female—standing in the central hub of the rift. Although I couldn't clearly see their faces from this position, the lesser shadow horns on the side of their heads unmistakably marked them as Kwesars. By the way they huddled together, they hadn't stepped into a phase shift by mistake and weren't trying to get back outside. I knew beyond a doubt that they were what I'd been hunting for all these weeks.

CHAPTER 17
KAIDA

The blue-scaled female rummaged in the medium-sized messenger bag dangling on her hip and retrieved a small piece of shadow obsidian. It looked smaller and more irregularly shaped than the shadow obsidian stones used to summon portals. She also took out a caster: a smaller, sleeker version of a nutcracker the size of a nail clipper. It allowed one to break a marked shadow obsidian stone to open a portal to the destination inscribed on the stone.

The two males—one green, one golden—stepped slightly away from her, and took on a ready stance. Meanwhile, the female placed the odd stone in the caster and broke it. The familiar thunderclap sound resounded, although muffled by the short distance between the triad and us. Sound didn't carry in the void.

A large portal opened before them. While it looked stable, its creation appeared to further destabilize the rift. The pathways connecting to the hub we were standing in were collapsing or reshaping themselves. Many became shorter, their shadowy dead-ends moving up closer to us, and many opening a window into the real world.

I strained to hear what the triad was saying, but their physical reactions and the green male's fist pump confirmed the summoning had yielded the result they had hoped for. It was a flawless portal, the destination close enough that I could see it as if peering through an open doorway. A purple mountain peak in the distance—whose name I couldn't remember—identified that destination as near one of their major landmarks.

"Only a couple of meters off," the male said with excitement. "You're getting really good!"

The female beamed at him. Then, together, they worked on dispelling the portal. Understanding dawned on me as they struggled to close it. They were Scribe apprentices, testing the inscriptions they'd performed on bad quality shadow obsidian stones that would have never met the approval of their mentors. Remembering how easily Cedros dismissed his portals with an absentminded flick of his wrist further underlined the power gap between their different classes. Surely the Gate Masters would have had a much easier time of it.

I gave one of Nero's tentacles a gentle squeeze as a thank you. He tightened his hold around me and rubbed his cheek against mine. This was the lead I needed. I continued observing in silence while they took turns cracking one of the stones they had marked. Each yielded varying results, from almost perfect to complete duds.

I was debating whether to call Cedros via my armband. As I couldn't communicate telepathically with him like he could with me, we'd taken to wearing armbands with a com system that allowed me to reach him at all times. The memory of Nero chasing me around the house that first day still traumatized me. The golden male cracking one of his last stones took that choice from me.

The apprentices cursed, all three of them shifting into their battle form—which was much smaller than Cedros's. The portal had opened onto a dark area bathed in purplish fog and filled with a swarm of aqrats. From what I could glimpse through the swirling vortex, they had been fighting over the carcass of some massive void creature. But the sight and scent of fresh prey commanded their attention.

As one, at least two dozen aqrats rushed towards the portal. Halfway through shifting, the three apprentices started breathing fire—normal flames, not shadow ones like Cedros had done—at the incoming beasts in the vortex. Simultaneously, they seemed to attempt to close the portal. Without hesitation, I tapped the emergency call to Cedros on my armband.

"No!" I hissed in a whisper, when I felt the tingle of Nero starting to shift us out of there. "Release me! Cedros is coming."

He hesitated for a second, but me activating the energy shield on my armband while grabbing my blaster forced his tentacles to release me. That broke the stealth aura that had hidden us from view. The golden male noticed us, shock and horror descending on his now fully draconic features, just as he was vanishing from view. Almost at the exact same time, the other male and female also vanished.

I realized my terrible mistake as the aqrats burst out of the portal into the rift's hub. With the Kwesars having phase shifted out of here, the beasts switched their focus on Nero and me. I never thought the apprentices would cut and run, leaving me behind to face this mess. But then, they hadn't known I'd been here until they were already mid-shift.

I opened fire on the aqrats, but Nero activated his insanely badass beast mode. The shadow dweller's size quadrupled in a blink, his tentacles glowing with an almost blinding purple light, while electricity crackled at their tips. The potent static energy had my hair standing on end, and a cold shiver ran down my spine when he emitted a terrifying roar that even the void couldn't dampen.

Purple lightning shot out of the tips of his tentacles, striking a dozen aqrats at least. Those who had the misfortune of getting hit in the face never realized what killed them. Their heads exploded like overripe watermelons. Others ended up with massive gaping wounds or severed limbs. But even as more of them pressed into the small space, Nero grabbed them and the wounded with his tentacles, effortlessly tearing them in half like one would a piece of paper. He discarded them like so much trash while chomping the head of another right off with one bite of his insanely enormous mouth.

Barely twenty seconds had elapsed, and yet corpses were already piling up. Things were happening so fast, I felt as if I was moving in slow motion as I fired at the creatures. I was turning my blaster towards a handful of aqrats rushing towards a nearby pathway opened onto the outside world when Cedros came bursting out of one of the shadowy walls of the void, already in his battle form.

In the time it took me to fire two more shots, Cedros had already assessed the situation. He flicked the portal closed with a wave of his hand while smashing two creatures trying to exit into the real world to a pulp with his tail. The battle ended in a blink, with Nero grabbing the last aqrat, holding it helpless in his tentacles, then ate it alive in four huge bites.

I swallowed hard, feeling a little creeped out as I looked at his crazed and nearly feral expression. The sphere that was both his head and body had grown bigger than two-thirds of my body. He glanced at me from head to toe with his glowing purple eyes, then at Cedros, before turning to the corpses on the ground.

Before I could say or do anything, Cedros scooped me up into his embrace, even as he was morphing back into his normal form. Behind him, Nero hovered over the fallen beasts, his tentacles splayed while electric tendrils shot out from their tips to crawl over the remains. Seconds later, the corpses began collapsing in on themselves, deflating into mummified-looking carcasses before vanishing into smoke.

"My Kaida, are you hurt?" Cedros asked, moving away from me just enough to examine me for any sign of injury.

I absentmindedly shook my head, stretching my neck to look at Nero over his shoulder. "What is he doing?"

"Are you sure you're not injured? Did any of them scratch you or inject you with their toxin?" he insisted.

"No. I'm fine. What is Nero doing?"

"Kaida, if toxin—"

"Cedros, I'm fine!" I exclaimed, interrupting him. "Stop worrying. Now, please tell me what he's doing."

Despite his obvious desire to insist, Cedros yielded and cast a glance at Nero. "He's siphoning their lingering life force to replenish the energy reserves he expended."

"Oh," I said, looking at the shadow dweller with awe as he was finishing draining the last corpses. "He saved my life. I made a stupid call, and he saved me."

"What happened here?" Cedros asked in a severe tone.

I quickly recapped what I had witnessed. When I told him about the apprentices phasing out of here, he lost it.

"They abandoned you?!" he shouted, displaying anger for the first time since I'd met him.

"No! It wasn't like that. They did not know I was here. When the aqrats showed up, I called you and got out of Nero's camouflage to help them fight. The golden male saw me just as he was vanishing. Since this is an unstable rift, I doubt they could have just waltzed right back here to assist me, even if they had wanted to."

While my words somewhat mollified him, they had definitely not appeased his fury.

"They still created this dangerous situation and fled," Cedros hissed, before pointing an angry finger at the open doorway onto the real world the aqrats had tried to go through. "This portal leads off-world. Had you not called me and stopped them from jumping out, aqrats would be roaming that land and decimating innocents!"

"What?! But... I can see outside! I thought common people like me could only see on the other side of a portal if the destination was nearby?"

"That is true with a common portal. But you could see on the other side of a master portal, one infused with tremendous energy. Did you not see the terrace of my lair through the very first portal I had sent for you and Kayog on the day you moved to Dramnac to be with me?"

I nodded. "Right. I had forgotten about that. But they are apprentices..."

"They didn't cast this doorway," Cedros explained, turning to look at it. "The portal they opened further destabilized the rift and caused a power surge in that specific pathway."

"So that's how those terrible off-world accidents have occurred," I said pensively.

As if summoned by my words, two young Ordosian children slithered into view on the other side of the portal. The Naga-like species—considered primitive by galactic standards, were only to be exposed to other worlds under strict guidelines. That the portal opened in an area where their children hung out indicated it was trespassing into their sacred lands. The thought of what slaughter could have ensued had the aqrats gone through made my stomach roil.

Both children jerked their heads left, no doubt having been called by someone. The smallest one with black scales pointed a finger at us—although more likely at the portal. To my shock, a tall black human female came into view. As soon as I saw the golden scales adorning her neck and arms, I knew who the woman was. I'd heard of the mess at the Great Hunt. She picked up the little Ordosian with black scales. He immediately wrapped the snake tail that served him as legs around his mother's waist, while she pushed the oldest child behind her protectively, her eyes scanning the portal with a worried expression.

Cedros immediately dispelled it.

"Fuck," I mumbled under my breath. "I'm going to need to warn the UPO. The Ordosians will not take this intrusion kindly at all. But first, we need to have another talk with Headmaster Aldyr," I said with a harsh voice while looking at the ground near the area where the apprentices had summoned the portals.

"Agreed. Can you recognize the culprits?" Cedros asked.

I frowned. "I'm not sure, to be honest. I never got a good look at their faces as they were sideways to me. The one I saw straight on was in his battle form. And the void dampened their voices too much for me to clearly hear them."

I walked the short distance to where the apprentices had initially stood and crouched to pick up a few of the shattered fragments of the stones they'd used. I stuffed them into an evidence pouch before turning back to Cedros.

"However, I have a good idea how to narrow them down. I'd been toying with a theory that turned out not to be far-fetched at all," I said. "Let's go have a talk with Headmaster Aldyr regarding his surprisingly talented new cohort, who is learning much faster than usual."

The Headmaster's midnight-blue scales took on a duller hue as he paled, listening to me recounting the incident I had witnessed. Although crestfallen, the absence of genuine shock and the worry on his face confirmed this was no news to him.

"You knew what your students were up to," I accused factually, my voice devoid of aggression.

The Headmaster stood from his stool, circled around his desk, and went to stand by the patio door of his office's terrace, looking down at the apprentices training. I didn't press him to answer, knowing he would in his own time.

"Poverty is a difficult thing, Miss Daigo," he finally said in a conversational tone, his back still turned to us as he continued to look outside. "You are new to our world. While my people may look happy and well-adjusted to you, we have our challenges, like most organized societies."

He turned to look at me, his silver eyes glowing against the darker shade of his scales.

"I know very well the challenges of poverty. I was an orphan in a crime-ridden refugee colony. If not for the opportunities to make a better life for myself that school and good grades gave me, I'd either be dead or a criminal myself," I said sternly.

"Then you understand why these ill-advised apprentices resorted to desperate measures," Aldyr said in a passionate tone. "This program is expensive and lengthy. For many of our pupils, finally starting to work professionally is the lifeline their families desperately wait for to make ends meet at last. There is nothing more devastating than for a promising apprentice to be forced to drop out because they can't afford a Miner to give them the quality stones they need for their training."

"I empathize with all of that. But there are security rules for a reason!" I interjected. "Innocents have died because your students tried to cut corners. And you said nothing!"

"Hold on!" he exclaimed vehemently. "We didn't know that our pupils were the cause. They don't have the kind of power necessary to open an off-world portal. Frankly, from your own recounting of today's events, I doubt the apprentices you saw even realized the full extent of what was happening and how a portal inside an unstable shift could cause the required power surge for it. Even *you* saw the doorway and didn't realize it led off-world until Shadow Lord Cedros told you."

"That may be true, but what they did was still irresponsible. Sure, the rift would eventually collapse, but had that window been into our world, my brothers and I would have been stuck cleaning up that mess. I wouldn't be surprised your pupils are the cause of the abnormally high number of roaming aqrats we've had to deal with in the Vessant sector. And you allowed it," Cedros countered.

"Like every other Headmaster before me," Aldyr snapped back. "I could lie to you, pretend like I did not know, and let the apprentices take the fall. That's what my predecessors have done when pupils were cast out of the program for getting caught using subpar stones. Notice that I said *subpar*, not *unsuitable*. But I refuse to keep hiding from the truth. It has never been a secret within the inner circles that Scribe apprentices often train with non-regulatory stones. Even the Council knows."

"What?!" Cedros exclaimed. "The Council is aware of these practices?"

"Of course they are. Some of their own offspring have done it," Aldyr said with a disgusted expression. He ran a hand over his horns before coming back to sit behind his desk in front of us. "It is all a stupid political and economic game that apprentices, especially commoners—are caught in. We've repeatedly asked for the right to normalize the use of faulty stones for training. We already supervise their summoning. Had they done what you witnessed earlier here in the Conclave, one of the Gate Master mentors would have swiftly dispelled the portal. No one would have been harmed, especially not off-worlders."

"So why the hell don't you?" I asked, confused.

"The Council refuses to make it legal," Aldyr spat out.

"But why?" I insisted, baffled. "It makes logical sense not to waste premium material for training purposes, if there is a cheaper, but safe, alternative."

"Economics," Cedros replied with contempt. "It would significantly increase the value of faulty stones, while decreasing the scarcity of proper shadow obsidian stones. As long as people have to juggle between using them for transport or burning them for their offspring's training, the prices stay up. But if every family no longer had to waste their stash of good stones for education, they would start hoarding them instead, and their prices would plummet."

"And that is only one of their concerns, an absurd one at that," Aldyr continued. "Sure, the price on shadow obsidian stones would go down, but that simply means demand would go up as more people could buy and use them instead of being forced to traipse around the black gate to save credits. But the real reason is that they want to slow down people's ability to elevate their plateaus."

"What?" I asked, wondering what that had to do with anything.

"Faulty stones are usually ground into shadow obsidian dust, which is used to elevate the plateau their lair is built on," Cedros explained. "Because they are faulty, there is usually a great amount of waste created. But not with a proper stone. A skillful Stone Master will perfectly grind every part of a good stone. If they become more affordable and more readily available, commoners will be able to acquire large amounts of dust quickly and elevate their status faster."

Anger surged through me, no doubt reflecting on my face. "And as you need less dust to climb at lower levels, the nobles want to prevent the plebs from ever catching up to them. So they create unnecessary scarcity and high prices."

"Yes," Aldyr said with a tired sigh.

"Be that as it may, what your students did was wrong and caused deaths. This needs to be reported. There needs to be consequences and, more importantly, it needs to stop," I said in a stern voice.

This was the part of my job I hated. There was no question in my mind that the apprentices had meant no harm. I also believed that, had they known, they would have stopped or taken greater security measures. They were fighting for a better future and living conditions for their families. Should they be cast out now or face criminal consequences, it would only perpetuate the circle of poverty and hardship for them and their loved ones. Yet, because of their actions, people had died. That couldn't simply be swept under the rug.

"I agree," Headmaster Aldyr said, taking me aback, having expected some major push back from him. "I fully expect you or the Shadow Lords to write a report to the Council. I will do the same. Just so you know, I will fight to save these apprentices from being expelled. While their actions may have been the trigger, those deaths were accidents, ones they didn't even know they'd caused. And I will fight to make safe training with faulty stones the new norm, even if that costs me my position. For now, I will go have a serious talk with all the Scribe apprentices."

CHAPTER 18
CEDROS

In the month that followed that momentous discovery, our collective reports to the Council created quite a stir, further compounded by the UPO's displeasure. It turned out that a far greater number of apprentices—*and* Scribe Masters—had been using faulty stones for portal summoning. The former had done so to speed up their training at a more affordable cost, and the latter to save on their stone consumption for personal needs.

While Kaida—with Nero's confirmation—had identified the three apprentices she'd encountered in the void, no criminal charges were laid against them. The main reason for this? Too many other people had either been identified as well or confessed to have also done this on a regular basis. Half of the current cohort of Scribe apprentices and Scribe Masters would have been incarcerated or banned from the profession. That several of them were nobles or their offspring greatly cooled anyone's eagerness into prosecuting.

I had mixed feelings about it. Like my Kaida, I believed it unfair that no justice would be found for the victims. On the other hand, aside from the fact that the Scribes appeared to have been genuinely unaware of the consequences, it would be impossible to pinpoint who had been responsible for which incident.

However, with all of this being made public, the population at large demanded a thorough revision of the shadow obsidian policies. The legalization of the usage of faulty stones—which the nobles and the Council had feared and tried so hard to prevent—would likely come to pass. The countless security measures put forward by their proponents were sound. But more importantly, they went a long way in pacifying the UPO.

We weren't dependent on or beholden to them in any way. After all, unless they mastered a method of creating portals of their own, they had no way of coming to Dramnac without our help. However, since my finding Kaida, my other Shadow Lord brothers who had not yet found their Ejayas were seeking closer interactions with off-worlders, and especially with humans. Kayog had hinted at a potential special collaboration between the Prime Mating Agency and the Shadow Lords. But that would only be possible if Dramnac was in good political standing with the UPO. Needless to say that my brothers and I were adding our own considerable pressure onto the Council.

Unfortunately, all of that drama hadn't gotten my Kaida any closer to figuring out who the mercenaries were. She compared it to looking for a grain of salt in a bowl of sugar—an absurd undertaking. Her superiors appeared to agree. When they semi-shelved that mission, my female took it as a personal failure. Despite both her employer and me telling her it wasn't the case, she kept thinking she could have done more.

But she had…

Aside from new incidents coming to an almost complete halt and the number of cases of roaming aqrats diminishing by half, Kaida's investigation had provided new trails. She had sent the Enforcers the remaining fragments of the faulty stones the apprentices had used in the rift. The analysis performed by their scientists not only indicated that they still contained residual power, but that it could also be artificially reproduced... to a certain extent.

They theorized that mercenaries had recovered some fragments in an accidental portal and had tried to recreate them. Additional conversations with the Veladeem Research Lab people further supported that theory as the stones artificially created by the Enforcers significantly resembled those the mercenary had sold them.

A specialized team had been assigned to identify every company and organization with the capacity and interest in trying to reproduce such stones. It was too big an undertaking for my Kaida alone. As much as she chafed at having that investigation passed on to someone else, she took solace in the fact that they still kept her in the loop on any progress they made.

In the meantime, my Ejaya had resumed her regular work as an Enforcer. At first, her going back to her world had terrified me. What if it reminded her of just how different life and customs were off-world? What if it made her homesick enough to draw her away from here? What if she met another male?

I had provided her with two stashes of shadow obsidian stones. One opened a portal directly at the Enforcers HQ, light years away from here, and the other took her right back here on the terrace of our lair. While this aimed at giving her a sense of freedom of movement, I made it a point of summoning her portals to and from work. I often entered the portal with her and made a display of kissing her goodbye, so there would be no doubt for any of her male coworkers that she was mine. It was petty and mostly unfounded, as her passion and affection for me seemed to deepen daily. However, until she committed to us and bonded with me as my mate, I would continue to feel insecure.

I'd been reading some more about humans, especially courtship. To my dismay, I'd discovered that the first book I'd been focusing on, *The Care and Feeding of Humans*, had actually been an ancient Delvenian 'pet care' guide. The advanced species had believed humans to be primitive creatures that made good, clean, easy to train, and low maintenance house pets. Why, by the Gods, would they still have that book in circulation and translated in various languages? Apparently, because they used it as an educational manual and cautionary tale for xeno-politics students, and anyone whose profession involved first contact with primitive species.

This new book, *The Romantic Gentlemen: A Human Dating Guide*, was deemed a bestseller on Earth and in many human colonies. Some of their rituals sounded unnecessarily messy and pointless, like the trails of flower petals. Others sounded rather impractical, like the candlelight dinners. Only three days prior, I'd devoured a full shajen in my battle form. The herbivorous creature was somewhat comparable to a buffalo. I wouldn't be hungry for a few weeks. As much as Kaida loved that I could take her shopping anywhere in the galaxy in a blink, she wasn't that materialistic. And that I didn't want her wearing clothes defeated the main purpose of shopping.

We regularly cuddled when watching romantic 'movies' together, or admiring the stunning Dramnac sunsets. We didn't go on romantic walks but did plenty of flights together, mostly with me carrying her. Although I appreciated the high-tech jetpack Kayog had given my mate, I much preferred holding her in my arms. I'd already gotten her a 'pet' and regularly brought her off-worlder treats, including strawberries dipped in chocolate. In fact, anything chocolate earned me major points with my mate. That had been one of the best suggestions from the book.

The bubble bath sounded good, but we didn't have baths. I was more than willing to build one in our lair, but intended to try an alternative tonight to see how my Kaida responded to it. The massage also felt like a good plan. Aside from its relaxing effect, it would make my female feel good, on top of giving me an excuse to touch her. However, for that too, I wanted to give it a special spin that would make it a unique experience.

I checked the massage hammers one last time. To think I'd come this close from majorly messing up when I went to acquire them. I'd almost bought a pair of clubs used by the humans' rhythmic gymnasts instead. These ones were heated and cushier to provide the ultimate foot and leg massages. When Kaida and I had watched the remake of an extremely old—and somewhat sad—human classic movie called *Raise the Red Lantern*, she had repeatedly wondered about how the foot massage the favorite concubine received would feel. She would find out tonight!

Speaking of which, Kaida would leave work any minute now. I had given her a special marked stone, telling her to join me there when she was done, as I might be late picking her up otherwise. She didn't question me. After all, we regularly went to the Kairns of Alja on Friday evenings, either to attend a Vayarka match, do an activity at the fair, or just hang out with my family or some other Shadow Lord-Ejaya couple by the orchard on the plateau. One of us arriving early would allow us to secure a good spot if watching the match or picnicking.

But I had a very different plan in mind.

I checked one last time that I hadn't forgotten anything, including utensils. Feeling both excited and nervous, I headed to the Spirits Cave to prepare everything. The natural formation—although slightly helped by architects—had many little chambers that provided complete privacy for couples. They needed to be reserved in advance, the price very reasonable and affordable once a year. However, any additional visit in the same year became extremely steep to discourage those who would simply use it as a regular romantic getaway.

Moments after I finished setting up the table, my com chimed. A quick glance at the interface of my bracer displayed a message from Kaida, stating she was on her way. Considering the great distance it had traveled, the message had been sent at least a couple of minutes ago, meaning she'd be here any second now.

Hearts pounding, I hugged the side of the cave, hiding in the darkness so that she wouldn't see me when she first arrived. My perfect night sight had allowed me to function without light. The stone would take my Kaida right at the entrance of this specific cave, bathed by the fading daylight of Oddran.

As if summoned by that thought, a portal opened with a muffled thundering sound. Through its window, I watched my beautiful female wave goodbye to her colleagues before entering it. Like all non-Shadow Lords, she couldn't see the other side of the portal like I did. So when she emerged on this side, Kaida stiffened to find herself in this unexpected location rather than the Kairns of Alja.

Lips parted in confusion, she tried to peer inside the darkness before casting an uncertain look over her shoulder at the portal. My poor female no doubt wondered if I'd accidentally given her the wrong stone. Not wanting to risk her jumping back into the vortex, I dismissed it with a flick of my hand.

Kaida jerked her head in my direction when my throat and chest glowed as I filled my heating chamber with hydrogen. I breathed out a soft stream of shadow flames at the ceiling, starting half a meter in front of her. Instantly, the microorganisms —somewhat similar to mushrooms that coated it—lit up in a wave. You would think a carpet of glowing pearls had unfurled overhead, lighting up the space.

My female gasped, her eyes widening with wonder. I extended a hand towards her. Her eyes still flicking this way and that, she approached with slow steps, taking my hand absent-mindedly as she took in the dreamy aura the glowing lights had given the space.

"Welcome to the Spirits Cave, my love," I said in a soft voice, drawing her to me.

"*This* is the Spirits Cave?" she exclaimed, finally focusing her stunned expression on me.

I stiffened, taken aback that she would know of it. "Y-yes. You've heard of it?"

She gave me a strange look, which shifted into a taunting expression. "You're not the only one reading about the weird other species in our couple."

I snorted. "Derakeens aren't weird. Humans are."

"Says you," Kaida replied teasingly, before kissing my lips. "I can see why your people come here to exchange their wedding vows," she continued wistfully. "It is breathtaking."

I swallowed hard, tension building in my back that she knew this place's main purpose. Sure, couples often came here merely for the magical experience of quality time together. But most came here to seal their engagement or formally exchange vows. I had intended to slip it in during the evening to see how she would respond to that possibility. After all, we hadn't discussed her becoming my mate in months since that first time.

To my relief, Kaida didn't seem distraught that I brought her here, appearing instead quite eager to find out what I had planned for us. I gladly obliged. Leading her by the hand, I breathed out more shadow flames, lighting up the rest of the space.

"Oh, my God! This is stunning!" my female exclaimed when the rest of the wide corridor we'd been walking in lit up.

The hallway flared open into an intimate four-square-meter space overlooking a pale purple river. The same dreamy glow bathed the room in the perfect light. In the center, a stone table laden with food awaited us.

"Sit, my Kaida," I said, pulling the stone bench for her, the plush cushion on top making it comfortable.

She settled down, her beautiful face split in a wide grin. I turned on some soft, romantic human music from a portable device. My female couldn't seem to decide if she wanted to feast her eyes on the various delicacies or on the spectacle of the bubbling river. Me scooping small portions of everything onto her plate forced her to pay attention to the meal I'd gathered for her.

"How did you get all of that?" she asked, a greedy expression settling on her features. "And how did you know these are all my favorites? I mean, how do you even know what they are?"

I puffed out my chest, feeling smug. "Simple, my Kaida. I listen when you speak. I memorize and take note when you don't look, then research. Your colleague, Maeve, actually helped."

"Maeve?! When? How?" Kaida exclaimed, stunned.

"I identified the species and planets that prepared the dishes you liked, but I didn't know their location. She not only provided me with the names of the best restaurants for each meal, but also with the specific coordinates so that I could portal directly there."

Kaida's eyes widened so much, they appeared on the verge of popping out of her head. "Holy cow! You mean you actually went to each planet to get these?!"

I gave her a slightly offended look. "Of course! Did you think I would settle for nothing than the best for my Ejaya?"

"You're crazy!" she whispered, awe and disbelief etched on her face.

I smiled. "For you, yes."

She batted her eyelashes and lowered a gaze with a soft, slightly embarrassed smile while her cheeks heated. It always warmed my chest to see that kind of blushing shyness from her, especially considering how wild she and I got at night.

"You're really too sweet for your own good," she said, cutting into one of the strange meats before her.

I had tried a few of Kaida's cooked dishes in the past. I would never get used to what I considered the charred taste of the meat, the weird spices and preparation. Just give me my meat, raw and bloody.

Watching my female eat things she loved always cracked me up. The faces she made, her delighted moans, or just the way she licked her fork to catch a last taste was just hilarious. I would never tire of providing for her. The Gods willing, I'd one day be providing for our younglings as well.

We chatted amiably while she ate, and I sipped on fermented beverages. I couldn't help another chuckle when Kaida finally gave up. Too full to eat another bite, she cast a miserable glance at the bounty of food remaining.

"Don't be sad, my Kaida. We can bring the rest home for you to eat later," I said, amused. I rose to my feet and started packing everything back up in the temperature-controlled containers. "No! You do not help with this. Your only task right now is to get rid of those pesky clothes."

Surprise gave way to understanding when she cast a glance at the river.

I shook my head with a smile. "No. We're not going into the Dancing Water just yet. First, we're going to visit the Sighing Chamber."

"The Sighing Chamber?" she asked with curiosity, while discarding her clothes.

I grinned. "You'll find out soon enough."

She glared at me, knowing I was deliberately teasing her. After she finished folding her clothes on top of the table, Kaida let me carry her towards the edge of the plateau. Her gaze flicked between the round hammers and flask clutched in my hands, and the bubbling water below the plateau.

"What are you going to do with those?" she asked warily.

My grin broadened. "You'll see."

"You're insufferable," she whined.

"And you're too impatient. Savor the moment, my Kaida."

She gave me another baleful glare. "You know I'm curious. And... Oh! I hadn't noticed this!" she exclaimed, noting at last the staircase at the end of the left wall of the cave, right before the two-meter drop to the water.

"I can't wait to see what you think," I said, stepping down the stairs.

The wall in front of the landing forced me to turn left, revealing a large natural room under the area we'd just been sitting in.

"What the heck is this?" Kaida asked in an awed whisper.

"The Sighing Chamber," I said proudly as I gazed at the room. "The ground is actually an organic membrane that naturally grows in this environment. It requires very specific conditions to thrive. Beneath it, there are vrojian rocks, a sort of hybrid mix of volcanic rocks and shadow obsidian. The heat from the rocks illuminates the membrane and steam trapped beneath it makes it undulate like this. And this soft whistling sound you hear is the sighs from some of the steam escaping around the edges."

"Okay, this is really cool! It wasn't mentioned in the stuff I read about the Spirits Cave."

I gave her an indulgent smile. "That's because not every Spirit Cave has a Chamber. As you're about to discover, the membrane isn't the only one to do the sighing in here."

Kaida's eyes widened, then smoldered. She gave the room an assessing look, clearly trying to imagine what kind of naughty things I had in mind. I grinned and put her down on her feet. Her lips parted in response to the warm feel of the undulating membrane beneath us.

"Hmmm, this is nice," she whispered, looking at the moving floor.

"And it's about to get nicer," I replied in a similarly hushed tone, my voice full of promises.

I placed the hammers on the ground, poured some of the massage oil into my palms and started applying it on her. Kaida opened her mouth, likely to ask what I was doing, but I silenced her with a kiss. She melted into it, allowing me to have my way.

By the Gods! Her scaleless skin was already naturally soft, but with the oil, it became like the finest silk.

When the first moan rose from her throat as I fondled her breasts, I couldn't help a chuckle. I would never tire of how responsive my female remained to my touch after all these months, and despite how insatiable I remained.

Breaking the kiss with much reluctance, I turned Kaida around, my lips tracing a path down her back seconds before my hands applied oil on it. It wasn't meant to make her skin slicker for a massage, but to enhance the benefits and effects of the membrane on her.

As was my wont, I nipped at her round behind. I was obsessed with those enticingly soft mounds, just like her breasts. As I reached her ankles, I finally forced Kaida to lie down. Her reaction to the warm, undulating waves on her bare back was immediate. A throaty moan escaped her. Lips parted, she closed her eyes with a blissful expression.

I couldn't decide if pride or lust burned the brightest in my gut that my plan was giving so much pleasure to my mate. Working its magic—further enhanced by the oil—the membrane quickly had my Ejaya completely languid, the heat and undulating massage seeping deep within her. Simultaneously, I resumed applying oil on her front. This time, it was both so that the steamy heat of the room would react with it, giving Kaida a greater sense of well-being, and as an excuse to caress her delectable body.

On my way down to her legs, it took every bit of my willpower not to bury my face between her thighs and feast. Her taste, her scent, the feel of her on my tongue acted like the most potent aphrodisiacs on me. They were my new drug. But coupling would wait.

Kneeling at her feet, I sat on my haunches and placed her feet on my knees. After giving them a proper massage with my hands, I grabbed the hammer and gently started tapping the sensitive points at the bottom of her feet, according to the meridians—or Chinese pressure points. My mate turned into a complete puddle under my ministrations.

When I finally collected her in my arms and sat her in my lap, she appeared completely groggy.

"I've died and gone to heaven. I'm flying with the angels right now," Kaida slurred.

I chuckled and kissed her lips. "Well, you need to come back down to Dramnac, my love. I have more plans for you… for us."

Still seeming too languid to hold herself up in my embrace, she gave me a 'are you crazy?' look. "If you're planning on dropping me in that boiling water, assuming I don't get fully cooked, I'll definitely drown."

I burst out laughing. "I won't let you drown, and the water isn't boiling. It's merely bubbling. This place is a semi-dormant volcano. That's why this Chamber and the water are warm. The vrojian rocks this cave is made of are a primitive form of shadow obsidian. It has occasional power surges. All around the basin, there are small tunnels through which the water streams. The power surges create suction in some of those tunnels and pressure in others, which causes the water to bubble."

An odd expression flitted over her features. All drowsiness apparently gone, Kaida gave me an intense look before asking her next question.

"Is it that pressure that causes the Spirits to dance?"

I hesitated. "How much do you know about the Dancing Waters?"

She shrugged and gave me an apologetic glance. "Not as much as I wish I did. I only read that Derakeens come here to exchange their wedding vows and ask the Spirits to bless their union. If they dance over the waters, then their union will be successful."

"That is correct," I said cautiously. "But the Spirits are really just a mix of steam and water that rise in spiraling columns because of power surges. If you breathe shadow flames at the river, the 'Spirits' will come forth. There is always at least a handful that appear. However, that number varies from one time to the next. The more of them dance for you, the happier your bonding will be."

"Is this why you brought me here? For us to bond?" Kaida asked in a soft voice.

I stiffened, my mind going blank and my tongue turning to stone. For the first time, I almost wished my mate hadn't grown so comfortable asking me whatever question crossed her mind, as I'd been encouraging her to. I'd been praying for exactly that kind of opening, and now that she had given it to me, I was going into panic mode.

I swallowed hard, then shook my head. "No. I brought you here so that you could experience the most romantic and sacred place for lovers on Dramnac. Do I wish tonight was our bonding night? Yes, absolutely. I love you with everything that I am and will never be whole without you. I can only keep hoping that, before our six months are up, you will deem me worthy of being the male you wish to spend the rest of your life with. Should that day come, you will have but a single word to say, and I'm yours."

She studied my features with an unreadable—but incredibly soft—expression. "Careful, I just might."

My hearts leapt in my chest. "By all means, do."

For an insane second, I believed Kaida would ask me to bond with her. I barely managed to hide my crushing disappointment when she asked me a different question instead.

"What exactly does Derakeen bonding entail? I couldn't find anything about your weddings," Kaida said with a frown.

"We do not have formal weddings like humans," I explained, my thumb absentmindedly caressing her upper arm while she looked up at me, her head resting on my shoulder. "Naturally, if we ever became mates, we could organize one for you, if you wished," I added quickly.

She smiled and shook her head. "It's really become more of a commercial con to get the newlyweds to start off their new lives either broke or with an unreasonable amount of debt. Granted, fancy weddings are truly beautiful, but it's still a massive waste of credits. There are simpler ways to immortalize that moment."

I nodded. "Agreed. For us, the bond is simply between the two partners. We exchange vows that can be as long or as short as we want. Usually, they are very short, only one or two sentences."

"Really?!" Kaida said, stunned.

I chuckled. "Yes. There is no need for long, flowery prose that may end up being nothing but wind and pompous noise. The true pledge is in your everyday actions and words. I will not promise you the moon, my Kaida. I will give it to you. And if it is beyond my means or abilities, then I won't have broken a promise and I will at least have taken you to the stars. You will never question my love for you, because I will remind you every morning, noon, and night, be it in words or in deeds. You will never have to fear anything, because should harm come your way, I will chase it away. Should you fall, I will *always* catch you. And if I can't do it myself, I will always ensure someone else can."

"Like my favorite brat, Nero," she said with an affectionate smile.

I snorted. "Yes, like that brat, Nero."

To my surprise, she cupped my cheek, her thumb gently caressing my lips. "Those vows were far longer than one or two sentences," Kaida said teasingly.

I stiffened, and my jaw dropped as I replayed my words in my mind. I hadn't meant to speak my vows, merely explain to her how fancy words and long speeches were unnecessary. My words simply aimed at giving a general overview of what I'd been doing—or at least had attempted to do—since her arrival on Dramnac. And yet, they definitely qualified as vows.

She smiled at my shocked expression and rubbed her nose against my snout. "I accept your vows and speak them right back to you. Although I cannot protect you the way you can protect me, I will always strive to make your life better and bring you joy in every other way I can. I do not need to wait for the six months to be up to know that I already have found the more-than-worthy male I want to spend the rest of my life with. I love you, Cedros. I'm *in love* with you."

The powerful emotion that surged through me nearly choked me. "My Kaida?" I whispered in a shaky voice. "Are you saying…?"

She nodded, her eyes glistening with repressed tears of happiness. "I want to be your mate, the mother of your children, and spend the rest of my life with you. Nobody has ever made me feel more seen, more loved, more valued, and more respected than you have. You've supported me in everything, even my career. You've encouraged me, and helped me become a better me, and freed me of the artificial barriers I'd been confining myself in. And you've made me happier than I ever thought anyone could be. Bond with me, Cedros."

A joy almost too much to bear nearly had my hearts exploding. I claimed her lips in a voracious kiss, to which she responded in kind. Before the last shred of lucidity escaped me, I broke the kiss, my gaze boring into Kaida's. She looked at me questioningly.

"One last thing, to complete the bond, I must bite you," I said, showing her my fangs.

"Bite me?!"

I nodded. "I will give you some of my nezarone hormones. It will create a physiological link between us. It is safe, and it will enhance you."

"Okay," Kaida said.

The word no sooner left her mouth than she was reclaiming mine. I hadn't fully explained the changes this would trigger, but it could wait. Giving in to the searing desire that had been burning deep within me from the moment Kaida had stripped out of her clothes, and especially when we started that massage, I crushed her lips with a passionate kiss.

While devouring her mouth, I laid her back down onto the undulating membrane of the cave. My hands were all over Kaida's body, caressing her and fondling her breasts that had become such an obsession for me. I broke the kiss, my lips tracing every line and curve of her beautiful face, then trailing down to her ear. I rubbed my snout against it before gently nipping at the earlobe.

I inhaled her intoxicating scent, always more potent right behind her ear, between her breasts and at the apex of her thighs. Inevitably, it sent blood rushing to my groin. My length ached to extrude, but I ignored it, despite the discomfort of its confinement. I didn't want to join with her right away. I would see her soar a couple of times first before I took her to the Dancing Waters for the blessing of the Spirits.

My mouth tasted and explored every centimeter of her soft, silky skin, which had mostly absorbed the oil. Being edible and flavorless, the oil in no way masked or altered the delectably sweet and salty taste of my woman. As my lips latched onto one of her quickly stiffening nipples, my tail gently caressed a path up her legs.

Kaida shivered and breathed in sharply when the tip of my tail started rubbing against her sex. I coated it with the slickness of her arousal while licking the tight little nub of her breast and the surrounding areola. My mate moaned, her legs parting wider to give me better access, and her back arching as she pressed her chest to my face.

Without stopping my homage to her breasts, I let my right hand glide over her flat stomach. It tickled her navel before pursuing its journey down. At the same time my fingers reached Kaida's sensitive little bundle of nerves, the tip of my tail probed her slit. A strangled moan escaped her as my tail sank deeper inside of her, and my fingers massaged her clit. I reclaimed her mouth, loving the taste of my name on her lips in between two rapturous moans.

Soon, my tail and my fingers had my female cresting. I swallowed her shout of ecstasy, my tongue mingling with hers a short while longer before I ended the kiss. One hand holding her nape still, I lifted my head just enough to stare at her gorgeous face dissolved in an air of pure bliss as my tail continued to move in and out of her.

The minute she began to come back down from her high, I resumed kissing her body, heading south towards my prize. To my shock, Kaida yanked my horns back, forcing me first to lift my head, and then to lie down on my back. I almost protested. I wanted to taste my mate, to make her fall apart on my tongue. However, a single look at her face made it clear she would have her way. I was usually dominant in our coupling, but I didn't mind occasionally yielding control.

She reciprocated what I had done to her, worshiping my body with her hands and mouth, making me feel like a god. In our three months together, my Kaida had discovered each of my sensitive spots, how to and where to touch me, how hard to scrape or bite my skin and scales to quickly make me fall apart. I thought her lack of claws would have been a detriment, but my female used her nails like a queen. I didn't wait for her to demand it before I extruded, groaning with relief at my liberation.

While my mate often liked teasing, prolonging the wait until she had me begging, this time she didn't torture me. I couldn't tell if the divine back massage of the membrane undulating beneath me had lulled my sense of time, but Kaida seemed to close her hand around my shaft immediately. Each stroke, each exquisite squeeze had growling moans tumbling out of me. When the blazing heat of her mouth closed over my length, I barely kept from spilling my seed.

Fire coursed through my veins as she sucked me in deeper and deeper while clawing at my pelvis with her free hand, driving me insane with lust. I cried out when she began to scrape her blunt teeth over the pulsating ridges of my shaft. Jaw clenched, my abdominal muscles painfully constricted as I battled the urge to climax, I pulled Kaida away from me. Her words of protest died in a startled cry when I impaled her on my shaft.

Head thrown back, her nails digging into my chest, my mate began to ride me in earnest. Wings spread, my own claws digging into the plump flesh of her behind, I vigorously pumped into her from underneath. Our moans and grunts mingled over the baseline of the Chamber's soft sighs and of the rumbling of the bubbling river.

When Kaida climaxed, her inner walls clamping down on me forced my orgasm from me. I quickly silenced my roar, my chest burning with the excess of hot hydrogen. But I needed to save all of my fire for the Spirits.

Even as my seed was shooting out into my mate in blissful spurts, I rose to my feet with one powerful flap of my wings. Holding Kaida tightly against me, my hips still thrusting into her, I flew to the edge of the Chamber. The opening under the stairs gave us direct access to the river, only a few centimeters below. Turning my head to the side, I breathed out my most potent shadow flames at the edges of the river, infusing the rock with shadows.

Even as I eased us into the water, the first 'Spirit' rose. The river wasn't deep, halfway up my chest, but would be right at the curve of Kaida's shoulders, if I wasn't still holding her up and pumping into her. I had wanted her to enjoy the spa-like experience of the warm, bubbling water of the river, but we were too busy getting lost in each other.

The warm massage of the roiling water around us, my female wrapped around me, caressing and kissing me, her tight sheath stroking my length in its greedy vise, the nezarone hormone flooding my bloodstream, and pleasure almost too much to bear nearly overwhelmed me. As our next climax built, my fangs further descended, and my heating chamber swelled with even more hydrogen.

Seconds before ecstasy swept us away again, I fired my shadow flames. Unlike true fire, they didn't burn or heat the water, only infused it with more power. As narrow columns of water swirled and twirled all around us at the surface—blessing our union—I buried my fangs into Kaida's neck. She cried out, her climax slamming into her at the same time that both my hormone and seed shot into her.

I threw my head back and roared, my vision blurring under the force of my orgasm. Kaida collapsed against me, eyes rolling to the back of her head, and her body shaking. As my nezarone coursed through her, enhancing her as well as each sensation she felt, she too drowned in a sensory overload.

My knot swelled inside her, further binding her to me. With the last of my seed spent, I held my mate tightly against me, my wings wrapped around us while the Spirits continued their joyful dance.

We were one.

EPILOGUE
KAIDA

Three weeks after bonding with Cedros, I was living my best life. I was head over heels for a male who all but worshiped me and treated me like a queen. I finally belonged to a family who wanted and loved me. And my career kept advancing, providing me with both the personal and professional sense of fulfillment and accomplishment I needed. Cedros always slightly worried that something could go belly up during one of my missions involving combat, but I loved how much he trusted in me being competent enough to get shit done.

Nothing pleased me more than catching bad guys. And these particular pirates had been a thorn in our sides for far too long. Trapped between the tractor beams of our three Enforcer vessels, the pirate cargo ship finally stopped its vain attempts at fleeing. Then again, Maeve hacking into their computer and taking over control of their vessel had gone a long way into convincing them about the wisdom of surrender.

We boarded their vessel, Tedrick and I taking point, while Oleg and Maeve covered our rear. The Nazhral captain Zilgo Nethe—a feline bipedal species—stood with his multi-species motley crew inside the docking bay. Unarmed, their hands raised, they didn't make a fuss as Oleg and I put magnetic shackles on them and patted them down.

"You're making a big mistake, Enforcers," Zilgo said. "The Cartel will not take kindly to you stealing their legitimate cargo."

"If the cargo is as legitimate as you claim, then we'll apologize, release you, and back on your way you'll go, along with all of your goods," Tedrick said in a taunting voice. "But you and I both know we're going to find all kinds of things that shouldn't be here."

"I look forward to your apology, human," Zilgo snarled.

Tedrick huffed, then turned to look at Oleg and Maeve, gesturing at the pirate crew with his head. "Take them to the brig while our friend Zilgo gives us a tour."

The Nazhral bared his teeth, his tail stiff, and his feline ears flicking with repressed anger. Under different circumstances, I might have itched to pet his fluffy tabby cat fur. However, I felt nothing but contempt for the ruthless male with a criminal file a mile long.

He first took us to the cargo hold. Tedrick scanned the mountain of crates and containers while I browsed the ship's manifest. At first glance, it all looked legit. But then, it always did. We were used to this old dance. These ships systematically had secret compartments and caches where they hid the really good stuff. The challenge was finding them.

By the time we finished with the cargo hold, Oleg and Maeve had rejoined us. We pursued our exploration of the vessel, looking for the illegal goods. As we cleared room after room, I started worrying they'd either successfully fooled us or truly had nothing shady happening this time. And then Tedrick saved the day when his scanner went off inside the captain's personal quarters.

Tedrick gave Zilgo a taunting smile and gestured with his head at the section of wall that had triggered his scanner. "Why don't you do the honors, old friend?"

Zilgo hissed at our squad leader like a feral cat, which only earned him an amused smirk from Tedrick and a chuckle from me. Mumbling and grumbling, the Nazhral tapped a few inconspicuous sections of the wall in a specific sequence, and an entire panel—the thickness of a security vault—opened, revealing a secret cache. It contained at least three kilos of Edocit Down—a misleading name, considering they weren't feathers but actual leaves that grew on the Dryad species under specific conditions.

"They were acquired legally!" Zilgo snapped, when Tedrick whistled at the impressive haul. "I've got the consent letters from the donors."

And impressive it was. ED, as it was commonly called, was a potent hallucinogenic and recreational drug that could also be turned into a lethal and untraceable poison. Edocit teenagers naturally produced them in large quantities, the delicate leaves blossoming in their vine-like hair. ED had become illegal in many places once reports of abduction began multiplying. The missing young dryads would resurface years later, looking aged before their time, once they'd stopped producing the valuable leaves.

However, as it was a very lucrative business, many Edocit families—whether poor or not—allowed their young to voluntarily sell some of their down. It either helped their financial situation or gave the teenagers a comfortable starting fund for their future. As long as the buyer could provide proof of legal purchase, he could trade those goods in peace on the planets and entertainment space stations that allowed it.

"If you have the consent forms, why did you hide your stash?" I challenged.

"Because I knew, if I left it out in the open, some annoying Enforcers or Peacekeepers would bust my balls over it," he snapped back.

A quick check of the documents he provided appeared to confirm this was indeed legit. It pissed me off to no end. My gut screamed there was more to this, and by the look on Tedrick's face, he also believed we were missing something.

"Well, I'm sure you'll understand if we temporarily hold on to your ED until we can verify that all the sellers you have listed here indeed sold these voluntarily, and that they are safe and free with their families," Tedrick said in an overly sweet fashion.

The Nazhral cursed up a storm in his language. I tuned him out as we resumed our inspection of the ship… in vain. Frustrated beyond words that we'd have to release these known criminals for lack of charges, we gave it a last hail Mary. If we could at least find some illegal upgrades to their vessel, we could get it impounded, putting them temporarily out of their shady business.

However, as soon as we entered Engineering, a wave of cold had me jerking my head towards the back of the room.

"What is it, Kaida?" Tedrick asked.

"Do you feel that?" I asked.

"No, what?"

"The intense cold coming from over there," I said, pointing in its direction with my chin.

Tedrick and my other two teammates gave me a baffled look. A glance at Zilgo revealed nothing, his face completely closed off. With determined steps, I headed towards the back, the cold intensifying, soon followed by a familiar tingling sensation.

"Oh, my God. There's no fucking way you're not feeling that!" I said, looking at my team with a mix of excitement and disbelief. I shook my head in annoyance when all of them continued to give me a confused look, then shifted my focus to Zilgo. "There's a hidden compartment behind that wall. Open it."

Although he visibly blanched, Zilgo lifted his chin defiantly and fisted his hands on each side of his body. "There is no hidden panel here. Scan, and you'll see. I cannot open something that doesn't exist."

My teammates immediately began to scan. By their troubled looks, their scanners showed nothing. But, in a way that I couldn't explain, I knew beyond any doubt that there was one. Especially since I could feel the treasure they had stashed there.

"I don't need a scanner to confirm it," I said in a harsh tone that had Tedrick frowning with worry. "You can either open the secret compartment, or I'll have one of our engineers cut this entire wall open. Your choice."

"You can't do this!" Zilgo hissed before turning to Tedrick for support. "You cannot damage a vessel without solid evidence or proof. There is *nothing* on your scanners because there is *nothing* here."

"There is a big stash of shadow obsidian stones behind that wall," I snapped, eliciting shocked gasps from my teammates. "I live on Dramnac, and I am married to a Shadow Lord. I *know* when I'm in the presence of shadow obsidian. Open. The. Fucking. Wall."

This time, Tedrick stepped forward. "You have five seconds to comply, or I'll get the engineering crew down here. And once we retrieve the stones, I will have them gut this entire ship to find anything else that you may be hiding."

Defeated, the Nazhral mumbled a series of curses under his breath that sounded like he was casting a hex on us. I nearly screeched with joy when the panel slid open, revealing two large crates filled with faulty stones.

"Your eyes are glowing," Tedrick whispered to me while the Oleg was taking our haul to our ship.

Stunned, I touched my eyes, wondering what the hell was going on. They didn't feel any different.

We seized the vessel and booked the entire crew for contraband. Tedrick gave me leave to go home and figure out what was happening with me while he sent a crew to the manufacturing facility Zilgo had confessed he'd picked up the stones at.

As soon as I got home, I related to Cedros what had happened.

He grinned with a smug expression. "It's our bond kicking in."

"What?" I asked, baffled.

"Our bond, my love. I will show you," he said, picking me up in his arms and flying us down to the black gate.

As soon as we landed in the main hub, he asked me if I noticed anything different about the portals.

I shook my head. "No. They all look the same as they always have."

"Really?" he insisted.

"Yes. Why? What should be different?" I asked, confused.

"Can you read the destinations?" he asked, ignoring my question.

I blinked, more baffled than ever. "Yes, of course. Why shouldn't—" And then it hit me. "My visor! I don't have my freaking visor on, and I can see the runes! I can read it all!"

He beamed at me. "The nezarone I've been injecting you with is enhancing you. According to Kayog, your vision should improve to the point you will see like we Derakeens do, including greater distance and night sight."

"Oh, my God! That's badass!" I said, bubbling with excitement. "I could feel the stones from so far away. Will I be able to phase shift like you guys do?"

He gave me an apologetic smile. "No, my love. This you won't be able to do. Don't be disappointed. It is a good thing, as it might otherwise have affected your ability to be my Ejaya."

"Right. My phasing would mess with you," I said, feeling slightly bummed out.

"But you'll get other, much better enhancements," Cedros added with a mischievous glimmer in his eyes.

"Really? Like what?"

"According to Kayog, aside from increasing your lifespan and regeneration abilities—making you heal faster and less prone to common illnesses—you should also develop telepathic and telekinetic powers."

This time, I squealed and threw myself into his arms, making him burst out laughing.

"Why the hell didn't you guys tell me I had all this to look forward to? Why did Kayog hide this from me?" I asked, baffled and feeling somewhat cheated.

Cedros sobered and gently caressed my face. "Because I asked him not to. I didn't believe I would want a human mate. But if that ever changed, I wanted to be sure you wouldn't consent to bonding with me simply to gain those abilities. And by the time I fell in love with you, I didn't want to tell you for fear you'd think I was trying to buy your love by dangling these powers before you."

"You silly male," I said, melting against him. "We were fated to fall in love. You are the best thing that's ever happened to me."

"As you are mine."

"Anything else I should know that you've been keeping from me?" I asked.

This time, the air of happiness on his face left me voiceless, even more than the words that followed.

"Yes, my Kaida. You are pregnant with our twins."

S itting on the couch in our living room, Arzoth's mouth latched onto my nipple, I cooed at our youngest son while breastfeeding him. I lifted my head to look at Cedros, sitting on the cushioned stool across from us. I chuckled at the baleful way he was staring at our little one.

"Stop giving him the stink eye," I said, amused.

"He's too greedy," Cedros muttered. "He never leaves me any."

I burst out laughing. "You're an adult, Cedros! You don't need breastmilk! It's for the baby!"

"You're *my* mate. That makes it *my* milk. He could share a little. I need it, too!"

"You are aware that the more Arzoth drinks, the more milk I produce, right? You should be grateful that he has such a healthy appetite!"

As if in response to his father's shameless whining, Arzoth finally let go of my nipple, his little mouth chewing while he slowly blinked, looking ready for a nap.

"There, he's done. Happy now? You can stop complaining."

"YES!" Cedros hissed, coming to crouch in front of us.

I placed my palm over his snout, preventing him from leaning in to suck on my slightly sore nipple. He gave me an outraged look.

"Not so fast. You burp your son first. *Then* I'll think about whether to give you the remaining milk."

He made a face, looking at me as if I was doing him dirty, but still took our son with infinite care. I placed a towel on his shoulder and watched him settle Arzoth in the right position before tenderly rubbing his back. My heart melted looking at them. I leaned in to kiss our baby's head before kissing Cedros. But loud screams outside cut that moment short.

"Oh brother," I muttered, racing to the terrace to see what our other little hellions were up to.

Cedros chuckled in anticipation as he slowly followed behind me. My shoulders slumped, and I rolled my eyes at the spectacle that awaited us. Sitting on one of the chaise lounges on the terrace, our daughter Theka was directing the abuse Nero was inflicting on our firstborns. The shadow dweller held each of the twins by one leg, dangling them over the edge of the plateau. Whichever one Theka pointed at, Nero zapped with the electric tendrils at the tips of his tentacles. Obviously, it was no more than a tickle, but my wretched daughter had mesmerized the shadow dweller and had him eating out of the palm of her hands.

"Theka! Cut it out!" I shouted, putting my fists on my hips.

Looking guilty, Nero immediately tossed my oldest sons, Kairzan and Kinshu, onto the grass. They jumped back onto their feet, looking at me for the redress of their grievances. Theka stood up, holding my gaze with the same type of self-righteous outrage as her brothers.

"They stole my treat box and won't confess!" she exclaimed, pointing an accusatory finger at her brothers.

I rolled my eyes. "They can't confess because they didn't steal it. *I* took away your box because you won't stop gorging on the treats instead of only having a maximum of two a day, like we agreed when your father brought them to you."

Theka scrunched her face before casting a 'oopsie' glance at her brothers. Then, brazen as always, she shrugged at them. "You still deserved it."

The boys gasped in outrage and broke down chasing after their sister. She squealed and half ran, half flew into the house. Lightning fast, Nero swooped in, wrapping himself around Theka and camouflaging her. The boys shouted at the unfairness of it all while hunting them both down, making use of their freshly acquired Shadow Lord powers.

As amused and annoyed as I felt, my heart tightened looking at my children.

"What is it, my love?" Cedros asked, noticing my mood shift.

"I don't want her to go on the Shadow Trail," I said, piteously.

"She'll be fine," Cedros said reassuringly, drawing me against him with his tail.

"But she's my only baby girl!"

"You sent out the twins and handled it just fine," he countered.

"And they were gone for two years!" I exclaimed.

"And they just came back safe and sound as young Shadow Lords, didn't they?" he argued.

"Yes, but she'll be all alone. At least the twins had each other."

"And she will have Nero. He worships her. You know he'll never leave her side. She'll be fine. Anyway, there's no guarantee she will become a Shadow."

Although I'd told myself the same arguments he was giving me, I wasn't ready to let go of my maternal worries. "She's a golden dragon, like all of our kids. There is a good chance she will become a Shadow Lady."

Cedros nodded, not impressed or fazed in the least, and looking rather smug. "That's right. One of the best Shadow Lords of this generation has sired them." He chuckled when I glared at him and kissed the tip of my nose. "She'll be fine, my love. Plus, we could always have another daughter."

"What?! I'm not trying to find a replacement. Plus, I've just gotten off of maternity leave. You seem to forget that we haven't shut down all of the illegal off-worlder fake shadow obsidian factories. Anyway, we already have four children."

He shrugged. "You said Theka was becoming a spoiled brat, and that she needed a baby sister so that she'd be less of a little princess. And four is nothing. Trinit and Rovain have six younglings."

"How many kids they have isn't a valid argument," I retorted, giving him a disbelieving look. "It's not a competition."

"It's not?" he asked, opening overly innocent eyes.

Just as I playfully elbowed him in the ribs, Arzoth emitted a resounding burp.

"There! Burb done!" Cedros exclaimed with excessive joy. "Now it's my turn to drink."

I burst out laughing while rolling my eyes in discouragement. "You're hopeless."

"I'm hopelessly lovable, and hopelessly in love with you, my Kaida."

I smiled, and melted against him. "I'm hopelessly in love with you too, my Cedros."

THE END

CEDROS

AQRAT

NERO

SHADOW STONES

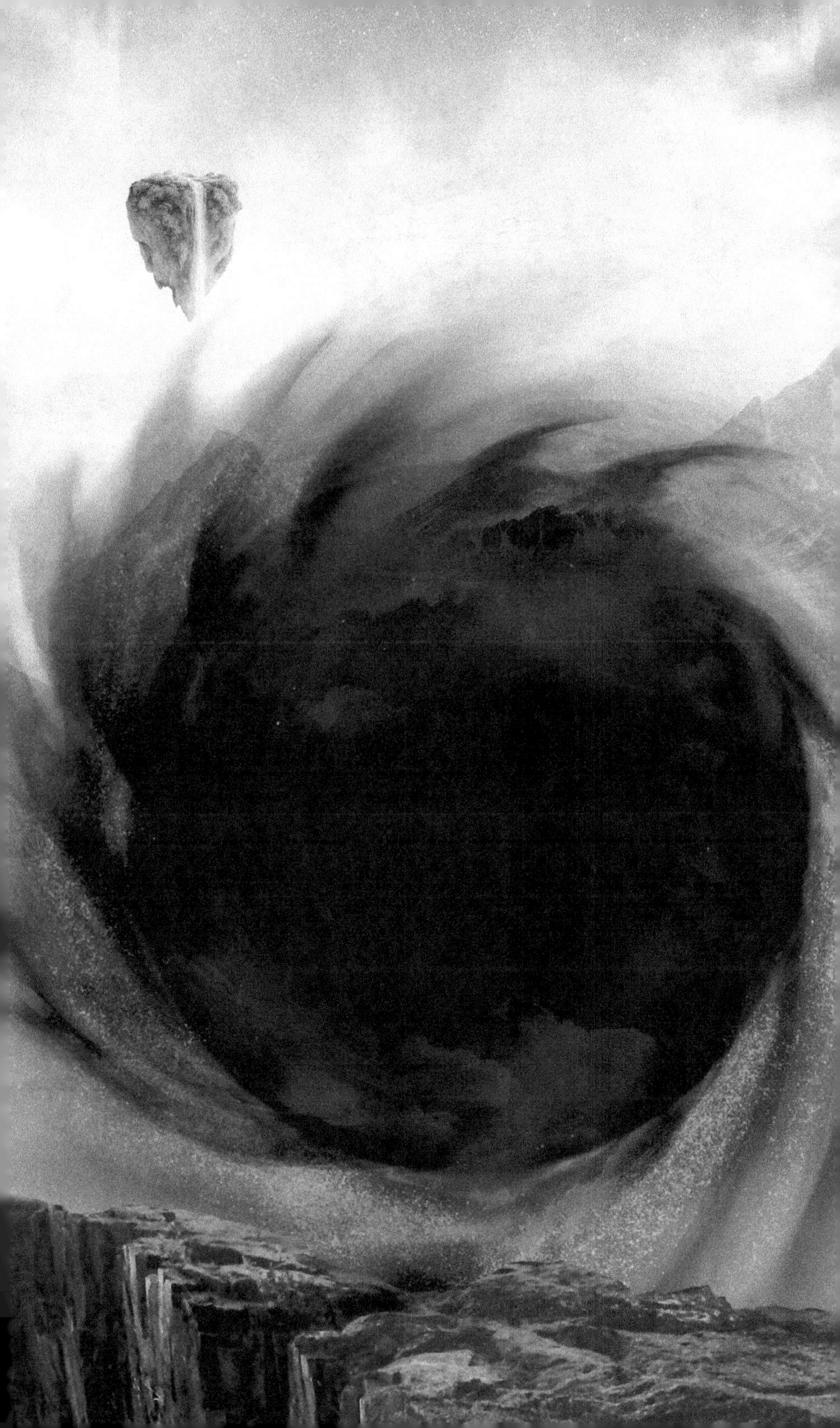

ALSO BY REGINE ABEL

THE VEREDIAN CHRONICLES
Escaping Fate
Blind Fate
Raising Amalia
Twist of Fate
Hands of Fate
Defying Fate
Imperial Fate

BRAXIANS
Anton's Grace
Ravik's Mercy
Krygor's Hope
Keran's Dawn

XIAN WARRIORS
Doom
Legion
Raven
Bane
Chaos
Varnog
Reaper
Wrath
Xenon
Nevrik
Rogue

PRIME MATING AGENCY
I Married A Lizardman
I Married A Naga

I Married A Birdman
I Married A Minotaur
I Married Wonjin
I Married A Merman
I Married A Dragon
I Married A Beast
I Married Krogal
I Married A Dryad
I Married An Incubus
I Married A Mothman
I Married A Catman
I Married Amreth
I Married Kayog

THE MIST
The Mistwalker
The Nightmare

BLOOD MAIDENS OF KARTHIA
Claiming Thalia

DARK TALES
Bluebeard's Curse
The Hunchback

THE SHADOW REALMS
Destined to the Wraith
Destined to the Reaper
Destined to the Lycan

VALOS OF SONHADRA
Unfrozen
Iced

EMPATHS OF LYRIA
An Alien For Christmas

OTHER
True As Steel
Alien Awakening
Heart of Stone
Oops! I Summoned a Liderc

ABOUT REGINE

USA Today bestselling author Regine Abel is a fantasy, para-normal and sci-fi junkie. Anything with a bit of magic, a touch of the unusual, and a lot of romance will have her jumping for joy. She loves creating hot alien warriors and no-nonsense, kick-ass heroines that evolve in fantastic new worlds while embarking on action-packed adventures filled with mystery and the twists you never saw coming.

Before devoting herself as a full-time writer, Regine had surrendered to her other passions: music and video games! After a decade working as a Sound Engineer in movie dubbing and live concerts, Regine became a professional Game Designer and Creative Director, a career that has led her from her home in Canada to the US and various countries in Europe and Asia.

Facebook
https://www.facebook.com/regine.abel.author/

Website
https://regineabel.com

Regine's Rebels Reader Group
https://www.facebook.com/groups/ReginesRebels/

Newsletter
http://smarturl.it/RA_Newsletter

Goodreads
http://smarturl.it/RA_Goodreads

Bookbub
https://www.bookbub.com/profile/regine-abel

Amazon
http://smarturl.it/AuthorAMS